ORACLE

· BOOK THREE ·

I SEE US

Library and Archives Canada
Doidge, Meghan Ciana, 1973 —
I See Us/Meghan Ciana Doidge — PAPERBACK EDITION

Tattoo page break by Inked By Chloe
Character illustration by Nicole Deal
Paperback design and quotes by Serif and Somnia

ISBN 978-1-927850-48-0

ORACLE

· BOOK THREE ·

I SEE US

MEGHAN CIANA DOIDGE

Author's Note:

I See Us is the third book in the Oracle series, which is set in the same universe as the Dowser, Reconstructionist, Amplifier, Archivist, and Misfits of the Adept Universe series. While it's not necessary to read all the interconnected series, <u>the ideal reading order</u> is as follows:

More books in the Archivist and Misfits series to follow. Reading list doesn't include the shorter stories interspersed throughout all of the main series, but more information can be found at www.madebymeghan.ca.

FOR MICHAEL

Only after we were an us was I able to fully be me.

INTRODUCTION

Here be an oracle. Despair all ye who seek her.
Magic will have its cake and eat it too.

Okay, well. So I was mixing metaphors.

I was new to the gig.

But as far as I could tell, there were three kinds of people. Those who wanted confirmation that they'd chosen the correct path. Those who wanted to deny there was any sort of destiny at all. And those who wanted to tear it all down.

So why was it always the third type that showed up at the door to my 1975 Brave Winnebago, dragging me into their power struggles and using my past against me — when I didn't even know what that past was?

Could I thwart the destiny that had been envisioned for me before I was born? Could I carve out a future filled with love and light with my chosen mate?

I certainly knew what I was capable of doing to survive. Beyond the past, through the present, and well into the future ... I'd see us.

ONE

"STOP SQUIRMING," I SAID. "THIS IS WHAT YOU came here for."

"It tickles."

I snorted. "Your life is fraught with inconvenience."

Henry chuckled, causing his chest to shift underneath my careful henna application. Again.

"Don't make me hurt you," I snarled, only half-joking.

"I bet you say that to all the sorcerers."

"Only the good guys."

"I'm not sure you're the best judge of that, Rochelle."

"Yeah?" I kept my attention glued to the fine line I was adding to a henna design I was painting on Henry's chest. "And what does that say about you?"

Henry didn't answer. I flicked my gaze from the pale skin of his left pec to his piercing cobalt-blue eyes, countering his judgemental silence with a sneer. He broke eye contact with me almost immediately.

I didn't blame him. I wouldn't want to be gazing into the weirdly pale-gray eyes of a diminutive oracle either.

Especially not one who was currently hunched over me with her nose only inches from my bare chest.

I returned my attention to the henna tattoo. It was my third attempt since January at finding an image or symbol that would help Henry not only tame the wolf within him — stopping him from transforming at all — but also harness the strength and agility that came from being bitten by a werewolf ... and surviving that bite.

I still thought it was an exercise in futility.

But, believing that I was capable of somehow imbuing my magic into the tattoos I sketched, Henry thought differently.

And as such, the newly-returned-to-active-duty US Marshal had flown all the way northwest from Arlington County, Virginia, to Summerland, British Columbia, where Beau and I were currently located. This was Henry's second trip to Summerland. He was only staying for a couple of days. Hence the reason I had my ass planted on the lime-green kitchen table of the Brave and my feet on either side of Henry, who was seated on one of the cushioned dinette bench seats only two hours after his arrival.

I rolled my neck but didn't take my eyes off the rich mahogany-red lines of the half-rendered image occupying the left upper third of Henry's chest. I'd added a coiled pair of handcuffs constructed out of barbed wire all around the clawed wolf paw I'd designed for my second attempt, which I'd hennaed on Henry last May. But the design had failed to stop his transformation under the influence of the full moon. We had to start over every time he transformed into his half-man/half-beast form, because the shifter magic overrode any mark I made. I wasn't exactly sure why I'd added the image of the cuffs this time. But it felt like the right next step.

My applicator cone was almost empty. I was still learning how to apply the henna smoothly, and found it got especially tricky when the cone wasn't full. But when I reached blindly for the second applicator I'd prepped, I knocked it across the table toward the open window. The Brave was parked in the middle of a grove of apple trees. Though the orchard grass was slowly dying in the heat of June, the trees were swathed with lush green leaves and immature fruit.

Henry reached for the applicator, risking smearing the wet henna on his chest. Again.

"I've got it," I snapped, leaning sideways and picking up the second cone without looking.

Henry hissed excitedly under his breath. I frowned at him, pulling my attention away from the design unfolding across his chest and following his gaze to my right.

The black ivy tattoo that normally curled around my right arm in a full sleeve was currently — and impossibly — projected about six inches away from my hand. The hand with which I would have sworn I'd grabbed the applicator. But it was the ivy, rather than my fingers, that were holding the second henna cone.

I blinked. Then I blinked again. I was fairly certain I wasn't having a vision, both because no white mist obscured my sight and because Henry could apparently see the disembodied tattoo as well.

"New trick?" the marshal whispered, as if he was afraid of breaking the spell. Or, rather, of interrupting the magic I was involuntarily wielding.

"Brand spanking new," I murmured, rotating the palm of my hand upward. The ivy curled back around my arm, depositing the cone applicator in my open hand before becoming inert once more.

"Do it again," Henry said.

I laughed, quick and heavy on the snark. I wanted to lose it. I wanted to scramble off the dinette and burrow into the well-worn sheets neatly smoothed over the mattress in the back of the Brave. I wanted to hide away. To ignore and deny the constantly changing landscape of my life.

Instead, I ignored the uncertainty and the fear trickling down my spine as I turned my attention back to the temporary tattoo, applying all my focus and the second cone of henna to the final lines of the intricate wolf paw I had been refining for Henry since he'd requested the tattoo almost a year ago.

I'd spent some time with Jade Godfrey — aka the dowser, aka the alchemist, aka the dragon slayer — five months ago. Not by choice, of course.

Jade laughed. A lot. She laughed at everything she couldn't control. Not lightly or offishly, but in acknowledgement that she couldn't control it. And she survived.

I wasn't going to develop a chocolate or cupcake obsession that I didn't have the funds to support. But I could co-opt her other coping mechanism. Jade laughed, so I tried to laugh.

"So the butterfly, the skeleton key, and now the ivy can all move independently?" Henry asked.

I nodded, adding a final curve to a claw before shifting back and letting my eyes go out of focus while I contemplated the design. I was still learning to trust my instincts when it came to wielding my oracle magic. Soft focus and patience helped me tap into those instincts.

"Blackwell was right," the marshal said.

"Blackwell was right about what?" I'd involuntarily clenched my toes, so I forced myself to relax my feet on the orange-and-brown fabric of the bench. I hadn't seen or heard from the sorcerer in five months. The mere mention of his name put me on edge.

"That the tattoos are your version of artifacts," Henry said. "Also possibly a form of personal shielding. One that makes people overlook you. Though you always stood out to me. Sorcerers generally channel their power through magical objects, touchstones, and the like."

"Like your handcuffs? Or Blackwell's amulet?"

Henry nodded. "Witches pull magic from the earth, channeling it through themselves." He shuddered as if the idea unsettled him. "Sometimes they use written spells, like a sorcerer. But often it's about intention rather than exact words. A sorcerer needs a focus. Always."

"Except I'm not a sorcerer." Trying to not think too much about it, I bent over Henry's chest again, allowing whatever will guided my hand to move me. I added a few more lines to the henna-sketched image, including extra points on the barbed wire and a crosshatched detail on the chain links that connected the two halves of the handcuffs.

"Yeah. Magic doesn't usually combine. An Adept inherits magic from one of their parents. Similar to dominant or recessive traits. With necromancy, it's even more specific, with only female children inheriting."

Necromancers. Great. That wasn't creepy at all. Though, after two and a half years, nothing about the Adept world really fazed me anymore.

"Which is why Beau is a shapeshifter like his mother and not a spellcaster like his dad."

"Also slightly unusual, though I'm not well-versed in shapeshifter lore. Tigers are a rare form of shapeshifting. Wolves are most numerous. So I would have assumed the trait was recessive, but I guess not."

"But I'm an oracle. And also some sort of sorcerer."

"Apparently."

I lifted my gaze to meet Henry's. He didn't look away this time. "And you think that's why Blackwell is interested in me."

"I guess that depends on how much he knew about you before you met."

"Well, since I didn't even know magic existed then, I'd say he didn't know much. Other than whatever the sketches he bought told him. That I was an oracle of some sort."

"Fair enough." Henry's Southern drawl thickened as it always did when he forced himself to be polite.

I smirked at him, then dropped my gaze to the tattoo again. I wanted badly to change the subject.

"Did you shave again?"

"I waxed."

"You should think about laser."

"Once you commit to a design and actually ink it, I'm hoping I can keep the chest hair."

I nodded. "Very manly."

Henry snorted, then silence fell between us. We'd spent hours like this, both here in Summerland and earlier in Portland, over the last six months or so. But Henry never complained about how long it was taking me to figure out the design, or how long I fiddled with each application.

"Question is, though," the sorcerer murmured, apparently not content to leave things be, "why isn't Blackwell training with you?"

I met his cobalt gaze for a brief moment. Then I swung myself off the table and slid standing to the floor. I crossed to pull a bottle of lemon juice out of the tiny fridge a couple of steps over on the other side of the RV. "I haven't heard from him."

Henry shifted up off the bench seat, stretching. Then

he reached for the cowboy hat resting on the counter to my far right. "And why is that?"

I shrugged, adding lemon juice to a small bowl of sugar and cloves already measured out on the countertop.

"Since when?" Henry ran his fingers along the brim of his hat, then set it in its rightful place on his dark-haired head.

"Since Westport." I carefully stirred the lemon juice into the sugar, making a thin but sticky paste.

"That's odd."

I looked over at Henry, deliberately and casually shrugging one shoulder as if it didn't bother me in the least that I'd been pretty much abandoned by Blackwell. Okay, 'abandoned' might be a strong word. But what else was I supposed to think after, like, twenty unanswered text messages?

"So ... you haven't seen him?" Henry was referring to my visions, not my actual sight.

"I didn't say that."

"So he's still alive?"

"As far as I know."

"Perhaps for the best."

"Survival usually is."

Henry snorted. "You know what I mean."

I didn't answer. I wasn't interested in discussing Blackwell with anyone. I wasn't interested in having friends in general, but Henry apparently had other ideas.

"You want to dry that in the sun?" I asked. "So I can do multiple applications of the lemon juice quickly?" Keeping the henna design moist to prolong its drying helped it adhere as darkly as possible to the skin. Once it was dry, rubbing it off carefully rather than washing it, then coating the design in oil kept it from fading too quickly.

"Sure. Just let me hit the head first." Henry crossed toward the bathroom tucked behind the driver's seat at the front of the Brave.

"Good thing you put on your hat," I said, attempting to tease him. "You never know what might happen while on the toilet."

The marshal flashed me a grin that had gotten much, much toothier since he'd been bitten by Kandy. "You never do know."

AFTER THREE APPLICATIONS OF THE LEMON-AND-clove mixture, Henry lay for a while in the sun to let the henna tattoo fully dry. He was sprawled out by our cheap resin patio table on one of a set of matching chairs. Beau had purchased the set from a thrift store just after we got into town. While he rested, I made potato salad. Even chilled, the hardboiled eggs didn't peel easily, but their ragged edges were barely noticeable once they were chopped and covered in mayo, sour cream, green onion, and paprika.

We'd been in the town of Summerland since the end of March. Because I was Canadian, I couldn't stay in the US for more than six months, though I'd pushed that requirement between the crap with Beau's family and the short leash the pack liked to keep us on. Beau and I had been planning a slow trip up north to the Yukon and Northwest Territories, but when we asked permission from the West Coast North American Pack to leave their US territory, Desmond had other ideas about what we should do while we were spending time across the border.

Being indebted to the pack had put a seriously tight tether on my need to be as free as possible.

Still, our current surroundings were idyllic, even far from the American west coast I'd fallen in love with. We were helping the Thompson family open a CSA orchard — community supported agriculture — along with a bed and breakfast. Eddie and Leanne were members of the West Coast North American Pack, as were their eleven-year-old twins. They had inherited the five-acre property we were currently camped on from an uncle the previous year.

When I was done making the salad, Henry wandered back to his cottage to grab a cold six-pack. His newly built, self-contained vacation rental suite was situated between a stand of slowly ripening yellow, greengage, and early Italian plum trees, and a smaller mixed grove of peaches, nectarines, and apricots that filled the front yard of the property's main house.

I locked the Brave behind me, taking a circuitous route through the apple orchard toward the driveway, then down to the lakefront beach.

Usually, the pack preferred to keep its members close to — if not actually in — Portland, where it was based. But the Thompsons were a special case. First, there was the potential for the property — revenue-wise and as a base of operation in BC away from the lower mainland and Vancouver Island where the witches held territory. And second, the twins were an anomaly, not unlike me. They hadn't inherited the shapeshifting abilities from just one of their parents. Leanne was a werewolf, and Eddie was a coyote shifter. But the twins were thought to be a mix of both species, even though they were too young to have transformed yet. Apparently, werewolf senses were honed enough to scent the twins' burgeoning magic. Crossbreeds of wolf and coyote were supposedly common enough in the real world. The Eastern coyote was a wolf hybrid that ranged all along the east coast of the US and Canada. But such things complicated the rigid structure of the pack. So the Thompsons had relocated to Summerland with the blessing and financial backing of Portland, putting the twins out of sight. Though not out of mind.

I paused underneath one of my favorite apple trees, peering up through the screen of leaves at its immature fruit. The trees in the older section of the orchard had lower boughs that arched just over my head, and upper branches that rose up well over twenty feet off the ground. Eddie was planting semidwarf fruit trees in the expanded and reclaimed sections of the property. Those ten-to-fifteen-foot-high varieties were easier to pick, and were cultivated to yield more fruit than full-sized trees.

Since we'd first arrived at the property, I'd been checking on the fruit every day. Eddie still wasn't entirely sure which varieties of apple were growing in this section of the orchard. He thought they were probably McIntosh, mixed with Gravenstein, Jonagold, Fuji, and Cox's Orange Pippin. But he hadn't actually been on the property since he was a boy. I had gone online to investigate all the apples he'd mentioned, and had been diligently looking for signs to distinguish one tree from another as they bloomed, then fruited.

I didn't miss the significance of our current campsite. I had a thing for apples. I'd teased Beau about agreeing to Desmond's 'commission' because of the location. But, all joking aside, I was fairly certain my thoughtful boyfriend figured that keeping me calm and centered would help with my oracle magic. So he had pretty much made sure I was surrounded by one of my most favorite things in the world, day in and day out. Which at least partially made up for the pack ordering us here to help the Thompsons' transition.

Well, Beau was helping, anyway. He was doing a ton of landscaping work and heavy lifting, while I fielded requests from the occasional random Adepts who showed up at the door of the Brave with little or no notice. Most of those were vetted by the pack, so it wasn't clear why they couldn't give me more of a heads-up. I also kept my Etsy shop as updated as possible. Most of my sketches still sold within forty-eight hours of listing. And not all of them to Blackwell. Actually, as far as I could tell from shipping addresses, the sorcerer hadn't purchased a single charcoal from any of my updates since January. Since the last time I'd seen him, in Westport with Jade.

Blackwell had stepped back from my life. Way back. And I knew why, but I wasn't sure there was anything else I could have done at the time to prevent it. I sketched what my magic willed me to see. And when Jade Godfrey had abruptly appeared in Westport, Washington, needing to find the path that would lead her to the kidnapped far seer, I'd shown her what I'd seen, which had gotten Blackwell involved.

And though the sorcerer had survived — according to the brief glimpses I'd had of him since then — his silence led me to believe it hadn't ended well.

Blackwell wasn't the forgiving or charitable type. He preferred that his investments were secure and firmly indebted to him, and to him alone. I had crossed that line by intentionally bringing him and Jade together, and risking his health and safety by doing so. Though I had no doubt the sorcerer would seek me out again the second it was profitable for him to do so.

Speaking of profit that had nothing to do with actual

money, whenever an Adept showed up to request a 'seeing' from me, they always brought an offering. As if I was some sort of agent for an ancient deity. It was seriously weird, but I was fairly certain it was the proper way of things. One of those rituals that helped Adept life run smoothly. And I wasn't rude enough to turn any offering down.

But I didn't ask any questions either.

I just did my job as an oracle.

Because if that wasn't what I was meant to do, they wouldn't have shown up at the door to the Brave in the first place.

Yes.

I believed.

I believed I was an arm or hand of destiny. Or maybe just one set of eyes among many other sets, including my actual mentor, the far seer of the guardians.

I hadn't seen Chi Wen in months either, though that wasn't at all unusual. According to Kandy, who Beau kept in text contact with, everyone who had been meant to survive whatever quest I'd helped them with last January still walked the earth, including the far seer. Sometimes the green-haired werewolf was as oblique as my mentor. But since I had no intention of getting involved any more than I already had, I didn't bother asking anything more beyond verifying that Kandy, Jade, Drake, and Chi Wen were okay.

Plus, magic was meant to be wielded. I felt that as a fundamental truth — that to deny the oracle magic would be to deny an important part of myself. Maybe even my soul. If I'd believed in that sort of thing. But higher powers and all that were out of my scope.

The seeings I did for my so-called clients were eclectic, and I didn't put any real effort into analyzing those visions beyond the time it took to share them, and to occasionally sketch some aspect of what I saw that drew my attention. Sometimes I wasn't sure if I was seeing the future at all. Maybe some Adepts needed clarity about the past.

The eggs I'd just used in the potato salad had come from chickens that were one of the offerings I'd received. They were a gift from a witch who had found me just a few days after we'd hooked up the Brave in the Thompsons' orchard. Four twelve-week-old pullets and a cockerel. Westphalian deathlayers, they were called. An exceedingly rare dual-purpose breed with gorgeous black-and-white feathers and vibrant red combs. Deathlayers were so-named because they laid eggs their entire lives, which — I had figured out via Google — was unusual. The dual-purpose part meant they were good for meat and eggs.

But no matter how insanely cool it might be to own animals called deathlayers, I'd had no idea what to do with the box of chicks. Fortunately, Leanne had gleefully taken to them, and we'd set up temporary housing for the birds in the garage of the main house while Beau built them a coop. The pullets had come into lay at the beginning of May, producing large white eggs. Leanne was planning on trying to hatch some chicks in the late fall, after the harvest was done and all the people who were members of the CSA orchard had their shares fulfilled. With the grand opening of the B&B scheduled for Canada Day, the new venture would have been up and running for four months by then.

Hatching chicks seemed crazy complicated according to my hastily compiled Internet research, but if Leanne wanted to give it a try, then good for her. I was just surprised at how attached I'd gotten to the birds. A pet that laid eggs was pretty cool.

Actually, any pet was seriously cool to someone who'd lost count of how many foster homes and temporary placements she'd been subjected to since becoming an orphan at birth.

My necklace with its huge raw diamond was the only thing I had that tied me to any sense of the family I was supposed to have been born into. The only thing that tied me to my mother — Jane Hawthorne, the Oracle of Philadelphia. And I only knew her name, title, and place of residence courtesy of the far seer. By the length of the necklace's thick rose-gold chain, it was an easy guess that she'd been much taller than my five-foot-three-inch stature, but I had no other idea of what she'd looked like. No sense of whether she'd shared my pale-gray eyes. Or if her hair had slowly turned white in her early twenties as mine was doing. It wouldn't even hold the jet-black dye I preferred for more than forty-eight hours.

Nor did I have any idea why my mother had been in Vancouver the day she'd died from injuries sustained in a car accident right before I was born.

I hadn't stayed more than a couple of months in one place since my nineteenth birthday, though moving on quickly wasn't always by choice. But after three months, the orchard, the surrounding five acres, and the beach along Okanagan Lake were starting to feel ... well, not like home, but normal. Even comfortably habitual.

I glanced up at the main house as I crossed into the section of the orchard dedicated to mature pear trees. The freshly painted, brown-sided rancher was perched two-thirds of the way up the property, which rose in a gradual slope from the main road.

Eddie Thompson was a brilliant gardener. The beds situated behind the house were already teeming with fresh lettuce, spinach, and peas. Tomatoes, zucchini, and cantaloupes were growing as well.

Leanne was the cook. She wanted the 'breakfast' part of the Thompson B&B to stand out. Summerland was a well-established tourist destination, so making a name against all the other B&Bs in the area was key. Though I had a feeling the Thompsons' guests would have a very 'Adept' vibe about them, and that the pack would specifically be sending a lot of business this way.

The 'bed' part of the B&B consisted of six brand-new cottages, ranging from four-hundred-square-foot single-room suites — like Henry's cottage — to the six-hundred-square-foot two-bedroom unit situated up near the top of the property in the cherry tree grove. Only five had been built so far, though. The Brave was occupying the sixth spot, whose concrete pad Beau had immediately claimed when we arrived.

I had also reserved the cottage nearest us for my friends Gary and Tess, who were arriving in a couple of days for the B&B's unofficial opening. It had a great view of the lake. The other three cottages were at the base of the property among the plum trees, in the middle of the acreage among the pear trees, and Henry's cottage near the stone fruit grove. Two of the four empty cottages were still in the final stages of construction, needing some paint, hardware, and light fixtures.

I changed course to walk between fifteen-foot pear trees that bore tags marking them as Bartlett, Bosc, and Flemish Beauty. Crossing slightly uphill underneath their already fruit-laden boughs, I caught a glimpse of my deathlayers. Technically, I was supposed to be heading down to the beach with my potato salad offering in hand for the communal barbecue Beau had planned for Henry's arrival, but I always checked on the chickens a few times a day. I liked the routine.

As I rounded the brown-sided chicken coop on my way to the wire-mesh run, the oracle magic hit me without warning.

My sight was whitewashed between one step and the next. My heart rate instantly spiked. I inhaled slowly and steadily, pulling oxygen into my lungs, then visualizing it running through my bloodstream and into my brain.

The whiteout in my mind's eye shifted, resolving into a thick fog I recognized. It was what sometimes marked out a vision as being particularly intense. I was still getting accustomed to the process, though. On top of dealing with the actual substance of my visions, it was a daunting task to glean and catalogue as much information as I could about my magic.

A few steps to my right, the rooster uttered a sharp cry, calling his hens to him. Wings flapped and talons scraped on the wooden ramps as the flock retreated into the safety of the coop.

I'd frightened them.

Or, rather, my reaction to the magic moving through the earth underneath my feet, channeling through my limbs, and settling into my brain made them wary.

Only I could feel and see this particular energy. Oracle power.

I tugged my necklace out from underneath my T-shirt. Wrapping my left hand around the large raw diamond, I whispered, "I'm here. I see. Show me."

The fog in my mind thinned, fading until it was a fine mist around the edges of my sight.

I was still in the orchard, among the fruit trees.

For a moment, I thought the vision had dispersed without showing me anything. Sometimes I got minor blips that way, like precursors to something bigger. As if the magic wanted or needed me primed.

Then I realized that the quality of the light was wrong and bright moonlight, not sunlight, was filtering through the deeply shadowed trees. I turned, scanning the trees in their careful rows. Nothing moved. I couldn't hear anything other than the soft comforting chatter of the chickens in their coop. Though the visions didn't always come with audio.

"Okay," I whispered. "I see."

The canopy of leaves above me was lush and green, the fruit well-formed and nearly ripe. Cherries. Not apples or pears or plums. The branches and trunks of the trees were thicker. Taller. I was presumably in the upper part of the property among the Bing, Rainier, and Skeena cultivars, and it looked to be the same season. But I had no idea whether the moment the magic wanted me to see was going to happen next week or a year from now.

Something shifted in the deep shadows. A spike of terror blossomed at the base of my skull, and I chided myself for it. It was a vision. Nothing could hurt me here.

In fact, the entire point of my visions was to stop bad things from happening. Well, usually.

But something was wrong — something felt off — about the darkening shadows on the trunk of the nearest tree. They were too dark, their edges too well defined. And they were too high up along that trunk.

If I'd been sketching the cherry grove by moonlight, I would have softened and shaded the pockets of darkness along the base of the trees. But this shadow leeched out around the front of one tree's smooth bark, and for a moment, I could have sworn I saw it suck all the vitality from that tree to leave only a gray, deadened husk behind.

"Not a shadow," I whispered. My brain screamed to comprehend what I was seeing. Pain seared through my temples.

The not-a-shadow had eyes. Crimson red slits burned within the darkness. A sharp-clawed, black-scaled, four-fingered hand grasped the tree trunk. It was as if the shadow was pulling itself into existence, manifesting within the orchard.

Not a shadow, though.

A demon.

The rooster crowed somewhere behind me, and I stumbled back from the creature as it appeared. My back hit the chicken coop and I collapsed to the ground. The rooster crowed a second time, fiercely claiming his territory.

The sound steadied me.

The visions were mine, and under my control. I wasn't going to run away from the darkness clawing into the reality unfolding in my mind.

"Rochelle?" a soft, childish voice asked.

The vision dissipated as quickly as it had hit. Though it left my actual sight hazy, I could see a towheaded eleven-year-old boy before me. He was grasping the Tupperware container that held my potato salad as if it might be precious treasure, presumably picked up along the path to the coop.

"Calvin." I tried to smile, conscious of the fact that I wasn't quite ready to stand.

"You dropped this," he said, squaring his shoulders and lifting his chin with a hint of fierceness. Though it was only June, his skin was already tanned a light golden brown.

My smile came easier. The steel wire mesh that surrounded the bottom of the coop and the run was cutting into my back, so I stood, finding that my legs held me without trouble. Apparently, my weakness was just a state of mind.

I brushed off my jeans. My necklace swung forward as I did so, capturing Calvin's attention.

His nostrils flared, scenting my oracle magic. His well-washed blue jean shorts were ragged around his knees, his T-shirt had been abandoned somewhere, and his green sneakers were covered in sand. I could smell the pineapple-and-coconut-scented sunscreen that had been applied so liberally it left streaks across his bare chest and arms. He'd been at the beach.

"Did Beau send you to fetch me?" I asked.

Calvin nodded without speaking.

I stepped forward, holding my hands out for the potato salad.

"I'll carry it," he said. "That's proper, right?"

"Sure."

He darted ahead of me toward the driveway that cut up from the road to the main house. Not sure if I was going to need to draw or not, I followed at a more sedate pace. I always had a sketchbook with me, but I preferred to work in the Brave. Out of sight of questioning eyes.

Calvin paused at the side of the drive, glancing back at me. He scuffed his sneaker in the gravel that edged the recently laid pavement.

I closed the space between us.

The child muttered something, but with his chin practically pressed to his chest, I didn't catch his actual words.

"Sorry?"

"Did you see something?" His voice was pitched just loud enough for me to hear him.

"Yes."

He nodded, then dared to tilt his head sideways to look

at me. His gaze fell somewhere in the vicinity of my eyes, though it was doubtful whether he could see them through my bug-eyed white-framed sunglasses.

"Something bad?"

"I'm not sure yet." I wasn't going to lie to him.

"Something about us? Something about Krista?" His twin sister.

"I didn't see her. Or anyone in particular, actually."

He nodded. Then with his duty as the ten-minute-older twin satisfied, he took off down the drive to the main road that ran alongside the lake.

Shapeshifters might be brave by nature. Even foolhardy. But even so, having an oracle living in their apple orchard was bound to trigger all sorts of territorial responses.

The entire family was wary around me.

But they adored Beau.

And who wouldn't?

OKANAGAN LAKE WAS SO LARGE THAT THE uninitiated might easily mistake it for an inlet or a bay of some adjacent sea. In the late afternoon light, the blue of the water was vibrant, almost blinding to my sensitive eyes. The landscape surrounding the lake consisted of gently rolling hills that were turning golden brown in the heat of early summer. Though according to the locals, it had been a slightly cooler year so far, and we'd been hit by an unexpected downpour the previous day. The breeze rustling through the surrounding grassland and across the sandy beach was dry despite the size of the lake, though, and was doing a great job of tangling my wedge-cropped hair.

Three cities occupied the shores of Okanagan Lake along its eighty-plus-mile length — Vernon at its northern tip, Penticton in the south, and Kelowna about a forty-minute drive north of us. In addition to Summerland, a number of other smaller communities also spread along the lakeshore.

Much of this area was wine country, and vineyard after vineyard had ousted heritage farms and orchards over the last two decades. The growing conditions along the lake were supposedly perfect for dry whites and a complex, ever-evolving Pinot Noir. Not that I'd ever tasted either. But it was pretty much all the predominately white, well-aged population of Summerland talked about, even at Tim Hortons or IGA. Both of which were within walking distance. Along with four different wineries, of course.

And not that I had any particular problem with older white people. Tess and Gary were two of my only friends, and they fell into that category. But Beau, with his gorgeous mocha skin and deep Southern accent, and I, with my Asian-shaped eyes and dual arm-sleeve tattoos, didn't inspire much chumminess from the neighbors.

But that was all cool, because I was seriously lacking in the small-talk-conversation department anyway.

Standing on the edge of the beach, I could see for liter-ally miles in all directions. The first time we'd wandered down from the house and dipped our toes in the water, Beau had grunted in pleasure and proclaimed the landscape 'perfect for spying danger from a long way off.' The grassy hills surrounding the lake were only occasionally punctu-ated by sagebrush and scattered ponderosa pine trees.

All the area needed to really pull off the look was

cowboys, cattle, and First Nations tribes, but I knew that such things had long been shoved way, way back into the annals of history. Those days had been conquered three times, in fact — first by the gradual settlement that had followed the early days of the fur trade and the gold rush, then by the orchards that had dominated the area by the 1950s, and now by the wineries.

And the conquerors always rewrote history, right? That was more than a rote saying for me these days. I'd seen it.

That was what happened when you hung around with really powerful people, even if you weren't the one doing the rewriting. Even if you were simply a tool that the people with the power used.

I shook off the inappropriately timed thought.

No one controlled me. No person, at least. I made choices. I was master of my own fate.

Well, as far as I knew. Because I was actually blind to my own future.

So, yeah. I'd spent some time on Google researching the area. Beau had the Wi-Fi installed the day after we set up the Brave.

I tugged my sneakers off one at a time before stepping onto the hot, dry sand. Calvin was already shoeless, apparently well adapted to the heat, and racing ahead of me. A dozen or so feet away, where the sand became harder packed, Beau and Leanne were fussing over the half-lit coals of a massive portable grill.

Calvin tossed the potato salad in the general direction of his dark-blond mother. Leanne caught the offering without turning her attention away from the grill. Apparently, werewolf reflexes were an asset when raising children.

The boy veered off, sprinting to the water's edge to join

his twin sister and his father, Eddie, who were paddling around in two large inner tubes.

Beau looked up, catching my gaze. His dark aquamarine eyes were brilliant against his sun-darkened skin. A lazy grin spread across his face, and my heart pinched. It was always this way when I hadn't seen him for even a few hours. I'd always thought people in love were supposed to get used to each other, or even bored, as months and then years rolled past. Familiarity faded into contempt, didn't it? But it didn't. I didn't. We didn't.

I might actually love Beau more than I had thirty seconds before. I wasn't sure how I contained all that emotion every day, but I did.

I smiled back at him as he paced toward me, meeting me halfway across the beach. I lifted up on my tiptoes to accept a chaste kiss. The loose sand was warm underneath my feet, comforting now rather than uncomfortable.

"Watch out for Ogopogo!" Calvin shrieked, evoking the serpentine monster that supposedly inhabited Okanagan Lake. He surged out of the water and attempted to knock his father off his tube.

Grinning even wider, Beau slung his arm over my shoulder as he turned around to observe the scene unfolding at the edge of the lake. More delighted shrieking and laughter exploded as Krista dove off her inner tube, then popped up on Eddie's far side. Wearing a light-blue bathing suit underneath green swim trunks, she was Calvin's exact twin except for her longer hair and slighter stature. United against their father, the two colluded to dethrone him.

I ran my hand down Beau's forearm in a slow caress, knowing that at any minute, the preteens would be calling for reinforcements and he would answer their summons.

"You had a vision," Beau said, flicking his gaze away from the happy family for a second. He could most likely smell the oracle magic still lingering around me.

"I did. But I've got nothing to report. Not yet."

"You don't need to draw?"

"Not yet."

"Beau!" Krista was standing knee deep in the lake, her hands on her nonexistent hips as she delightedly shrieked her second champion's name. She beckoned to him, each of her wrists boasting a half-dozen colored plastic bracelets, each one representing a charity the eleven-year-old actively represented.

Beau tugged off his bright-green T-shirt and pressed it into my hands before jogging over to join the group thrashing in the water. When he was in waist deep, he turned back, offering me a wink and a saucy grin before he dove into the lake.

I could watch Beau running shirtless on a beach all day. And keep watching when he returned all dripping wet, then threw himself down on a towel next to —

Henry cleared his throat behind me.

I spun, glaring at him.

He tipped his cowboy hat in my direction, then wandered over to Leanne and the barbecue. He was carrying the six-pack of beer, and had changed his blue T-shirt for a dark-green short-sleeved cotton shirt. I would have thought a cowboy would look out of place on a beach, but he didn't. But then, Henry was one of those people who seemed to just fit in anywhere and everywhere, like Beau and Jade Godfrey. The rest of us had to be comfortable on the periphery, or in the shadows.

A flash of my vision in the cherry grove wiped the late-afternoon sun-drenched scenery away.

I was suddenly starkly cold, watching a shadow that wasn't a shadow move among the fruit trees. Or, as best as I could figure, rip its way into our world through the fruit trees, from wherever demons originated.

A rooster crowed. Its cry was a mournful sound I'd never heard the deathlayer rooster make.

Then Henry laughed.

I was back on the beach.

Correction.

I hadn't left.

It had been a long time since a simple vision had distracted me so much that it made me lose touch with reality.

Beau was shoulder deep in the water with a towheaded, chortling twin over each shoulder. He was looking back, watching me. Concerned, but trying to not draw attention my way.

I shook my head slightly, assuring him I was okay. Then I willed myself to move toward Leanne and Henry.

No point in losing it until there was something to lose it over.

Like the fact that the grill was smothered in chunky, gag-worthy hotdogs. That was definitely something I was going to have to take exception to.

TWO

"I'm going to sleep well tonight," Henry said.

"Going to bed before dark is a sure sign of old age, marshal." I glanced over at Henry, noting that my black butterfly tattoo had chosen this moment to flit from my left wrist and dance around the brim of his cowboy hat.

We were meandering back from the beach, cutting right from the driveway and past the chicken coop while the Thompsons headed all the way up to the main house.

"You forget I'm three hours ahead."

I snorted. "The sun will be barely set in two hours."

Henry chuckled. "It's not my fault that it wanes late in this part of the world."

My butterfly tattoo took off, flitting through the apple trees between us and into the clearing where the Brave was hooked up. Henry must have caught a glimpse or hint of it, because he missed a step, then slowed his pace. Either that or his beer buzz was weighing down his feet.

The trees parted before us.

A woman was waiting outside the door to the Brave.

She'd apparently just knocked, and was smoothing her dark auburn-dyed, bobbed hair as she took a step back.

Henry stood motionless at the edge of the apple grove, tilting his head slightly to look past the lower branches at his eye level.

I stopped next to him. I could walk through the orchard without needing to stoop. So there was one advantage to being short.

The woman by the Brave didn't feel dangerous to me, but Henry's magical senses were much more refined than my own. My butterfly tattoo danced around her head, then flitted over her sharp nose. I hadn't quite figured out why the butterfly did what it did yet, except that it drew my attention to Adepts. But only some Adepts.

The auburn-haired woman waved the black butterfly away as if it were any other bug, then shifted impatiently as she tried to get a peek into the RV through the dinette windows.

The butterfly flitted back to me, settling on my wrist with only a whisper of a touch.

An amused smirk spread across the marshal's hat-shadowed face.

Great. I had yet to figure out why Adepts of one magical persuasion inherently didn't like Adepts of other types. Jealousy, maybe. Power plays, for certain.

Anyway.

Let the Adept games begin.

Beau stepped into the neat row of fruit trees directly opposite us on the other side of the clearing.

I stopped myself from looking over my shoulder, though I would have sworn a second before that he'd been right behind us. He'd been piggybacking both Krista and Calvin up the driveway, pausing for a brief moment to let them jump off his back before following us through the trees.

"You're a long way from the road, witch," Henry said.

The so-called witch flinched as she whirled to face us. She was in her late twenties, with skin the color of honey and standing about five-foot-six in sleek black leather Oxfords. Her tailored navy pantsuit, porcelain-white blouse, and sleek black briefcase were completely out of place in Summerland. She should have been sweating buckets, but she appeared perfectly cool. With the sun barely touching the horizon, the evening air was too warm for layers or long sleeves.

She squared her shoulders, relaxing her face into a carefully neutral expression while she ran her eyes over Henry. Assessing him.

"Greetings, sorcerer," she said, not sparing me a glance. "I'm seeking an oracle of Hawthorne descent. Do you know where I might find him or her?"

"Open your eyes, witch," Henry said.

The stranger grimaced, then glanced around the clearing. She didn't pivot far enough to spot Beau among the fruit trees behind her. She also apparently completely dismissed me.

"Well, that's flattering," I muttered.

Startled, the witch focused in on me finally. Then she frowned deeply. "I'm here on business, and have no interest in games."

"I've been standing here the entire time," I said, holding my hands out in a 'here I am' gesture.

"And shielded," the witch spat, her cool composure slipping.

Henry chortled.

"What?" I snapped.

"The tattoos. Like I said. Personal shielding." He stepped forward with his hand extended toward the witch. "Henry Calhoun."

"Ember Pine, of the legal firm of Sherwood and Pine. No relation. The Seattle branch," she said with a lift of her chin. She pointedly ignored Henry's hand. "And I believe you are a United States Marshal, Mr. Calhoun. A tidbit you should perhaps lead with ... for legal purposes."

"Why?" Henry dropped his hand. "Aren't we going to be friends?" There was something seriously threatening in his affable tone.

Ember glanced at me, then back at Henry. She'd slipped her free hand in her pocket. I wondered if she was carrying a weapon of some sort.

Despite his ever-present cowboy hat, Henry was dressed casually in deference to the heat, and presumably to his being on vacation. I would have been surprised if he'd attempted to fly across the Canadian border with a gun, though maybe that wasn't an issue for police officials or perhaps the marshal kept his weapon magically concealed. But I knew he'd have his magical handcuffs on him. And no one could avoid those cuffs once Henry targeted them.

"I'm getting eaten alive by bugs," I said, opting to defuse whatever situation was brewing in the peacefulness of the orchard. Adept games really weren't all that amusing once magic started getting flung around. Plus, with the Brave and the apple trees in the line of fire, I had a vested interest in moving this meeting forward.

"Are you the oracle?" Ember asked.

"Are you a lawyer?" Beau's deep, lyrical voice cut through the slowly deepening darkness of the trees behind the witch.

She flinched again, cursing under her breath as she

whirled around. Beau stepped into the clearing, pausing about ten feet away from the witch. Though he could cross that distance in a blink of an eye if he needed to.

"What do you want with an oracle, lawyer witch?" Beau asked. "And what brought you here specifically?"

Ember took two steps back, putting her back to the Brave and deliberately smoothing the hand that had been concealed in her pocket over her suit jacket. Perhaps indicating she was unarmed and had no ill intent. She was trying to gain control of the situation, but she'd made a tactical error. A few of them, actually. Faced with three Adepts of unknown strength, putting her back to a door when she had no idea if anyone was in the RV was a bad idea.

She was either fearless, really out of her depth, or seriously good at bluffing. I would have bet on it being the latter, and I made a note to myself to avoid ever getting locked into a contest of wills with her.

But as a result, I instantly liked her, though I tamped down on the feeling. I didn't go around liking people too often, and I had a reputation to uphold. I figured aloofness worked for an oracle, and since being reserved came naturally to me, there wasn't much point in trying to fight it. Choosing to be open to fate and destiny didn't mean I was any different than I had been before I knew magic and the Adept world existed.

Ember settled her completely composed gaze on Beau to her left. "A 1975 Brave Winnebago parked on land ostensibly owned by the West Coast North American Pack isn't all that difficult to track, Mr. Beaumont Jamison."

"Why were you looking in the first place?" Henry asked. "What's it to you?"

"The oracle is under my protection."

Ember eyed me. "You keep interesting company."

"Yeah, so I've heard. Can you get on with it so everyone can either stand down or kick you off the property?"

Ember opened her mouth to retort, presumably planning on saying something about her ability to hold her own ground. But after another glance at the three of us, she shut it and nodded curtly. "I have a legacy package to deliver to the descendant of Jane Hawthorne, the Oracle of Philadelphia. Are you she?"

A chill ran down my spine. "Why now?" I asked calmly, instead of freaking out at the mention of my long-dead mother's name.

"You're a cold case," Ember said smugly. "I specialize in cold cases."

"She means she's trying to make a name for herself," Henry said. Though his tone was more neutral than malicious.

"I didn't think big-time sorcerers went in for fortune-tellers," Ember said snottily.

"If you think you're standing before some hack wielding a crystal ball, I suggest you get your eyes checked," Henry said. "Or is it that your witch senses are so weak you can't tell the difference?"

Ember clenched her jaw. For just a moment, her deep-brown eyes flared blue. Then she eased her grip on her briefcase and offered Henry a curl of her lips. More of a smirk than a smile.

The marshal chuckled quietly, tipped his hat in my direction, and pivoted back the way we'd come toward his cottage.

"I repeat, you keep interesting company, oracle." Ember gazed after the retreating sorcerer.

"You know, friends in high places," I said mockingly.

"No," she said, returning her attention to me. "I don't know."

"Shall we go in?" I didn't wait for an answer as I crossed toward the Brave.

Beau shot forward to open the door for me, not too subtly forcing Ember to stumble backward as he did so.

He towered over her, grinning.

She blinked up at him owlishly.

I smothered a snort. Beau was pretty enough to render even self-important lawyer witches mute.

I stepped up into the Brave, flicked on the lights, then slumped into a huddle on the far bench seat of the dinette. If I was going to get a dump of information about my mother, I wanted to be in my safe place. What orphan wouldn't?

Ember followed at a slower pace, taking in every inch of the faded-yet-still-garish orange, brown, and lime-green interior as she crossed through.

Beau closed the door behind the witch with a soft click. He never sat in on any of my seeings, and I surmised that he also didn't want to crowd the witch. Plus, with his shifter senses, he could hear everything from outside anyway.

I dug a piece of charcoal out of my satchel, then placed the bag beside me on the bench seat. Tucking the charcoal into the palm of my left hand, I tugged my mother's thick-linked rose-gold necklace out from beneath the collar of my T-shirt. The raw diamond settled between and just below my breasts. Its magic was a soothing echo of my own power.

Ember watched my preparations for our conversation with a carefully neutral expression.

I took off my sunglasses, folding and placing them on the table next to the wall. Then I looked up at the witch expectantly.

She didn't flinch at the sight of my uncovered eyes — bonus points for her — but she didn't look quite so poised any more.

"I don't want a reading," she said. Her thin tone further betrayed her nerves, and she grimaced as if she wished to take the statement back.

"I figured that out. What with you being a lawyer and mentioning my mother." I refused to give in to the smirk threatening to overtake my expression. No matter how weird it was when Adepts feared me, I was going to be professional and polite. Well, my version of those things, anyway. "I won't tell you that you're going to die."

Ember looked aghast. "You've seen me die?"

"No ... I ... That's the joke, isn't it? The thing the psychic says ..."

Ember smoothed her features, placing her slim black leather briefcase onto the dinette and sliding into the bench seat across from me without another word.

Everything always went sideways when I tried to be friendly. I really shouldn't have bothered.

Ember dialed a combination into the lock on the briefcase, lifted the lid, and shuffled some papers around.

"Did you see me coming?" she asked without looking up.

"Not you," I murmured. "At least I hope to hell not."

She glanced up at me sharply.

"I don't see my own future."

The witch nodded, as if she should have known that pertinent piece of information already. "Right."

After trailing her gaze across my dual arm-sleeve tattoos, she returned her attention to the briefcase and placed a handmade envelope on the table between us. Its parchment surface was the color of weak tea, and it was closed with a burgundy wax seal. Something even deeper red was smeared across the rune-embossed wax, but I didn't recognize it or the symbol.

From the briefcase, Ember then extracted a children's jewelry box wrapped in floral-printed paper, a four-inch-wide copper ring, and a tea light. She set them all on the table, then closed and placed her briefcase on the floor.

She lifted her brown-eyed gaze to mine. "Ready?"

"Sure." I had no idea what the hell was going on, but Beau and Henry wouldn't have left me alone with the witch if they thought she was dangerous.

Of course, we were all fallible.

Me, deeply so.

Ember clicked open the jewelry box to reveal the expected plastic ballerina and peach-pink satin lining. A couple of my foster sisters had owned little boxes like this one, filled with worthless baubles and stuffed in a single garbage bag along with every other worldly possession whenever it was time to move on from one home to another, or back and forth to their birth parents. I didn't own a single piece of jewelry, other than my mother's necklace. This box was empty.

"Recording," Ember intoned seriously.

I almost laughed. Then the ballerina started twirling. I'd expected the witch to wind up the box to produce some sort of mechanical lullaby. But none played.

Ember then placed the tea light within the copper ring. She snapped the middle finger and thumb of her right hand over the wick and the candle lit. A wash of magical energy kissed the bare skin of my arms, and for a moment, I would have sworn that my tattoos rippled in response.

Ember frowned down at the copper ring, then gave it a slight twist.

"What is that?" I asked.

"It's supposed to be a sound barrier spell." She spoke without looking at me. "Localized to the immediate area. So the table and the benches only. For privacy. We can hear out, but others can't listen in."

"Oh." The tattoos settled down as if quieted by my acceptance of the spell.

"Ah, there," Ember said, confused but attempting to maintain her professional demeanor. Or perhaps she was always distant and somewhat aloof.

Not that I minded. I wasn't the squeal-and-hug type myself.

The witch lawyer turned her attention to the envelope, carefully tapping one thick edge so that it was perfectly aligned between us.

"Beau will come in if he can't hear us."

The witch nodded. "Then he will see that I mean no harm."

"Most people don't. But that's no guarantee."

"True. Shall we begin?"

The door to the Brave opened, and Beau climbed into the RV. It didn't dip with his weight. He'd been practicing moving soundlessly, along with somehow controlling the distribution of his weight, for over a year. It was some sort of shapeshifter stalking/hunting technique he was learning from Audrey and Kandy. He met my gaze over Ember's shoulder.

"All right?" he asked.

I could hear him despite the 'privacy spell,' but I nodded instead of speaking, assuming that he couldn't hear me.

Ember frowned without turning to look at Beau, then cleared her throat, as if speaking for the jewelry-box recording device rather than to me. "My name is Ember Pine. I represent the firm of Sherwood and Pine, who house the legacy papers of Jane Hawthorne, Oracle of Philadelphia."

"Okay."

"I'm recording this conversation for my own personal record. The recording will be automatically wiped in twenty-four hours, or at the time of my death."

"That's ... extreme."

"Our client confidentiality extends to the heir of the Hawthorne estate. Do you understand?"

"What's said here stays between us. I'm not as dumb as I look."

"You don't ..." Ember shook her head, then continued. "I have to say these things."

"I'm all ears."

"What is your name?"

"Legally? Rochelle Saintpaul."

"And your Adept name?"

I eyed the witch across from me, suddenly not too sure about giving up all my secrets. Beau prowled past us, brushing his fingers against the silence spell sealed over the dinette.

Ember ignored him. "Do you need a secondary oath?"

"Excuse me?"

"Do you want me to swear another oath as to my —"

"No." I interrupted the witch before any magic could somehow attach to her words and bind me to her. "I'm not interested in any magical bonds."

Ember lifted one thinly plucked, gently curved eyebrow. I was fairly certain she dyed them to match her hair, though I hadn't known that was a thing.

Beau plucked a box of Oreos out of an upper cupboard,

then leaned back against the shelving unit just behind my shoulder. He started tossing the cookies up in the air one at a time, catching them in his mouth.

Ember refused to be intimidated by this display of eating skill. "The weight of the magic would rest on me. I'm an expert in contract —"

"No. It would still be tied to me. So no."

"Accepting the legacy will also tie to you. In fact, that's the only way to accept it. You'll have to prove your relationship."

"I have no proof. Just hearsay."

"So you are the daughter of Jane Hawthorne?"

"So I'm told."

"When did she die?"

"Shouldn't you know?"

"Legacy magic isn't that precise. The bequeathal was delivered to our vaults at the time of Jane Hawthorne's death, but there was nothing tying it to you specifically. Nor is there any magical recording of the events of your mother's death."

"If she's my mother."

"Shall we see?"

"How?"

"Only a direct descendant can break the seal." The witch fished a tiny jeweled knife out of her front suit pocket, raising it toward me. I wondered if this was what she'd had her hand on earlier when faced with the three of us outside the Brave. I doubted the blade would be capable of even scratching Beau.

Beau slammed his hand down on hers, crushing her fingers and the knife to the lime-green Formica. I hadn't even seen him move toward us.

Ember gasped.

The candle snuffed out. All the energy that had been slowly flowing around us snapped, dissipating in an instant.

Ember gritted her teeth, looking up at Beau and meeting his fierce gaze without flinching. Then she slowly lifted her free hand, reached across her pinned arm, and flicked the lid on the jewelry box closed.

So it wasn't just bluffing. The witch was fearless.

"The seal can be broken only by blood," she said calmly.

"No," Beau said.

"Blood magic?" I asked.

Ember turned her gaze on me, correcting my supposition snootily. "Legacy magic."

Beau snorted.

"Do you know differently, shifter?" Ember asked, meeting Beau's gaze again.

He smiled at her. Or, rather, he bared his teeth. The witch blanched, but didn't drop her gaze.

"Want to say something else stupid?" Beau asked sweetly.

"If Rochelle is who I think she is, then I'm bound to aid her in any way I can. To oversee her inheritance and protect her legally in any way needed."

"Why now?" Beau growled.

Ember swallowed. "The file fell to me when one of the partners passed last year. And there have been recent inquiries. Repeated inquiries by multiple parties through official and unofficial channels. They were ignored, as was legal and proper, but the possibility of a living heir came to light."

"By who specifically?" I asked. "Other ... relations?"

Ember flicked her gaze to me, probably not missing the

way my voice had wavered. "Not of your mother's bloodline."

"What does that mean?" Beau snarled.

"It means that no one had legal standing to access the file," Ember said with mounting frustration. "We're doing everything out of order. There is a process to these things, a way to broach and convey information. To ease a client —"

"I'm not that kind of client," I said, interrupting the witch before she started lecturing us on magical protocol. "I like things to be clear and straightforward."

"Until you prove who you are, I cannot address any of your questions. Not in the way you want me to, or with the level of detail required."

Beau lifted his hand off Ember's. She dropped the knife on the table and rubbed her freed fingers.

"One drop of blood?" Beau asked. "On the seal?"

The witch nodded.

Beau held his hand out to me, palm up.

I looked up at him. "This doesn't change anything ... whatever is in this envelope doesn't change anything between us."

"Of course not," Beau said. "Still, it's a choice. Your choice."

"We don't have a great track record with family."

Beau snorted.

I placed my right hand into his. He flipped it over, running his thumb across my palm and down my wrist.

A lovely flush of pleasure followed in the wake of his touch. Then his magic prickled against my skin and the tip of his thumb lengthened into a wickedly hooked tiger claw.

Ember moaned, then instantly muted herself as she cast her gaze to the table before her. She'd just figured out what level of shapeshifter she was dealing with. Henry must have been right about her magical senses not being terribly sharp. Most Adepts were carefully polite around Beau. Funnily enough, except for the fortune-teller dis, the witch had been more wary of me since she'd figured out who I was.

That didn't bode well for whatever was in the envelope.

I pressed my forefinger against Beau's manifested claw before I could think too much about it. Blood bloomed, then I felt the pinch of pain.

I disengaged my hand from Beau's and hovered it over the sealed parchment. "Do I have to say anything?"

Ember shook her head. "Just touch."

I pressed my bleeding finger to the seal, then swiftly removed it before it could grab me, or explode, or whatever magic thing it was going to do.

Beau handed me a folded paper towel. I pressed it to my bleeding finger.

The seal on the parchment cracked.

Ember sighed with great satisfaction.

"You get paid on commission, eh?" Beau asked snidely, passing me a Band-Aid and tugging the paper towel out of my hands.

"An estate fee. Yes," Ember said coolly.

I eyed Beau. It was rare for him to be ... well, not exactly rude, but definitely on the edge of it.

The parchment unfurled, revealing a smaller white envelope within its four wings. 'Rochelle Saintpaul' was printed across it in clear, precise, black-inked letters.

"Your mother died after you were born?" Ember asked. "But you didn't take her surname?"

"She died at the moment of my birth."

"But then how ..." Ember trailed off, then met my gaze. She was wondering how my mother could have known my name before I was even born.

I smiled, the expression tight against my teeth. "Oracle, remember?"

"She wouldn't have been able to see her own future, you said."

"But she could see mine. Can I take it?"

"You need to, in order to open the entire legacy package."

I didn't exactly know what that meant, since there wasn't anything else within the unfurled parchment. But I wasn't going to refuse a letter from my dead mother.

I plucked the white envelope out of its wrapper, but didn't immediately rip it open. I wasn't going to read it in front of a stranger. Even one who claimed she was my lawyer.

Magic fluttered and flowed across the previously blank envelope parchment, lifting it about two inches off the table. Then glowing letters and symbols inked in dark blue began to appear in streams of lines across its front and back. Hundreds of lines, thousands of words. The printing was so tiny I couldn't read a single one.

Unable to hide her eagerness, Ember lifted her briefcase onto the table and tucked the now-ink-covered parchment into it. She retrieved the copper ring and the snuffed-out tea light.

"Oh," she said, flipping the jewelry box open. "Resume recording." She met my gaze, then her eyes dropped to my hands and she frowned slightly.

Unaware that I was doing so, I was pressing the letter from my mother against my heart. I lowered my hands until they rested on the table, but I didn't manage to loosen my grip on the envelope.

"Do you know where your mother was buried?" Ember asked officiously.

"She was cremated ... by the government. She had no identification on her."

"And her remains?"

I shook my head. The question made me uncomfortably aware that I hadn't ever asked anyone that question myself. Simply surviving foster care since birth had kept me preoccupied enough on its own.

"City? State? A necromancer of power might be able to summon her shade if there is any dispute."

"Who would dispute ... and what?"

"I'll let you know once I get access to everything. City?"

"Vancouver, British Columbia, Canada."

"Ah, Godfrey territory."

"Is that a problem?"

"No, it's good. They'll have access to a necromancer powerful enough, if needed. A strong coven always attracts other capable Adepts."

Ember snapped the jewelry box shut and slipped it back into her briefcase.

"That's it?" I said.

"By the look of things, there is a lot to go over," Ember said. "It will take me a number of hours to retrieve and collate everything. Then possibly a couple of days to put together a file, so I can brief you coherently. There will be paperwork for you to sign. By the amount of detail revealed on the parchment, the legacy is more extensive than I was aware."

Beau snorted derisively.

Ember's eager expression hardened, but she didn't respond to his scorn. "And I'll need to sleep. I booked a room at the Summerland Waterfront Resort, just in case."

"I already asked Leanne to make up the bed in the

cottage I finished today," Beau said. "It'll be a good test run for the B&B."

Ember nodded. "Fine. I prefer to be near."

"You don't have to know what's in this, then?" I was still holding the white envelope too tightly. I eased my grip.

"No. Not unless you need me to know."

"And the blood on the seal?" Beau asked.

"Inert," Ember said. "As well, I'm oath bound to Rochelle now. So I couldn't harm her even if I wanted to."

"But others could take a sample of what you have collected."

Ember lifted her chin. "They could try."

"Now isn't the time for bravado, witch. We've faced foes and magic you couldn't even imagine."

"Are they after you now?"

"Not that I know of," Beau said.

"But life changes," I added. "Quickly."

Ember nodded. "The magic in your blood was used in unlocking the spell. It's dissipated."

Beau grunted, satisfied by the witch's answer.

Ember tugged a cellphone out of her pocket, unlocked the screen, and slid it across the table to me. "Your number?"

I added myself to her address book without comment, then sent a text to myself to confirm the connection. When it was done, Beau led Ember from the Brave.

I glanced down at the envelope that bore my mother's handwriting. The once-pristine-white paper was covered in smudged, blackened fingerprints. I had forgotten that I'd been rolling a piece of charcoal in my left hand for comfort.

I WAITED FOR BEAU TO RETURN BEFORE I OPENED what I was assuming was a letter from my mother. The regular-sized envelope wasn't sealed. My mother had simply tucked the flap inside, rather than licking the glue strip. The paper within was folded into a rectangle and looked to be about an eighth of an inch thick.

Beau stepped back into the Brave, immediately shutting out the dark of the night and turning the aftermarket lock on the door. This was one of several generations of locks, actually. The latest of which had been replaced in January after a run-in — literally — with Jade Godfrey.

He hesitated after taking a couple of steps inside, gazing at the envelope in my hands. Then he ran his hand over the back of his head and sighed heavily. "I don't like it."

"I know."

He nodded, closing the space between us and leaning over the dinette to brush a kiss against my lips. I lifted my face to his, wrapping my left hand around the back of his warm neck and feeling his magic dance underneath my palm.

"You haven't opened it?" He pressed another soft kiss against my parted lips.

"No."

I sucked lightly on his lower lip, then released him. I was comforted by his presence, but still totally anxious about the missive from my mother.

"Scoot over."

I dropped my satchel on the floor behind my feet, obligingly moving over so Beau could squeeze himself into the bench seat beside me. He had to wrap his right arm across the back of the seat and leave his left leg in the galley in order to fit next to me. I was completely sandwiched between him and the window. So it was perfect.

Without thinking much more about it, I slipped my thumb under the flap of the envelope and pulled it open. Then I freed the folded paper inside.

Unlike the utilitarian envelope, the paper of the letter was thick, similar to the pages of my more expensive sketch-books. The folds looked soft, not crisp, as if it had been opened and refolded many times.

I opened the letter.

Except it wasn't a letter. It was a black-inked drawing of a woman standing on a rocky cliff of some sort, with her hair blowing around her face and a cloak billowing behind her. The woman — a superhero, really — was holding a wicked-looking whip. It curled down from her right hand and snaked across the ground as if it were something alive. Her left hand was raised, holding aloft the wide chin of some terrible, black-scaled beast. She looked crazy powerful with the creature half-wound around her. Its claws — talons, really — had gouged the stone at her feet. But she was looking off into the distance, not at the demon before her.

"Holy crap," I whispered.

"Is that a demon?" Beau's arm had tensed across my back. He sounded as though he was forcing himself to speak.

"Yes." Though I was confident in my identification of the scaled beast — having seen demonic creatures in my visions before — I wasn't thrilled to be presented a drawing of one from my long-dead mother only hours after having a vision of a demon appearing in the orchard. Though I wasn't sure it was the same creature, a coincidence seemed unlikely.

"This is a ... do you think this is a vision?" Again, Beau sounded pained ... shocked and dismayed, maybe.

But I only had eyes for the inked drawing.

"Maybe." I peered down at the rendering, willing myself to see every little detail all at once. My heart was thumping — but almost happily. I'd never seen another oracle's vision. The woman was gazing into the sketched valley that lay below and beyond the cliff on which she stood. Every inch of the inked drawing was incredibly detailed, from her grip on the whip to the broken rock underneath her booted feet to the tiny evergreen trees way off in the distance. I could never render this level of clarity with charcoal, which lent my sketches a dreamy, arty quality. This vision was as sharp as reality.

"Huh. Do you think this looks familiar? With the mountain peaks beyond the deep valley?"

Beau didn't answer.

Then I noticed the tiny lettering in the bottom corner of the sketch.

Rochelle.
I'll love you forever.
– J.H.

"J.H.," I whispered. "My mother drew this."

"Yes." The single word sounded as if it had been squeezed from Beau's lungs.

"For me."

"Yes."

"Do you think this is her? I mean, supposedly she couldn't see her own future, but —"

"No."

"But why include it in the —"

"Rochelle."

"What?" Something was wrong with Beau, but I couldn't tear my gaze from the drawing. What if it disappeared if I looked away? What if there was something within it that I was supposed to see? Some message from my mother?

"Rochelle." The sharpness of Beau's tone cut through my enthralled mind.

I looked up at him, cranking my neck hard left in order to meet his gaze. His dark aquamarine eyes searched my face. He looked desperate … scared … but also thrilled?

"Beau?"

"Look at it again."

"I was looking!"

"Look again."

I glanced back at the drawing, searching for whatever was weirding Beau out.

"You think this is … something bad? Someone who might try to hurt us?"

"I don't know."

"I don't see what you see."

Beau reached around my neck, grabbing my right forearm lightly and drawing my hand back until my fingers rested underneath my mother's inscription.

"I still don't get it, Beau," I said, getting testy. "Just tell me."

"I'm trying, but …" He swallowed audibly, then pressed a kiss almost harshly against the side of my brow. "See the period after your name?"

"Sure. She knew my name. That's weird, but —"

"No. She was titling the sketch. The second part is the note to you."

"Titling the sketch? That's —" My gaze flew upward to the woman's face. To her subtly slanted eyes. To her bluntly cropped hair rendered in black ink but which might also be any color, including white. Like my hair. "— crazy ..."

I jerked away from the sketch, desperate to ignore or deny all the clues crashing together in my head.

"This isn't a self-portrait. Your mother wasn't part Asian. And you already said you think it's a vision. Of you."

"It can't be, Beau."

"It is."

I looked at the superhero — or maybe supervillain — etched in ink on the repeatedly folded paper before me. "She carried this with her for a long time."

"Yes."

"Does it smell like magic?"

"Yes."

"Like my magic?"

"Similar, but not the same."

"Because I'm not just an oracle."

"No."

I tore my gaze away from the drawing, looking at Beau for some sort of respite. I locked my hands together, fighting my sudden mad desire to seize the vision rendered in black ink and delivered to me by way of a magical legacy package, then tear it to shreds.

"It can't be," I repeated inanely.

"It is."

"There are no tattoos, Beau!" I cried. Then I slammed my hands over my mouth to swallow the sob of emotion threatening to explode from my chest.

Beau carefully pried my hands away from my face. Awkwardly in the cramped space between us and the table, he tilted my head up to accept his kiss. My spike of panic eased.

"It's you, Rochelle," he whispered against my cheek. "The woman in the drawing is you. I recognized you immediately."

"No." My protest sounded weak, even to me.

"But she changed you somehow. Your mother. Like you do, when you try to counter a vision. Maybe that's why you don't have any tattoos in the drawing."

"You think ... you mean ... if she hadn't died ... if I'd been raised by my birth family ... that this is who I would be?"

"I don't know. I don't know. If this was your vision, how would you interpret it?"

"It's a warning," I whispered. "It's some sort of warning. Otherwise, why put it in the legacy package?"

"Maybe."

"But the woman ... she's so powerful ... so strong ... and powerful ... and dark. So, so dark."

"Yes." Beau whispered it as if he'd been waiting years to hear me say those words, to acknowledge myself that way. "Strong ... and crafty. The kind of Adept even shapeshifters would cross the street to avoid."

I shoved the drawing away. It slid across the lime-green Formica of the table, tipped over the far edge, and slid out of my sight.

Then I turned to Beau, awkwardly half-rising out of the bench seat, sprawling across his lap, and wrapping my arms around his neck.

He met my desperate kiss with an equal intensity, half-lifting and half-dragging me away from the dinette to the bed at the back of the Brave.

We began in a tangle of limbs and clothing, kissing each newly exposed section of sensitive skin. Then stripping away each remaining layer, until our souls lay bare next to each other in the aftermath of bliss.

Words would come later. We'd figure out what the sketch meant later. We'd move on, or forward, or wherever we wanted to go or be.

Together.

I didn't know what future — thwarted or not — had been captured in my mother's drawing. What she'd reached out from the grave to tell me. To show me. What I was supposed to do with that information, either now or in the near future.

But I knew the present.

I knew every breath, every sigh, every touch, and every spasm of ecstasy in Beau's arms.

I knew it to be the utter truth — past, present, and future.

I LEFT THE COMFORT OF BEAU'S SLEEP-HEAVY ARMS in the deep of the night, scooped up my mother's vision captured in black ink from underneath the table, and carried it and my phone to the bathroom. After quietly shutting the door and flicking on the light, I took a picture of the drawing without examining it any further.

Then I texted the image to Blackwell.

This isn't my mother.

I sat on the toilet and waited for a response.

I didn't have to wait long. Even after five months of silence, I knew the sorcerer wouldn't ignore this message.

>*No. It isn't.*

Who is it?

I wanted to see if Blackwell would confirm what Beau thought, and what he'd pretty much persuaded me to be true. That I was the woman rendered in the drawing. Then I wanted to know everything the sorcerer hadn't been telling me. Every secret he'd kept carefully readied for just the right occasion, the perfect leverage.

Blackwell wasn't evil, but he wasn't good either.

And apparently, neither was I. Not in the future my mother had set down in ink and somehow delivered to me only hours after I'd seen a vision of a demon — possibly the same demon — tearing through the fabric of reality in a grove of cherry trees.

>*And this isn't your sketch.*

No. It isn't.

> *I'd have to see it in person.*

Hedging his bets, as expected.

First it's time you tell me what you know.

I waited longer this time, confirming that whatever Blackwell had been keeping from me, whatever his connection to my mother was, he didn't want me to know it. Or he wanted to carefully control his revelations.

>*Where did you get it?*

I'm not trading information. Tell me what you know.

More time passed. I stretched out my legs, pressing my feet against the back of the door. I was sleepy again all of a sudden, as if my brain could handle only the tiniest drips of information without needing to shut down.

>*Where are you?*

I thought about answering. About giving him the address in Summerland, then stepping outside to greet him in the dark of the night. But instead, I turned off the bathroom light and returned my mother's drawing to the dinette table.

My phone lit up with two other text messages as I was finishing a glass of water.

>*Rochelle?*

>*Face to face would be better for this conversation.*

"Yeah," I whispered. "I guessed that already."

I turned off my phone and crawled back into bed with Beau. Tomorrow in the daylight would be soon enough for more revelations. Plus, I was still pissed at the sorcerer. I wasn't a fan of being abandoned. And whether he saw his absence as such or not, I didn't care.

THREE

ROCHELLE.

A thick, low fog was rolling through the grassy patches between the trees, and clinging to my ankles as I walked through the orchard. I had never seen fog manifest like that before. It didn't get foggy in Vancouver very often, but when it did, it put the entire city into whiteout. That held true for most of the places we'd camped along the US northwest coast, similarly close to the ocean.

I glanced up at the sky, peering through thick, leaf-covered branches above me just as a cloud obscured the half-full moon. By the height of the dark trees, I assumed I was wandering through the cherry orchard. But I couldn't see any other distinguishing characteristics in the dark.

Which seriously called into question why the hell I was wandering around outside at all, let alone on the upper edge of the property so far from the Brave.

I paused.

The night was mild but not overly chilly. Perhaps I'd needed air? Though putting on some clothing would have been a great idea. Panties and a tank top were just inviting the bugs to a buffet.

A figure was standing with his back to me among the trees.

Dark hair, dark suit, pale skin.

Blackwell.

My heart thumped once, painfully. Why would the sorcerer be in the orchard in the middle of the night? Why would he show up without texting first? How did he even know where we were?

Blackwell tucked his hand up behind his back. Darkness was pooled in his palm.

Not darkness. Magic.

This wasn't a midnight stroll in the fog.

This was a vision.

A vision within a dream? Was that why I was surrounded by fog, not the mist that usually accompanied visions? Was I sleeping? Was that why I felt more present? Like I could feel the dry night air on my bare arms?

Rochelle. A deadened whisper echoed through my mind. The noise reached through my dream and imbedded itself into the darkest recesses of my soul. The voice was full of possessiveness. Though my name sounded overly articulated, as if the speaker was just learning to speak.

Blackwell whirled around, but he didn't look directly at me. He was looking at something beside me. His face blanched.

I turned my head.

The demon was standing next to me.

Me.

And it was looking at me, not at Blackwell.

It had clawed its way from the page on which my mother had rendered it and somehow appeared in this dream — this nightmare that might also somehow be a vision.

Fear rolled through my belly, but I refused to acknowledge it. This was a vision. I was in control of my magic. Well, at least in the sense of understanding that no harm could come to me within a vision. I was to observe and record.

Observe and record.

The demon tilted its head so that I was gazing directly into its black-smudged, crimson-orbed eyes. It was like looking into the pits of hell. If I'd believed in that sort of thing.

I forced myself to maintain eye contact, absorbing as much detail as possible. The creature was constructed out of scaled shadows, or maybe coal-colored smoke. I wasn't sure how I was going to draw it without more defined edges and —

The smell of death hit me. Curdled, spoiled, copper-tainted old blood. I'd never smelled anything like it before, yet I knew exactly what it was.

Death. Doom. Destruction.

"Run, you fool!" Blackwell shouted. Then he flung his deadly orbs of magic at me.

I threw my arms across my face, twisting away but unable to run.

And sat up in my bed, far from the cherry orchard and with Beau at my side.

"What is it?" he murmured.

A breeze tugged at the curtains across the window at my feet. The predawn light was touching the interior of the Brave. The rooster would be crowing in a few moments.

The remembered smell of carrion drifted across the bed. My stomach curled.

"A dream," I whispered. "Just a dream?"

"A vision?" Beau shifted up on his elbow.

"It couldn't be." I freed my limbs from the light cotton sheet I'd pulled up at some point in the night, more for comfort than warmth. I hung my legs off the edge of the bed, scrambling to gather my thoughts into some rational form. "I can't see myself. And I was in the dream. Me and Blackwell ..."

I omitted the second appearance of the demon, but only because I was trying to sort through the sequence of events. Had I experienced a vision while dreaming? Or influenced by my mother's drawing, had I somehow inter-mixed the two?

Beau caressed the small of my back. The comforting span of his hand was almost the same size as my waist.

The smell of carrion hit me again. My stomach revolted, and I gagged.

"What the hell?" Beau cried. "Crap. Something died in the orchard."

He climbed off the bed, sliding his warm, naked body past me as he snagged clothing from the shelves.

"You smell that?" I asked.

Beau tugged on a pair of boxers, then parted the curtains of the tiny window over the kitchen sink. The dim light washed across his smooth, muscled chest as he peered outside.

"You smell that?" I repeated.

"Yeah. It's okay," he said, turning to the door. "Not sure why I didn't notice it before it got this rancid, but I'll bury it now so we can get back to sleep."

He was halfway out the door before I could call him back. "But, Beau ... that smell ... that smell was in my dream."

He glanced back at me. "You probably just incorporated it," he said, though I could hear his concern.

I nodded. Then my left hand started to itch.

I lifted it, staring down at the offending palm as if I could discern some truth from the lines imprinted across my skin.

I looked up at Beau. "I have to draw."

"A vision, then."

The statement hung between us. Then I nodded, reaching for a T-shirt of Beau's and my satchel.

He muttered something under his breath. Then said more clearly, "I'll be right back."

I nodded, slipping the shirt on before crossing to the dinette with charcoal and sketchbook in hand.

Beau, still only in his boxers, stepped out of the Brave to search for a dead animal that I already knew didn't exist.

My magic told me so.

Except how could Beau have smelled it, then?

The oracle mist rolled across my mind's eye, taking my actual sight with it. I touched my sketchbook, smoothing my left hand across a pristine page. I would sketch and the dream would be untangled from the vision. I would get a glimpse of the actual future. Then I would figure out what needed figuring.

Time to draw, not time to think.

My magic told me so.

A ROOSTER CROWED.

No. My rooster crowed.

His muffled calls often woke me at dawn, after which I would lie in bed and listen to Beau breathing beside me. I'd visualize the deathlayer perched on his roost in the cozy interior of his coop with his hens all cuddled around him. The rooster would flap his wings, pumping his lungs full of air. Then he would thrust his breast forward and crow.

He claimed the dawn this way, defining his territory. It was a sound of comfort. Of permanence. Maybe even of home.

The rooster crowed again, its call pulling me out of the grasp of the oracle magic.

I was sitting in a warm pocket of early-morning light, but I was still completely blind.

Beau must have opened the curtains.

I could feel him nearby. Energy thrummed through the air to and from him. He was worried.

"You didn't find anything," I said.

"No. The smell just dissipated."

"Blackwell's coming."

"When? Here?" Beau's tone was sharp. "He doesn't know where we are. Does he?"

"No. Still, he's coming here, according to the vision. I'm going to shower."

"Can I look at the sketches?"

He always asked, even though I always let him. I loved his consideration.

"Yes. I haven't refined them yet, though. So I'm not sure what I saw. If it was a vision combined with a dream of my mother's drawing, or what." I rubbed my hand across my face. I was tired despite having just slept for hours and just needed a moment, or even better, a week to think through everything. Ember. The legacy package. My mother's vision. My visions of the demon. "Either way it's the same demon, I think."

I shifted out from the bench seat, perfectly oriented in the Brave despite the fact that I was still blinded by the white mist that accompanied every vision.

But Beau reached out for me, guiding me toward him rather than the bathroom. I wrapped my arms around his shoulders and pressed my cheek into his chest.

"You got dressed," I said with a playful groan of disappointment.

He laughed huskily. "Easily remedied."

I ran my hand up his back, feeling the energy of his magic settle. The smell of carrion manifesting in a vision, then occurring in the real world only to dissipate without explanation ... Well, that was crazy on a level we hadn't experienced yet. He didn't like feeling out of control. But then, neither did I. I just had more practice at it. At least, with my mind and my magic.

My life was a different story. No one told me what to do or where to go anymore. Too many of my twenty-one years had been controlled by others.

But maintaining that level of control now was really only possible because Beau and I were both essentially motivated by utter selfishness. Putting each other's wants and needs above all else.

I sighed as I disengaged from my delectable boyfriend. "I should shower."

Beau nodded. Even without being able to clearly see his face, I could tell that his mind was already on the sketches spread across the dinette.

So I showered.

Life didn't stop, right? It didn't slow down so I could catch my breath. All I could do was be ready for the next vision. The next set of clues. The terrible fate waiting to unfold.

So I might as well be clean and dressed in comfortable clothing.

No, life didn't stop. Not even when a demon whispered my name in a vision. Not even when an oracle wasn't supposed to be able to see her own future — if that was what was happening with the demon. Not even when the lines of reality started to get blurred. Again.

Yeah, it wasn't a dream.

Steady onward.

WHEN I CLIMBED OUT OF THE SHOWER, BEAU WAS still hunched over the dinette with my sketchbook open before him, comparing one of my newest sketches to my mother's inked drawing. I couldn't see which sketch had captured Beau's attention so thoroughly. Bent over with his hands on either edge of the table, Beau completely blocked the galley back to the bed. And my access to clothing.

"I agree. It's the same creature as in your mother's drawing," he said without looking up. "Same demon, or whatever."

"It could still be a coincidence, Beau."

"Look at the jaw and the eyes. I can't figure out if the thing looks like an overgrown lizard crossed with a weasel, or what. Some kind of bird of prey crossed with a goat."

I toweled off my hair. I'd thought I was ready for this conversation. I wasn't. But there was no way to avoid it. No reason to avoid it. At least, no good reason.

I pressed past Beau, who obligingly shimmied forward without lifting his gaze from the sketches. I caught a glimpse of the sketch he was comparing with my mother's drawing. It was a detail shot of the demon's head. The moment right before it had whispered in my mind. Right before it called me by name. At least, I think that had been the demon's terrible, soul-destroying voice that I'd heard.

I shivered.

Beau looked up. His brow was lined with concern.

Scared of admitting what I almost knew to be the truth already, I thought about waiting for more information, for more clarification. But Beau and I didn't hold things back from each other. "It knows my name," I said, forcing myself to speak firmly while I grabbed clothing from the shelves beside the bed. "Unless I somehow mixed up my ... uneasiness about my mother's drawing with what the oracle magic was trying to show me. The demon spoke to me."

"It spoke to you? Out loud? In English?"

"Actually ... I'm not sure. I'm not sure, Beau." Despite my best efforts to be rational, my voice was strained.

"It's okay. We're figuring it out. That's what we do, right?"

"Yeah." I forced myself to smile. "Yeah."

He grinned and my expression became more genuine. It was just a vision. A warning. Warnings could be heeded.

"It's the tilt of the head that really sells the resemblance," I said, tugging a pair of perfectly worn blue jeans on over fuchsia lace panties. "But what if I was influenced by seeing my mother's drawing last night?"

"It doesn't usually work that way, does it?"

"I'm not sure I have anything to compare it to." I clipped on a matching bra and yanked a black T-shirt over my head. "I've never had a vision while sleeping. Not one that I recognized as a vision, anyway. I've never studied another oracle's vision, let alone one from my dead mother."

Tugging my necklace — which I wore even when showering now — free of my T-shirt, I crossed closer, leaning over Beau's shoulder to get a better look at the drawing he had open in my sketchbook.

"It'll be too warm today for jeans," Beau said absentmindedly. "High of eighty." He reached back to cup my ass. "Twenty-seven degrees, I mean." He corrected his weather report for my Canadian understanding of temperature.

"I'll change after breakfast."

He nodded, moving my mother's drawing closer to the corner of the table nearest to me. "She loved you," he whispered, brushing his fingers over the tiny lettering in the corner of the sketch.

"She ... she loved the idea of me, I guess." Though I tried to keep them light, the words got caught in my throat.

Beau tugged me into the haven of his arms, effectively pinning my back against his chest and my lower stomach against the edge of the table. It was a tight squeeze, but I didn't complain.

"She could see you, Rochelle," he said, tapping the lettering lightly but emphatically. "She loved you."

A tear rolled unbidden down my face, but I wasn't sad. I wasn't terrified. I was just full. So full I had to release something. "You think so?"

"I know."

I nodded, brushing the tears threatening to blur my vision away. Then I slid my mother's drawing to the side so I could examine my own sketch. "So. A demon."

"Yep."

"We'd better get Henry to look at these. After I refine

them further. See if he can identify it. Though I'm guessing not. A cowboy with magical handcuffs and a mighty sense of the ethical doesn't meld with demons. In my mind, anyway."

Beau grunted in agreement.

"And I guess we'd better tell … someone … someone in authority."

"Not yet," Beau said.

"Why not?"

"Just not yet."

"Beau," I whispered, already knowing what he was going to say and dreading his answer. I was dreading confronting anything having to do with the demon at all, actually. "What are you thinking?"

Beau reached over, dragging my mother's drawing back so that it covered my open sketchbook. He stared at it without speaking for a long time. Then he whispered, "Maybe … maybe it's your demon."

"My … that's insane," I said, trying to convince myself as well as him. "That can't be. Just because you think that's me in my mother's drawing —"

"It's you."

I pivoted, turning so I could look him in the eye. He stepped back to give me room to move, leaning against the kitchen counter and settling his hands on my hips.

"Demons are … evil."

Beau nodded thoughtfully, but he didn't break his gaze from mine.

"And I'm not. And I'm not going to be. The demon, if it even is the same one, might have been tied to the woman in the drawing somehow, but I'm not her."

"I know. So let's just ask some questions first."

I half-turned, rapidly flipping through the charcoal-smudged drawings in my sketchbook. "The leaves look the same on the trees as they look right now. With the immature fruit and everything. This could happen tonight."

"Not tonight." Beau leaned past me to flip the pages back to a different sketch. It showed a wider view of the cherry trees, with Blackwell's profile in the foreground and the cloudy evening sky above. "See the last quarter moon? It's smaller, waning more than it is now." Beau had spent the weeks we'd travelled back from Mississippi to Portland with Henry and Kandy, studying moon cycle charts. They'd been concerned about the marshal transforming with the full moon while we were on the road.

"If it's an accurate representation."

"The visions usually are," Beau said grimly.

"How many days, then?"

"Two? Maybe three? If it's even this year. And if we don't do something to change it."

"Events are apparently unfolding," I said wryly.

Beau snorted at my attempt at humor. "You texted Blackwell, right?"

"Last night. But I didn't tell him where we were."

Beau flipped through the sketches again. He found one that depicted Blackwell almost hidden in the trees to the far left, while the shadow of the demon's head half-manifested on the far right of the page. I didn't remember seeing them positioned together in my mind, which lent credence to the notion that I had mixed up the details of a vision with a dream. Or, rather, a nightmare of the future my mother had envisioned for me.

"Send him this one."

"It's not done."

"Send it. He should see it, unfinished or not."

"Then what?"

"Then breakfast. I'm starving."

I nodded, dutifully reaching for my phone even as I hesitated with my other hand hovering over my mother's drawing. Then I picked it up, carefully folded it along its already well-worn lines, and tucked it into the inner pocket of my satchel.

I glanced over at Beau, questioning my decision to put my mother's drawing away.

He nodded, agreeing.

We would get Henry to consult on my sketches, to help us interpret them. But I wanted to hold the future my mother had envisioned for me hostage for a little while longer.

Maybe it would never be.

No matter what Beau thought, I certainly couldn't see any aspect of myself in the fierce woman with the whip, who was somehow aligned with the demon on the cliff. And I wasn't sure I wanted Henry to see me that way either. Not yet, at least.

Plus, I was pretty sure I had no idea how to even hold a whip, let alone wield one. So the world was safe from a whip-wielding me.

For now, I needed to just assume my mother had thwarted that future somehow.

Funny. I had texted her black-inked drawing to Blackwell without a second thought the previous night. As I took a picture of the sketch I was going to send him now, I thought about what that said about how I perceived both the sorcerer and myself. Both of us were capable of seeing the many shades between black and white on the good-and-evil scale. Possibly too well. There was a comfortability in that connection that I didn't share with anyone else. Again, I wasn't sure that was a good thing.

WE'D BEEN WANDERING UP TO THE MAIN HOUSE for breakfast around 8 a.m. for the previous week. As a test run of the 'breakfast' part of B&B. Leanne was still trying to get me to bend my no-meat policy with her homemade pasture-raised chicken sausage. But though I had no issue with eating eggs from our hens, I still drew a firm line at killing animals for food.

She had warned me about the fifty-fifty possibility of hatching cockerels once she began trying to expand the laying flock in the fall. Cockerels couldn't just hang out in the orchard. They'd kill — or at a minimum, maim — each other fighting over the hens. So they had to be raised for meat. But ethical meat, as Leanne called it.

I wasn't sure Beau and I would be sticking around that long, though. Even if technically they were my chickens. Even if I was getting slowly accustomed to the idea of being connected to ... something. Something other than the Brave and Beau. Though I couldn't quite imagine towing chickens at the back of the RV.

Leanne and Eddie were quietly chatting and moving about in the kitchen as we crossed around the house, then climbed up onto the back patio, passing alongside the extensive garden that filled the upper yard as we did. A white sunshade had been pulled out from under the eaves, casting welcome shade across the long, grayed-cedar trestle table that took up most of the brown-painted wooden deck. Screened sliding doors led through the eating area and into the large kitchen beyond. Leanne was bustling back and forth setting various dishes on the table. Smaller round slat tables of similarly grayed cedar were squeezed into opposite corners of the deck, both set with tilted white umbrellas.

Henry had claimed the center of the trestle table, sitting with his back to the kitchen and poring over a local real estate paper. He'd circled three properties on the front page.

Ember was well situated at the table farthest away from the sliding doors and Henry. She'd swapped out her power pantsuit for a pale peach silk blouse, a cream linen A-line skirt, and gold-beaded sandals. She appeared to be working her way through a small mountain of papers that she'd fanned out in stacks along the edge of her briefcase, then had trapped there by closing the lid. It was an easy guess that this arrangement avoided losing any documents to the light breeze. Or to the two eleven-year-olds who were prone to jumping into motion without warning.

"Beau!" Krista shouted, launching herself off her seat on the bench opposite Henry and into Beau's arms. Zero to sixty and all that.

I sidestepped, barely avoiding getting hit in the face by a flailing limb.

Beau caught the girl in midair, threw her up in a spin, caught her a second time, then set her down on her feet, facing in the opposite direction.

Krista nearly collapsed in a fit of giggles. Seven days and counting. Apparently, this game never got old.

Calvin hopped up from the trestle table, holding a buttermilk pancake aloft in either hand.

"Food. Hands," Leanne snapped, stepping out through the sliding doors. She placed a jug of fresh-squeezed orange juice next to the platter of pancakes in the middle of the large table.

Calvin spun back, dropped the pancakes onto his plate,

and carefully wiped his hands on his cloth napkin. Then he raced over to Beau and exchanged a complicated fist-bump handshake that ended in a manly round of backslapping that would have left me face down on the deck.

"Good morning," I murmured, reaching for the juice and circling around to settle in beside Henry.

"Rochelle," he said without looking up from his paper, "the witch has been waiting for you."

"I was going to come to the Brave —" Ember said.

"But I redirected her." Henry took a swig of his coffee.

"I am her lawyer."

"We've already had this argument."

Ember snapped her mouth closed on whatever she was going to retort, and took a prim sip of her tea instead.

Krista and Calvin returned to the table with Beau in tow. He settled onto the wooden bench opposite me, with a twin on either side. Calvin practically had to climb over the table to reach across and retrieve his plate.

"I have the first round of papers for you to sign," Ember said, eyeing Beau.

"First round?"

"Yes. The estate is rather ... complicated." The witch lawyer side-eyed Beau for a moment longer.

He lifted an eyebrow in her direction. She dropped her gaze and the subject.

Apparently, the witch had some sort of issue with Beau. That was unusual. And pretty amusing.

I smirked at him.

He grinned back, plucking a plate from the top of the stack at the end of the table. He dropped two pancakes onto the plate, then held it out to me.

Krista watched this exchange intently.

"Thank you," I said carefully.

"Butter? Maple syrup?" he asked.

"Yes, please."

Seemingly satisfied that the niceties of society were being upheld, the twins reapplied their attention to breakfast.

I topped up Henry's coffee, then poured a mug for Beau. The sorcerer grunted his thanks as Beau snagged the creamer, then practically dumped its entire contents into his mug.

For a moment, we were one big happy family.

And though I was way on the outside fringes of that family even here, I didn't have any urge to run away — declaring my freedom and my right to choose.

Compared to the life I used to lead, that was seriously weird.

"The estate appears to hold three properties so far," Ember said, excitedly muttering more to herself than anyone else. "I'd like to get them transferred into your name as soon as possible. But I'll need you to select your primary residence, for property tax purposes. Among other things."

A knot twisted in my belly. The sounds of happy eating abated. Beau lifted his dark aquamarine eyes to meet my tense gaze. He slowly chewed whatever bite he had in his mouth, stretching his leg underneath the table and pressing his ankle against mine.

Leanne carefully placed a platter of sausages and bacon near Beau, tousling Calvin's hair as she headed back to the kitchen.

"What's an estate?" Krista asked, blinking at all the quiet adults.

Henry carefully folded his paper, then placed it beside his empty plate.

I took a sip of orange juice. My pancakes were steadily

getting cold, but I didn't feel up to wielding my knife and fork.

Ember looked up from her notes, as if just coming to the realization that no one had responded to her. She glanced around. Then looked at me.

"Money. Property. You know," I said, answering Krista. "My mom left me some stuff in her will."

"Oh," the towheaded twin said. "Your mom died?"

"Yeah." I took another tiny sip of orange juice, attempting to behave normally. My mind was a blank, though. After the first spike of uncertainty, I felt oddly disengaged from the conversation — and even more so from the very idea of an estate, or property, or my mother's last will and testament.

Legacy. The Adept referred to all of that as a legacy.

"I'm sorry," Calvin said.

I looked over at the boy and nodded.

"I'm only about halfway —" Ember said.

"Not the time or place," Henry interrupted cordially, reaching for the sausages.

I locked my gaze back to Beau's.

Estate. Property. Three properties. At minimum.

"The Hawthornes are an old family," Henry leaned in to murmur to me, though any and all shapeshifters in the vicinity would be able to hear him anyway. "I gather you're the last living descendant."

I kept my gaze on Beau. My throat was tight, and the twist in my belly had turned into a weighty lump. His face was placid, but his eyes were full of compassion. I could feel his warmth even through my jeans, though our ankles were barely touching.

"How do you know?" I asked Henry, forcing myself to speak calmly.

"I've looked into it," the sorcerer said. "I was ... interested in the possible connection. I'm sure Blackwell has as well." He eyed Ember questioningly, but the witch didn't look up from her papers.

"When?" Beau asked. "When we met?"

"After. It took some digging, and I wasn't actually sure I'd found anything at all. No proof of relationship. Otherwise, I would have said something."

"Adepts stay off grid easily enough," Beau said, speaking to me. Coddling me.

"I already knew I was an orphan, Beau." I shifted my attention to my cold pancakes.

Leanne exited the kitchen again, carrying a platter of scrambled eggs and fried tomatoes. She was swiftly followed by Eddie. The werewolf and coyote shifters joined us at the table, and even Ember ignored her paperwork for a moment to partake in the huge breakfast.

Beau shifted, hooking his foot behind my ankle and bouncing my leg playfully. I smiled down at my perfectly fluffy, perfectly tasty eggs, reminding myself that the trappings of life didn't really exist for Beau and me. Not unless we chose to let such things in.

"So you aren't legally married?" Ember asked.

I paced the length of the cleared trestle table, wishing I was anywhere but trapped on the back patio with the witch. It felt as though we'd been shuffling papers for hours, though it likely hadn't been much more than forty-five minutes. "No."

Oblivious to my frustration, Ember continued needling me with questions. "I'll have to check the Canadian statute. Have you shared a fixed address for more than six months?"

"Define fixed," I growled.

The witch glanced up at me. She was wearing a pair of gold horn-rimmed reading glasses that magnified her eyes oddly. She opened her mouth to answer me, but I cut her off.

"Just spit out whatever you're trying to say. I'm not interested in ..." I waved my hand to indicate the mass of papers and their accompanying questions.

"We should draw up a relationship agreement," she said. "It's like a prenup. For your protection."

"No."

"All right," Beau said, wandering around the side of the house, then jogging up the short stairs to the patio. "Henry's looking at the sketches."

"Sketches?" Ember echoed. "Do you ... draw your visions?" Her weirdly magnified gaze fell to my tattoos.

"I'm not interested in any relationship agreement," I said, more to Beau than Ember. "End of conversation."

Ember huffed out a sigh, then returned to her papers. "As far as I can tell at present, the houses in San Francisco and Philadelphia have been sitting empty, but were magically sealed upon your mother's death. The last acquisition before your mother's death is an apartment in Vancouver ..." — she consulted another set of papers — "... So maybe it was a rental property, unless ..." The witch trailed off awkwardly.

I looked away, leaning back against the railing with my arms crossed. I let my gaze settle on a grouping of mature weeping willows that stood on the south side of the house. They'd probably been originally planted to provide shade.

"Unless my mother bought it with the intention of living in it but never got to the moving-in part," I said. "You know, because she died."

Ember pursed her lips and tapped her gold metal pen on the table. "I can investigate the dates further. But the documents appear to have been filed only a few days before Jane's death. Perhaps it was a transfer of ownership … or a payment of some kind."

I looked up at Beau. "So what was the Oracle of Philadelphia doing in Vancouver?"

"Adepts relocate all the time," Ember said. "The Godfrey coven is —"

"Why now?" I'd asked the witch that question before, but I wanted the full answer this time. "My mother has been dead for over twenty-one years. Why is this all happening now?"

"No one knew —"

"I thought a missing person can be declared dead after, like, seven years or something." I was aware that my voice was becoming strained but unable to fully stop it from happening.

"Not Adepts," Ember said quietly. "Adepts live long, often solitary, lives. And there aren't many oracles. They usually align themselves with a coven."

"But my mother married a sorcerer."

"Actually, I'm not sure they were legally married. Again, that's not uncommon for …"

I covered my face with my hands. My brain felt as if it might be melting from too much information, too quickly. Though I hadn't sought or even really needed to know any of it, it was still a lot to absorb.

Ember reverted to paper-shuffling mode.

"Write all this down," Beau said.

"Excuse me?" Ember asked.

"In a report. You can do that, can't you?"

"Yes, of course. I had every intention ... I didn't realize this would be so ..."

"Now you do."

I dropped my hands from my face. "And you'd better go back to Seattle."

Ember gathered up her papers, looking utterly aghast at my suggestion. "There are important documents that need to be signed."

"They've waited twenty-plus years. What does a few more months matter?"

"Months? No. Things are in limbo now. Bank accounts have to be unfrozen. The properties need to continue to be maintained."

"You might have mentioned that before you had Rochelle trigger it all, witch," Beau growled.

"I didn't know how extensive the legacy would be."

"You knew oracles were rare," Beau said. "What were the chances that the legacy package wasn't worth a trip to Canada and more than a couple of weeks of billing? You knew that a legacy like this, if you were right, would cement your place in your damn law firm."

Ember raised her chin. "This is my job. I'm not going to apologize for it."

"Then try some compassion."

"Rochelle has my oath."

"And you have a lot of billable hours. Hell, this is a lifetime of work, isn't it?"

Magic shifted across the patio as Ember scrambled to

her feet. Beau's energy and the witch's power clashed, rippling across my skin uncomfortably.

"That's enough," I said. "I'm fine. Just break it down for me a bit more, please. Then we'll figure out what to do with it all."

"I would advise —"

"Later," I snapped. But then I softened my tone. "Please. Later. There are other things going on here. I'm not sure you should stay."

"Do you know of ... have you seen a direct threat against me?"

"No, but —"

"Then I'll see you through this," Ember said.

I swallowed my frustration, concerned that the witch would be more of a hindrance than a help. And possible demon fodder. But I didn't know how magic worked. Maybe the witch was supposed to be here. Maybe that was why she'd shown up out of the blue.

"Thank you," was all I said.

"We should set a meeting," Ember said. "I'll need a few more hours before I have a solid understanding of the breadth of the legacy. Shall we say after lunch? Two o'clock?"

"Fine. Good." I felt relieved by the offered reprieve. And a bit cowardly as a result. "Please text me if you need more time."

"I will." Ember snapped her briefcase shut. Then, with a glance in Beau's direction and a nod to me, she hustled off the patio toward her cottage with her phone already to her ear.

I reached for Beau, tangling my fingers through his. We stood like that for a moment without speaking, a ton of unanswered questions hanging all around us but none of them immediately important.

I could hear Eddie humming somewhere nearby, probably out in the huge garden behind me. I couldn't see him past a wall of well-picked green-pea vines, though.

"Henry's in the Brave?" I finally asked.

"Yeah." Beau rubbed his thumb across the butterfly tattoo on my left inner wrist. "Did you hear back from Blackwell?"

"Not yet." I squeezed his hand, stepping closer. "Take me somewhere?"

"Somewhere?" Beau said, wagging his eyebrows at me.

I slid my hand around his waist, then down to grab his ass. "Yeah. Somewhere."

"I know just the place."

I STARED UP AT THE TREE HOUSE PERCHED AT least fifteen feet off the ground in between three massive, sloping weeping willow tree branches. It had been newly painted in electric blue. "That ... doesn't look particularly safe," I said.

"Did you want to be safe?" Beau caressed the back of my neck.

I laughed, ignoring the shiver of desire running down my spine. "Yes."

He chortled, stepping past me to tug on a length of rope looped over a lower branch. A rope ladder tumbled down, its wooden rungs also looking freshly painted. And the bright-yellow ropes knotted through holes bored in each end of every tread were definitely new.

"I finished fixing it up yesterday." Beau winked at me, playing it up. "With plans to bring you here already rolling around in my mind."

"What about the kids?"

"They've got some sort of outdoor survival day camp on Sundays." Beau reached out for my hand. "Climb up in front of me."

"In case I fall?"

"Nah. So I can ogle your ass."

I threw my head back and laughed. Then I reached for the nearest rung and climbed up into the tree house without further protest.

Inside, the light filtering through the open window barely illuminated the tiny wooden table and the chairs tucked into one corner. One of the chairs was painted red, while the other was blue.

I stooped slightly as I crossed to the window, though I knew I wasn't in any danger of hitting my head. The breeze stirred the light-green waterfall of willow branches hanging all around us, and I caught a glimpse of the roof of the Brave, way down the hill and to the left of us. Closer in, I could see the peaked roof of the cottage Henry was occupying, just below the peach and nectarine trees.

Beau and I were practically hidden away from the world. Though only if I ignored the fact that all the Adepts on the property could most likely track us with their magical senses.

As Beau pulled the ladder back into the tree house, he couldn't stand upright. Not even remotely. Even crouched over the opening in the floor, his body filled almost every inch of the available interior space. He grinned at me as he piled the ladder off to one side.

"Blankets in the cupboard," he said.

I looked around, spying an all-but-hidden cupboard beside an empty bookshelf built into the wall perpendicular to the table and chairs.

I opened the cupboard and pulled a light-blue fleece blanket off the top shelf, turning back to find Beau already sitting against the far wall. His legs practically stretched across the full width of the floor. From the second shelf, I grabbed a square pillow printed with a yellow lightning bolt and a quote from Harry Potter — *I solemnly swear that I am up to no good*.

I'd never actually read any of the Harry Potter books or seen the films. Fantasy never had been my thing. Given how my own life had turned out, as an orphan discovering she had magical powers, that was maybe a little ironic.

I threw the pillow and the blanket at Beau. "Planning on a nap?"

He caught the soft projectiles, immediately tucking the pillow behind his head. "Good plan," he said closing his eyes with a satisfied sigh. "Someone woke me up too early."

My stomach dipped at the reminder of what had woken me that morning. I turned back to the cupboard to grab a second pillow. This one was printed with the quote, *Mischief managed*. Beau had found the pillows on Etsy for the kids. They were a great choice.

"Rochelle," he whispered.

I met his earnest gaze.

"I'm here. Always."

I nodded. "But let's forget it for a few minutes?"

"Minutes? I was hoping for at least an hour."

I threw the second pillow at him. He laughed, then

tossed both pillows into the corner and reached up to do the same with his deep-blue T-shirt.

"Those jeans look too hot," he said huskily.

"Yes," I said, as earnestly as possible. "It's a terrible problem in need of immediate solving."

A grin curled across his face. My heart skipped a beat. I removed my sunglasses, placing them out of harm's way on the bookshelf. Then I pulled my T-shirt off, making sure to arch my back a little more than necessary.

Beau's grin widened. "Nice bra."

I nodded, deadly serious. "And my underwear matches."

"Show me."

I hooked my thumbs in my waistband at the sides of my hips. Then I ran them just underneath the fabric to meet at my navel, toying with the top button over my zipper. I bit my lip. "I'm not sure."

"Oh?" Beau asked, raising his eyebrows.

I undid the button on my jeans, then tugged the zipper down about an inch. Just enough to reveal the lacy top edge of my bright-fuchsia underwear. "Yeah, I mean, what if someone hears us?"

Beau nodded sagely. "Always a possibility when sharing property with a bunch of shapeshifters."

I kicked off my sneakers, shimmying my jeans down over my hips. I made a show of bending over much farther than necessary to pull them off over my feet. "Well," I said, still bent over and peering at Beau through the hair that had fallen over my eyes, "you'd better not do any screaming."

I dropped to my hands and knees. Beau was out of the rest of his clothing before I'd crawled the three feet into his lap.

I might not have been beautiful or what some would

consider pretty. But for Beau, I was sexy. And that was all that mattered.

He unclipped my bra with a swift, practiced move. Then he latched on to one of my nipples, then the other, as he divested me of my pretty panties.

I settled down over him without further preamble or playful chatter. Neither of us needed any more warming up.

Beau gripped my hips, immediately accepting my rapid and rather unsteady rhythm. When he and I had first gotten together, he'd liked to be in control. Above all else, he didn't like to be rushed. But I'd convinced him that multiple goes were a good thing. And that a practiced performance wasn't necessarily better than a tight, quick improv. Just different. And just as fulfilling.

My well-primed and desperately needed orgasm bloomed from low and deep inside me, lapping up over me as delicious, uncontrollable shudders. I flung my head back, ceding the rhythm and stroke to Beau, and allowing the wave of bliss to wipe my mind of any other care. If only for the moment.

>*I'd like to discuss the sketches. Are you nearby?*

>*I have a few more questions for you to answer before we meet. Should I text them or just come by the RV?*

>*Could you help me put the final coat of sealer on the bathroom tile in the cherry grove cottage this afternoon?*

Our phones started buzzing with text messages ten minutes into the nap that had ended our lovemaking session. Henry, Ember, and Eddie all wanted our attention. By mutual unspoken agreement, Beau and I ignored them all, opting to doze in the willow-sheltered tree house for a bit longer.

Beau's breathing was deep and lengthy underneath my hand, which was lazily splayed across his chest. I'd tugged the fleece blanket underneath me, so that I was lying on half of it and partially covered from the waist down with the other half. But Beau was sprawled out naked, almost touching the opposite walls with his head and toes. Well, he was naked except for the side of his body I was curled along.

"I thought being nomads meant we could avoid responsibility ... and family," I murmured into Beau's chest. "Though the family part is new for me."

He grunted, agreeing with me but still slumbering.

Unfortunately, once woken, I couldn't drift off again. "Do you think the visions are tied to the legacy thing? The timing sort of lines up."

"Maybe." Beau ran his hand down my arm to cup my ass. "We'll know soon enough."

"Yeah ... and apparently I'm an heiress," I said, clumsily shoving the awkward topic into our blissful moment.

"Apparently."

"Does that bother you?"

"Nope."

"Money comes with strings."

"Maybe."

"You're being terribly verbose," I groused.

Beau chuckled quietly. "I'm here for as long as you want me, Rochelle. Money, no money. Demons, witches, sorcerers ... responsibilities. I'm here."

"I hate it when you phrase it like that. As long as I want

you. Like anything else is even an option. When you know it isn't."

Beau rolled toward me, so that I was partially cradled underneath him instead of beside him. He kissed me lightly, almost teasingly. Then, not touching me anywhere else, he increased the intensity and length of the lip lock until I was breathless — and more than a little primed for a second round of lovemaking.

My phone buzzed again.

Beau growled, pressing his forehead against mine.

I sighed, then pushed against his chest until I could look him in the eye. "I don't like the paperwork crap. Every time I sign something, I feel like I'm losing a piece of myself."

"I know." Beau kissed me lightly, then rolled over onto his back to gaze thoughtfully up at the slatted ceiling. "But I think it's more like you're gathering pieces, you know? Of the puzzle. Of you before you were born. And it feels heavy because it's not simple."

"I don't think my life was ever particularly simple."

"But you knew your life. You knew what to expect, and how to act. And now you're embracing your magic. And, I guess, your heritage."

I closed my eyes, breathing through the rush of unaccustomed anxiety that his words had unleashed. "I don't want to be her," I whispered, feeling tears threatening at the back of my throat. Again.

"Her?"

"In the picture. The drawing from my mom."

"You already aren't her. Your mom somehow saw to that."

"By dying."

"Yeah, I guess. Though I doubt that was her overall

plan. Otherwise, why would she have bought an apartment in Vancouver?"

My phone buzzed again. Beau sat up and reached across me to grab it, tapping my password in with his thumb.

"Henry?" I asked.

"Yeah. He's got to look into something. He'll meet us back at the Brave in an hour."

I nodded. Pressing a kiss into Beau's neck, I hid my face against his warm chest, warring with my emotions.

"I hate not having all the information," I said. "It's so difficult making decisions while I'm still waiting to figure out all the options. Never mind making the right decisions."

"We never do have all the information. Not until it's all said and done."

That was terribly true. "Only glimpses," I whispered.

"Yeah. But we know this." Beau ran his fingers down my arm, tracing the coiled path of my barbed-wire tattoo. Then, lifting my arm, he pressed a kiss against the butterfly tattoo on my wrist.

Energy prickled between us.

Magic.

Our combined magic.

I smiled at him. "Yeah. We always know this."

FOUR

"Henry's on his way."

Beau's text messages had been on fire all through the late morning and into lunch. I gathered that he was in communication with the pack and Kandy, as well as Henry and Ember, running interference while I refined my sketches from last night's vision.

I was going to have to cope on my own for the afternoon, though, because Beau needed to get back to helping Eddie prepare the cottages for the grand opening.

Someone knocked on the door to the Brave — two quick double taps.

I looked up from the sketches I had spread out all over the lime-green kitchen table. "Well, that was quick."

Beau placed a cautioning hand on my left shoulder. A moment before, he'd been lying on the back bed. He was frowning in the direction of the door, which told me it wasn't anyone we knew knocking. And apparently he hadn't heard anyone else approach, which was exceedingly odd.

I opened my mouth to call out to whoever was there.

Beau shook his head at me, then padded almost silently to the nose of the RV. The curtains were half-closed on the open window next to the door. He placed his hand on the sloped paneling overhead, leaning over the window and breathing through his slightly open mouth. Trying to scent the air.

"Adept." He murmured so quietly that I barely heard him. "Sorcerer. Different sorcerer."

Shapeshifters could identify Adepts by the scent of their magic, as long as they'd encountered them before. It was a trait I would have loved to share, but I only occasionally sensed any magical energy from even the most powerful people. Even more rarely, I might catch a glimpse of a color that seemed to represent an Adept's magic, like the green that rolled across Beau's eyes, or the golden hue of Jade Godfrey's hair, or the blue-black orbs that Blackwell wielded.

Beau glanced back at me, nodding toward the table. Taking his cue, I gathered my loose sketches into a pile, then tucked them underneath my sketchbook against the wall.

Beau waited until I was done. Then he opened the door.

I stayed seated. This was our new routine when dealing with the occasional random Adepts who had been showing up at the Brave.

"I seek the oracle," a woman said from outside.

Beau didn't answer, eyeing the woman from across the threshold. I didn't recognize her voice, nor could I see her. But pressing my face against the window to get a glimpse down the exterior side of the RV seemed undignified for an oracle. Or anyone over twelve years old.

"Who sent you?" Beau asked.

"I come as a supplicant," the woman said smoothly —

and not particularly reverently, despite the weirdness of the assertion. "With an offering and without ill intent. Certainly, you can smell my honesty, shifter."

Tension twisted through Beau's shoulders. Whoever the woman was, he didn't like her, and people Beau didn't like on an instinctive level were few and far between. But now we'd met two of them in two days, Ember being the first. Though I was fairly certain his dislike of the lawyer witch was due to her upsetting our lives rather spectacularly, rather than any perceived malicious intent. But I had no idea what was ticking him off about the woman currently standing at our door.

"Will you let me pass?" she asked, her tone on the edge of derisive. "Or must all supplicants kneel before you?"

"I am one of the oracle's protectors," Beau said. "One of many."

"I would think you would be enough."

I couldn't tell whether or not she was being sarcastic.

"What I am, sorcerer," Beau said threateningly, "is not stupid. You might speak the truth, but you stink of insincerity and guile. Nor have you proclaimed the connection or recommendation that brought you here."

"Show me any Adept who doesn't couch their words and conceal their thoughts when seeking out an oracle."

Beau snorted, then looked over at me. I could see he was thinking furiously, putting some sort of action plan in place.

His caution was making me edgy. I'd never thought about what I might do if an Adept came for a seeing who I didn't want to touch, or even meet. This part of the oracle business was totally new to me. And it wasn't as though I was advertising my services. The few witches and shapeshifters who'd found their way to me had been referred, mostly by the pack. Meaning they'd been vetted, at least to some degree.

Beau glanced around the Brave, coming to a decision. "The oracle will be out shortly," he said without looking back at the woman. Then he shut the door before she could reply.

I frowned questioningly.

Beau lifted his hand to silence me as he pulled out his phone. His thumbs tapped out a rapid series of text messages as I slid out from the dinette, reaching back for my sketchbook and charcoal.

"Get a new one," he whispered.

I looked up, confused. He was still texting, so I stepped back and pulled a clean sketchbook and a new set of charcoal from the shelves beside the bed.

"Hoodie," Beau said.

"What?" I hissed. "It's too hot for a —"

"Long sleeves, then."

I glared at him.

Beau closed the space between us in three quick strides, pressing his mouth against my temple and speaking softly. "You don't want this woman to know anything about you. Glasses, long sleeves, tuck your necklace in."

"Geez, Beau." I reached for a thin, light-gray top with long sleeves to swap out for my crew-neck T-shirt. "Overkill much?"

"No." He pulled at my collar, feeding the necklace down beneath my shirt.

I batted his hands away, pulling off the crew-neck T and pulling on the grey shirt over my tank top, which automatically tucked the necklace underneath it. If I tugged on them, the sleeves of the new shirt would stretch down past my wrists. It was also loose enough to not show the outline of the chain and its diamond.

"If she's as powerful as you think, she'll feel the magic of the necklace," I whispered.

"Fine," Beau hissed. "But she doesn't have to see it, or your tattoos. And she's powerful, all right. More powerful than Henry or Blackwell. Or maybe both of them combined. You know how I know? Her magic is faint. Completely diluted. Camouflaged."

"But not more powerful than Jade or any of the dragons."

"Yeah, no," Beau said. "But they aren't here, are they?"

I ran my hands up my arms, feeling a chill despite the warmth of the air. "Should we ask her to go? Say I won't see her?"

Beau looked grim. "No. You need to see her."

"Why?"

He shook his head. "You need to see her ... clean. Without my input or bias. And I don't think you ask this sort of Adept to leave. I hope I'm wrong. But Henry is on his way. And Ember."

"You're texting with Ember?"

"What? No. Henry is."

"Well, that's interesting, eh?" I wagged my eyebrows at Beau playfully.

He stifled a smile as he pressed a swift kiss to my lips. A bunch of the tension filling the tiny kitchen of the RV seemed to ease.

Beau broke our embrace. Crossing to the front of the Brave, he opened the door and looked back at me.

I grabbed my fresh notebook and followed, confused but willing to trust his instincts. Jade and Drake were so powerful that I could feel them from inside the Brave when they were just standing at the door. But I couldn't pick up anything from whoever was bothering Beau.

Shielding my eyes from the sunlight despite my sunglasses, I stepped down out of the RV behind him. I couldn't see anyone beyond his broad shoulders until he stepped off to the side, toward the patio table and chairs. We'd been planning to eat lunch outside, but I'd gotten obsessed with fine-tuning the sketches instead.

Beau's unwavering attention was trained on a woman standing with her back to us in the shade of the apple trees, a dozen or so feet away.

She was tall and terribly slim. Dark-haired and — really oddly, considering the weather — wearing what appeared to be a black cloak. The butterfly tattoo was motionless on my wrist, so apparently it didn't inform me every time someone magical showed up.

The woman turned to look at me. And as she did, some kind of shock or energy tightened my chest, but trapping all my breath rather than squeezing it out.

As if I knew her.

Or should have known her.

Or maybe even as if I really didn't want to know her.

She was Asian. She looked old enough that her long, straight black hair had to be a dye job, but I wasn't sure how old exactly. Her skin was even paler than my own, and wrinkled in a way that let me know she frowned a hell of a lot more than she smiled.

"Oracle," she said, with an accent that sounded slightly more British than North American. "Were you expecting me?"

She smiled smugly, as if she thought I'd laugh at her lame joke.

I didn't.

She frowned as if momentarily disconcerted. Lifting a thin hand whose lines still weren't enough to give a clear sense of her age, she touched the edge of a platinum brooch pinned and half-hidden underneath the left side of her cloak.

I knew that gesture. Blackwell made it unconsciously all the time with his amulet. As did Henry with his handcuffs, and Jade with her knife.

The brooch was some kind of magical artifact. A touchstone.

I kept my hands away from my necklace. Though I was suddenly desperate for a bit of the grounding that contact with the diamond usually gave me.

"You're not what I was expecting," she said.

"I get that a lot."

"My name is Kai Win." She paused, as if waiting for a big reaction to her name. It took me a second to remember where I'd heard 'Kai' before. Chi Wen had told me my father's name was Kai Lei. So this woman had the same first name as my father? That wasn't weird at all.

"Rochelle."

Beau lifted the patio umbrella over the table, angling it to create a pocket of shade. Then he crossed into the shelter of the trees near the back of the Brave. Almost out of sight, but still very much present. My own personal guardian. It was a role we traded, though honestly, I thought Beau did a better job of it. Of course, it helped that he could turn into a seven-foot fanged monster with three-inch claws that could slice through steel. My sole defensive trick was much more up close and personal, and it didn't come with an amped-up healing factor.

Win stepped out of the shadows, never taking her gaze from me as she approached. "You don't know me."

"Should I?"

"You keep company with sorcerers."

Interesting. But if Blackwell or Henry had sent her for a seeing, why not say so outright? "Is that where you got my name?"

"No."

Closer up, I could finally make a guess at her age. In her sixties, if not older. Her eyes were gray. A much deeper shade than my own, but still disconcerting.

I didn't look away.

"Rochelle Hawthorne," she said musingly, pausing a few steps away from me.

"If you wish."

"Rochelle Hawthorne ... Kai," she said.

My belly hollowed out. This woman was claiming me in some way I hadn't quite figured out yet. Kai Win ... Kai Lei ... Wait. In China the family name came first ...

"You may call me Win. I am your grandmother."

Dread flooded through my system. The brand-new package of charcoals snapped within my suddenly tense grip. I stared at the woman before me, knowing she spoke the truth without needing to use any sort of magic.

Dread.

Not joy.

Shouldn't I feel some sort of joy? Some sort of missing connection finally fulfilled?

I reached up and removed my sunglasses, staring at her unflinchingly despite my troubled thoughts.

A slow smile spread across her face. She looked ... satisfied.

"You forgot Saintpaul," I said, sounding dangerous even to my own ears. "You know, for the hospital where I was abandoned. Rochelle Saintpaul ... the orphaned oracle raised by nonmagical strangers in foster care."

The smile fell from Kai Win's face. I could actually see her recalculating.

"You'll find I'm not a fan of people trying to redefine who I am." I put my glasses back on. The day was too bright. Plus, I liked the feeling of having a layer of something between us. As if protecting my eyes was fundamentally important around my so-called grandmother, for multiple reasons I hadn't yet begun to sort through.

I turned away, stepping into the shade underneath the umbrella. I met Beau's gaze as I placed my sketchbook on the table. His face was a thunderstorm of emotion. I offered him a smile to tell him I was okay. For now.

He nodded.

I sat down, facing my supposed grandmother. My legs felt rubbery, watery. But that was a weakness I wasn't willing to show. Not in front of a predator who had come to me in the guise of a relative. Because whether that was true or not, I was so not into the whole 'long lost parental figure sweeping in and us becoming one big happy family' crap.

We lived in a world filled with magic. There was no way my grandmother couldn't have found me if she'd wanted to.

"I didn't know you existed," Win said, as if reading my mind. "I have long tried to access your mother's estate. So when you claimed your legacy, they informed me."

She sat down across from me, graceful and unfazed. Then she shifted her chair so it was completely out of the sun. Her cloak came with a hood I hadn't seen before. The fabric of the garment was a more delicate weave in the sunlight than it had appeared when she was standing in the shadows. I wondered if that indicated some sort of magic.

"Okay," I said, placing the crushed charcoals beside the empty sketchbook on the table. Building another barrier between her and me.

"You draw," she said. "As did your mother."

Since that was pretty obvious, I didn't bother answering her. Actually, I didn't have a single thing to say to her. That was odd, wasn't it? Maybe I was in shock. Except I could still feel that sense of dread frissoning in my stomach.

"This isn't going well," Win said. "Perhaps I shouldn't have just showed up. Perhaps a letter would have been better."

"Perhaps."

"But I've been ... you are my only family."

"My father is dead, then."

"Yes. Lei is dead. Over twenty-one years ago now."

I'd been fairly sure, based on my conversations with the far seer, that my father was dead. Though my mentor could often be exceedingly obscure, and didn't have a great sense of time. But I'd figured if Kai Lei was alive and kicking and didn't give a crap about me, then I wouldn't give a crap about him either.

"And I didn't even know your mother had died," Win said, continuing to spin her story. "Not with any certainty. Only that she was missing. I figured out which firm oversaw her estate. But, not being a blood relative, I couldn't gain access to any more information than that. Not even where or when or how Jane died. I didn't even know you existed."

"That's weird, isn't it? That you didn't even know she was pregnant? Or even where she was when she died? It's like you weren't close to her at all."

My grandmother eyed me from across the table. She touched her brooch again. Now that I was closer, I could see that it was in the shape of a wreath of diamond-sprinkled platinum ivy, about two inches in diameter. She wore no other jewelry I could see.

An ivy brooch.

Ivy. Like the tattoo on my right arm.

And her cloak. Something was bothering me about it. I'd seen it somewhere before, but I couldn't remember where. Maybe in a vision?

No.

My mother's drawing.

The woman in my mother's drawing was wearing a cloak. The woman who Beau thought was me.

Suddenly, I was desperate to be sitting anywhere but across from Win. I didn't want her to know about me or Beau or the Brave.

My grandmother was staring at my hands. I followed her gaze down.

I was gripping my sketchbook as if it were some sort of weapon. I hadn't realized I'd picked it up. My long sleeves had ridden up, just enough to see the edges of my tattoos where they began at my wrists.

I eased my grip on the sketchbook.

"This is too much for you," Win murmured. "I forget what it is to be young." She lifted her chin, directing her attention to Beau over my shoulder. "I understand this ... place is a hotel of some kind."

"A bed and breakfast," he said warily.

"Yes. Would you secure me a room? A cottage?"

"Rochelle?" Beau asked, seeking permission to fulfill my grandmother's request.

I nodded without looking back at him.

"Perhaps we can meet for dinner?" Win asked. "That gives you a few hours to get used to the idea of ... me. And sort through your questions, of which I'm sure you have many."

Henry stepped out from the fruit trees a dozen feet behind Win. His demeanor suggested he was choosing to reveal himself, as if he'd been watching for a while.

Win shifted her gaze, looking over my other shoulder.

I turned my head slightly. Now Ember was standing six feet away from Beau.

"Your other protectors have arrived." Win sounded amused. She stood, having to step back to avoid losing an eye on the low umbrella. Apparently, I didn't get my diminutive genes from her side of the family.

"Please allow me to escort you," Henry said, as pleasant as always.

Win looked at me expectantly. I really didn't want to agree to dinner. And I really didn't want her anywhere near the Brave. Even though I had no idea why.

"There's a Dairy Queen up on the highway," I said.

Win frowned, then repeated, "Dairy Queen?" as if she'd never said those two words together before.

"It's a fast-food place. But good. Ice cream, fries, you know."

Win raised her pencil-thin eyebrows. "Ice cream," she echoed. Not unkindly, though. Just perplexed.

I gathered she didn't get out into the real world very often. The cloak was a dead giveaway. "Seven o'clock. Tonight."

She nodded, turning her attention to Henry. "Kai Win, sorcerer. Regent of Guangdong, Macau, and Hong Kong, among other territories."

"Henry Calhoun, sorcerer. United States Marshal. Director of the North American League."

"Ah," Win said. "I've heard of you."

"But I haven't heard of you. Nor the title of regent, not when used by a sorcerer."

My grandmother chuckled but didn't answer.

Henry's smile faded. He tilted his head, causing the brim of his cowboy hat to shadow his eyes. "Asian sorcerers do tend to keep to themselves," he said. "But Rochelle has other powerful friends from that region."

Win's smile widened. "It's good to hear that my granddaughter is so well protected. But then, people are drawn to power for many different reasons. Aren't they, sorcerer?"

Henry clenched his jaw. Apparently, my grandmother had a brilliant knack for getting under the skin of even the most easygoing Adepts.

So that was one trait we had in common.

Win gestured for Henry to lead. After touching the brim of his hat in my direction, he turned stiffly away, crossing back through the trees.

My grandmother followed, pausing as she stepped into the shade and looked back at me. "Send Mot Blackwell my greetings," she said. "I look forward to renewing our acquaintance."

And there it was.

Blackwell knew my grandmother.

And I was completely certain he'd known my grandmother the entire time he'd known me. Question was, why didn't he tell me? For my protection? Or for his?

Beau touched my shoulder lightly. I hadn't heard him approach. Ember brushed past us, following Win and Henry to just beyond the trees, then stopping to stare after them.

"Does her magic smell like mine?" I whispered the question, pressing my hands over the raw diamond nestled underneath my shirt.

Beau hunkered down beside me. He reached for the seat of my chair, rotating it out so that I was facing him. "No."

I wrapped my free hand around the back of his neck, then just sat in silence with him for a moment. Feeling his magic dancing underneath one hand, and the comforting energy of my necklace under the other.

"It's too much all at once," Beau said. "She was right about that, at least."

I nodded, not ready to speak.

"Who is Blackwell?" Ember approached us with her arms folded defensively across her chest.

"Did you know she was coming?" Beau ignored her question, his voice edged with a snarl.

Ember shook her head. "I knew there was a distant relative trying to gain access to the Hawthorne files. That someone not of the Hawthorne bloodline had submitted a standing inquiry, seeking contact with Jane or any heirs. I surmise, now, because your parents weren't legally married, all Kai Win could do was claim a connection through her son. She renewed her request a month after I got your file, as she did every year. That, along with a couple of third-party inquiries, was what drew my attention."

"How about why?" Beau asked.

Ember looked pointedly at me.

I snorted. "That woman is no long-lost grandmother looking to feed me milk and cookies."

The witch laughed. It was a sharp sound, and possibly the first sign of humor she'd expressed since her arrival. No matter how twisted and inappropriate for the moment.

"She's a piece of work, all right. But most sorcerers go in for flash and ceremony. The cloak, the dampened magic, the territorial claims. Ignoring anyone they deem beneath them."

Right. Win hadn't spared Ember a single glance, nor offered an introduction.

"And witches don't?" I asked, but out of actual interest rather than the usual need to be confrontational.

"Witches gather magic from the earth. Organically, if you will." She waved her hand in the air. "Draw a circle, light a candle, and access the energy. But sorcerers need a tie, a conduit, so they collect and carry items of power. Hence all the posturing."

"Like items created by an alchemist?"

Ember looked pleasantly surprised. "Yes. And spells, of course. Some sorcerers have the ability to write spells that give them a certain level of access to magic, but some spells are passed down from generation to generation. Or from master to apprentice. Witches don't need words, but sometimes they do use them for focus."

I glanced to Beau, who was listening to our exchange intently. "She's not here to harm me?"

"Not that I could pick up," he said.

Ember scoffed. "She's not an idiot. Who wouldn't want an oracle in the family? There's, like, only one or two per generation, per bloodline."

Neither Beau or I said anything in response. She glanced between us, then twisted her lips wryly. "So neither of you is going to answer the question about this Blackwell?"

"Sorcerer," Beau said.

"Ah, hell. Another one?"

I laughed. I couldn't help it. Apparently, being prejudiced against other Adepts was a focused way to live your life. You always knew who to avoid, at least.

Ember chuckled to herself. "Let me know if you need me again. I assume we're pushing our meeting off?"

"Please," I said.

The witch nodded, then set off toward her cottage.

I settled my gaze on Beau. His aquamarine eyes appeared lighter in the sunlight, creating a stunning contrast to his skin. He had darkened with all the outdoor work he'd been doing.

"So," I said. "You want to go with me and my scary grandma for ice cream later?"

He grinned. "You ain't getting rid of me so easily." But then he sobered quickly, looking off in the direction Henry had taken Win. "He'll put her in the cottage on the far upper edge of the property, near the neighbors' fence. We just finished painting it yesterday and sealing the tile today. It still reeks."

"Near the cherry tree grove?"

"Yeah."

My stomach soured slightly.

Beau watched me closely. Then when I didn't elaborate, he asked me, "Why?"

"The vision with the demon was among the cherry trees."

"But with Blackwell, not Win. And maybe not even these particular trees."

I nodded.

"So when Blackwell gets here, tell him to stay away from Win's cottage."

"Easy peasy, eh?"

"Yeah, isn't it always?" Beau reached for me, running

his thumb across my cheek so lightly that I could barely feel it. "Are you okay?"

"I will be. One revelation at a time."

He sighed. "I better check on Henry."

"I doubt she's going to tie him up and eat him. Not before dinner."

"Yeah." He straightened up from his crouch, my gaze following him up. "Plus, I figure you should talk to Blackwell alone."

"Why? I don't keep anything from you."

"No. But he likes to."

Beau caressed the back of my neck, then wandered off in the direction Henry had taken through the orchard.

I watched him go, even after I couldn't see him any longer. Then I pulled out my phone and stared down at the last text message I'd received from Blackwell.

>*Face to face would be better for this conversation.*

He hadn't responded to the sketch I'd sent of the demon and him in the cherry orchard. I wondered if it had spooked him. I wondered if he'd decided my visions weren't worth the risk they seemed to pose for him. That would be a completely rational reaction.

Maybe I shouldn't push to get him involved any further than I already had.

Maybe I didn't need the added complication. The added questions. The added betrayal I had a feeling was looming behind his silence.

Because that was what all friends and family eventually did, right? Betray each other? Even if I discounted my childhood as an anomaly, I didn't have to look any farther than Beau's family to confirm that assumption.

I tapped out four words onto my screen.

My grandmother says hi.

Then I hit send.

It seemed easier to just get it all over with at once. Then I could get on with my life with Beau in the aftermath.

Plus, Blackwell was going to show up either way. Magic had already told me so.

And I had a feeling a vision of a demon that knew my name was going to be difficult to thwart. Especially since I wasn't supposed to be able to see my own future at all.

IT TOOK BLACKWELL EXACTLY THREE MINUTES TO appear in the clearing, about two feet from the Brave's passenger-side front tire.

No text message reply.

No request for my location.

He just appeared, wearing his typical pinstriped charcoal suit, white dress shirt, and smooth black leather Oxfords, with pools of dark magic gathered in both hands. Armed for a fight. But he found only me, sitting at the patio table. Waiting for him.

He pivoted slowly, thoroughly scanning the sunlit trees all around us. His dark hair and pale skin were in sharp contrast against the bright green of the leafy canopy.

The magic dissipated from his hands.

The hair on my arms settled. Unlike with my grandmother, Blackwell's energy was undeniable. It was crazy to think that I'd met people even more powerful than the sorcerer. Crazy to imagine that more powerful Adepts even existed.

"How do you know her?" My voice was sharp, almost nasty, cutting through the warm afternoon air.

Blackwell looked directly at me, then. His gaze dropped to the new sketchbook and the crushed package of charcoals on the table. "Where is she?"

"Settling into a cottage," I said. "Can you tell she's been here?"

He shook his head.

"She's the sneaky sort, eh?"

The sorcerer barked out a laugh, then ran his hand through his hair. I'd never seen him do anything so vulnerable or emotionally telling before. And for some reason, the feeling of dread that Beau's soothing touch had settled amped up again.

Blackwell approached the chair opposite me, but then hesitated to sit. He glanced around again, uneasily.

"You thought you were popping into a fight."

He locked his dark gaze on mine, twisting his lips. "That is when you usually call me."

"You appear unharmed," I said, my pissiness breaking through my attempt at being coolly collected.

"No thanks to you."

"Do you think Jade would have looked at those sketches and not come for you?"

My question hung between us. But I didn't need to hear his answer. No matter what had happened in the aftermath, it was better that I'd brokered the deal between Blackwell and Jade in Westport last January after I'd had a vision of them together. I knew it. And he knew it. Jade hated Blackwell. I'm not sure I could have stopped that vision from coming to pass. I'm not sure I was meant to stop it. But I was damn sure that the sorcerer, as powerful as he was, was no match for the dragon slayer.

"Let's walk," he said, glancing around uneasily again.

"Did you bring your wallet?"

"Why? Do you have sketches to sell?"

I laughed harshly. "Oh, there are sketches. But I was thinking about donuts first."

I stood up, gathering my sketchbook and charcoals as I headed for the door of the Brave to retrieve my satchel. "There's a Tim Hortons on the corner at the highway."

I didn't bother waiting for his approval. Blackwell wouldn't have shown up if he wasn't planning on sticking around for a while.

WE DIDN'T TALK AS WE STROLLED THROUGH THE apple and pear trees toward the driveway. I checked the chicken coop for eggs as we passed, but there weren't any to collect yet. The rooster side-eyed Blackwell — and made me realize how remarkably similar his black eyes were to those of the sorcerer — then crowed after us as we continued on to the driveway, then turned onto Lakeshore Drive South.

I touched the bottom corner of the Thompson Orchard B&B sign that Beau had finished varnishing and hung up a couple of days ago. It swung slightly as we brushed by.

"Pack territory?" Blackwell asked stiffly, as if he couldn't stand speaking to me.

"I guess so."

"Can I expect to run into your pet enforcer?"

"Who? Kandy?" I asked with a sneer. My own anger was also still too close to the surface. "Why?"

Blackwell reverted to his silently stewing mode as I turned left onto Solly Road and we started to wind our way up to the highway. The houses on either side of us spread upward in a gradual incline from Okanagan Lake. Flowering bushes and the occasional overgrown fruit tree dotted large lots filled with half-dead, though still neatly trimmed, grass. Most of the houses were older but well maintained. A couple had pools. No sidewalks. Few fences.

It was a nice neighborhood.

Wandering through Summerland in his suit, Blackwell stood out like a sore thumb. I took off my long-sleeved shirt and stuffed it into my satchel, opting for my tank top and hoping the sunscreen I'd applied liberally that morning hadn't completely worn off.

"I get why you're mad." I'd finally simmered down enough to broach the subject further.

"You broke our contract, Rochelle. 'You will not knowingly endanger my life.' A fundamental clause."

"That was your 'friends' stipulation, Blackwell. Plus, I wasn't putting you in danger. I mitigated that danger."

He huffed out a sarcastic laugh.

"You're going to deny that you're the big, powerful sorcerer with all the resources and answers? That you've known about my grandmother this entire time?"

That took the smile off his face.

We turned on Macdonald, then zigzagged back onto Solly Road again. It was warm in the full sun, but not unpleasant. Well, not yet. Thankfully, it was only a thirty-minute walk or so. Spending the bulk of it in silence was better than arguing constantly.

A few cars passed slowly, pulling farther onto the other side of the street than they really needed to in order to get by us.

Like I said, it was a nice neighborhood.

"I don't have all the answers," Blackwell murmured.

"But you have well-founded guesses," I said. "Things you've been keeping from me. Possibly for my own protection?" I was giving the sorcerer an out. It wasn't like I wanted to wander around all day, or week, or month feeling all betrayed.

He didn't answer.

We continued up the slope from the lake. The sun was hot on my shoulders. I kept my gaze ahead of me and didn't fight the deep valley of silence between us.

The sound of traffic increased as we rounded the final curve that led to Highway 97. The red-and-white Tim Hortons sign stood out against the wide blue sky up ahead.

Cars were suddenly whipping by in front of us. The hot air of their wake lifted my cropped hair, then pressed it across my sunglasses.

Blackwell glanced around. "Crosswalk?"

I shrugged. "Just wait."

The light turned red, traffic slowed, and I darted across the highway.

Blackwell swore in a melodic language I didn't recognize, then followed.

I laughed. It was funny, an all-powerful sorcerer being afraid of four lanes of traffic in a tiny Canadian town. I paused to wait for the light to change and the walk signal at the next corner. Despite the prominent placement of the sign, the Tim Hortons was actually tucked behind a Vietnamese restaurant.

"Maybe Asian would be better," I muttered.

"Better for what?"

"Dinner. With my grandmother."

The walk signal flashed and we crossed the street.

"I doubt she'll eat," Blackwell said.

"Why not?"

"Fear of poison," he said grimly. "A lot of them are undetectable by magic. Not being magical themselves."

I looked over at him, startled. "My grandmother thinks I want to poison her?"

"Of course not." He smiled tightly, without any humor or joy. "I wouldn't mind some pho, though. Is it any good here?"

I swallowed, suddenly aware that I'd been mouthing off around people and things I didn't understand. "I ... I wouldn't know the difference. Beau likes it."

Blackwell nodded thoughtfully. "Let's look at the menu on our way back." Then he shrugged out of his suit jacket, folding it carefully over his arm as he casually set a course for the Tim Hortons ahead.

I followed at a slower pace. I was fairly certain the sorcerer had just threatened to poison my grandmother. And I wasn't sure I actually wanted to know why.

AFTER WE SETTLED ONTO THE DARK-TAN VINYL bench seats of a booth next to the front windows with our drinks and boxes of donuts, the other customers stopped glancing uneasily our way. My tattoos drew more attention than Blackwell's suit, but even in the air conditioning I was still too warm to pull my long sleeved T-shirt back on. I wasn't really all over donuts, but I thought Beau and the kids might like them for a snack later on. The restaurant was only half- full.

"Tell me about my mother."

"I never met her."

"But you know my grandmother."

"I did."

"What does that mean?"

"That we haven't seen each other for a very long time."

I scoffed. "I know you're only thirty-four or thirty-five, Blackwell. You told me yourself last year. How long could that be?"

He twisted his lips in a wry smile, then sipped his coffee.

I wouldn't have thought Blackwell would be sitting across from me in a booth at Tim Hortons in Summerland, BC, if he wasn't prepared to answer questions. But apparently I was asking the wrong questions.

"I'm surprised you take milk and sugar," I said. "In fact, shouldn't you be drinking tea?"

He smirked at my attempt to lighten the conversation. "That's a British stereotype, not Scottish."

"There's a difference?" I asked flippantly. But I grinned to soften the insult.

He snorted softly and took another sip.

"You came," I said.

"You texted."

I raised my eyebrow at him. "I've been texting since January. I texted you this morning, but that wasn't enough to get you to show up."

"You texted about something important."

"Something intriguing."

"Indeed."

I opened the large box of donuts sitting next to a smaller box of Timbits on the deep-red laminate table, selecting an old-fashioned glazed after careful consideration.

"Not the apple fritter?" Blackwell asked.

"Later. Though I'm not sure how much actual apple there is in it."

"You'll need the comfort."

"You really think my grandmother is going to hurt me?"

"No. Not you."

"Who, then? You?"

"Possibly. Though I'm still an asset to her."

"You said she hasn't seen you in years."

"She hasn't needed to see me in years."

"You're talking in riddles!"

I swallowed my outburst almost as quickly as I'd made it. But still, Blackwell glanced around. No one was paying any attention to us, though. Most of the steady stream of customers were getting their coffee and donuts to go.

Closing my eyes for a moment, I attempted to gather my thoughts.

"It's a series of difficult subjects," the sorcerer said. "Which I need to talk around."

"Meaning you can't trust me with them?"

He shook his head sharply. But just once.

"That you think will ... upset me?"

"Possibly. But after Southaven, I believe you can handle it."

"But you didn't think that before."

"You were in a fragile state when we first met."

"I thought I was insane," I hissed.

Blackwell spread his hands in an 'as I was saying' gesture. Then he assessed the box of Timbits. Selecting a chocolate glazed, he popped it into his mouth and carefully wiped his fingers on his napkin.

I contemplated strangling him.

He offered me his typical tight-lipped smile.

"Because I stabbed Cy," I said, casting my voice low. "Now I've proven myself to you?"

"You think I would be more impressed by your mental state because you were able to kill a man?"

I opened my mouth to argue the murder charge, then gnashed my teeth. "Yes," I finally hissed back.

Blackwell laughed. A deeply satisfied, quiet chuckle. "Yes," he said.

He took another sip of coffee, then placed it down and turned it so the logo faced him. The cup was perfectly centered on the table. Blackwell was sitting perfectly centered on the two-seater, dark-tan vinyl bench.

He was anxious, as if there was something he wanted to say but couldn't.

"Just tell me," I whispered. I focused on his long fingers resting on the lid of his cup, not looking at his face. "You know I won't judge you."

"I know you won't."

I removed my sunglasses, then. I lifted my gaze to meet his dark eyes.

He nodded. "Do you know what a geas is?"

"No."

"Do you know what a gag order is?"

"Obviously."

He waited for me to connect the dots.

"A geas is a magical gag order?" I asked.

"Of sorts."

"Under pain of death?" I joked. Not even remotely amused, Blackwell raised an eyebrow in response. "What are you saying ... that my grandmother placed a geas on you?"

He didn't answer.

"Did someone force a magical gag order on you?"

"You can't force a geas."

I huffed in frustration. "A deal, then. You like deals."

Blackwell's lips quirked. "I do."

I thought about all the questions I had. I thought about all the answers Blackwell had.

Then I thought about it as if it were a game.

"Did someone other than my grandmother place a geas on you?"

"Not one currently in effect."

I wasn't completely sure what that meant, but I moved on instead of backtracking. "Why would someone need to place someone under a magical gag order? To share information and not worry about anyone blabbing?"

"Usually."

"Why not just stay silent? Conversely, why accept the gag?"

Blackwell leaned forward. "Some information is worth making deals for."

"Like ... first-look access to an oracle's visions?"

"Yes."

"Can you talk about my mother?"

"I can, but I know very little about her specifically."

Stymied, I paused to nibble on my donut.

"Did you bring any sketches?" Blackwell asked.

"No. The sketchbook I brought is a new one."

"Why?"

"Beau didn't want my grandmother knowing too much about me."

"He picked up that you were related?"

"No. Just didn't like her. Actually, I don't know for sure."

"Smart boy. What about on your phone?" Blackwell's tone was casual. Too casual. He wanted to talk about a sketch he thought I had on me.

I fished the phone out of my pocket and opened the Photos app. The last two images were the ones I had texted to him. My sketch of Blackwell and the demon. My mother's drawing.

Tapping on my mother's drawing, I swallowed hard and turned the phone to face Blackwell.

He smiled. The expression actually reached his eyes, as it almost never did. As if he was proud of me.

"Do you ..." My voice was caught in my throat. "Do you know who this woman is?"

"You. Unrealized."

My stomach bottomed out. "You think this is the future?"

"What else does an oracle draw?"

"I mean, you think this is still to come?"

Blackwell shrugged one shoulder. "You tell me. What would your mentor say?"

He meant Chi Wen.

I realized my hand was shaking. I put the phone down on the table. Blackwell placed his fingers gingerly on the screen, then zoomed in on the photo. Enlarging the section where the woman ... where I ... was cradling the demon's chin.

"No tattoos," I murmured.

"No. But the same demon." Blackwell flicked his thumb against the screen, swapping one sketch for the other. The demon in the cherry orchard.

I forced myself to answer. "We think so. I think so."

"Did the vision come before or after you opened the legacy package?"

I frowned. "How did you know I opened anything?"

Blackwell waved his hand dismissively. "Kai Win has been trying to track it down since your mother went missing. To figure out what Jane had been up to in her final days. I assumed that was why she was here."

I glared at him a bit longer.

He huffed out a laugh. "I don't have the Brave magically bugged."

"Then how did you know where I was? You just appeared without instructions or pictures."

"Fine. I do have the Brave tagged. Just not for sound or images."

I narrowed my eyes at him, because I had to do something other than glare.

"We're getting off track." Blackwell tapped my phone again, flipping back to my mother's drawing. Then he looked at me pointedly.

I wasn't sure what he wanted me to ask. "Do you know the demon?"

"No."

"Do you know ... the location?"

"No."

"Have you seen anything about this picture before?"

Blackwell smiled. Then he tapped his nose in a very human, very nonmagical sort of gesture.

"Have you seen this picture before?" I held my breath.

"Not this exact one."

"But one like it."

"Yes."

"A drawing of my mother's."

"Yes."

"Of ... me."

"Yes."

"Where?"

Blackwell smiled slyly. "Who did you meet for the very first time today?"

My heart rate amped up. "My grandmother has a drawing like this?"

Blackwell didn't answer, and I figured that meant he probably couldn't answer.

"She said she didn't know I existed."

"I would imagine that is the truth." Blackwell spoke carefully, as if testing out the words. Trying to get around the geas, maybe?

"But she knew I was a possibility? How did you see the sketch? Where exactly? Did she talk about it? About me?"

Blackwell gritted his teeth, then shook his head.

I changed tactics. "Why was my mother in Vancouver? She'd bought an apartment there a few weeks before her death."

Blackwell leaned back in his chair, thoughtfully rotating his cup and staring out the window.

"Did you ..." I choked on the question, but I knew I had to ask it. "Did you have something to do with my mother's death?"

Blackwell sneered. "At fourteen? Why not ask if I'm your father?"

"Are you?"

Blackwell huffed out a derisive laugh. "No. To both questions."

My grandmother was standing outside the window. She appeared suddenly and without warning, standing only inches away from the glass to our left.

Blackwell flinched.

Startled, I choked ... on nothing.

Win smiled at us. The expression looked utterly genuine. And it scared the crap out of me. Then she turned to walk toward the entrance.

I looked at Blackwell, utterly aghast and briefly worried

that every person in Tim Hortons was about to be eradicated from the earth. I mean, he'd pretty much just threatened to poison Win and —

The glass entrance door opened, allowing a whoosh of warm air into the restaurant.

Blackwell slipped out of the booth to step forward.

I thought about hiding underneath the table.

I could feel Win approaching. I hadn't sensed even a trace of her magic outside the Brave, but I could feel her now. As if a low-grade electrical storm had just dropped by for a dozen donuts. All the hair stood up on the back of my neck.

I swiveled around rather than keeping my back to all that energy, watching as my grandmother strode toward us. Her cape rustled around her ankles as she moved. But no one else — no one nonmagical, I supposed — glanced her way. I wondered if she maintained some sort of personal cloaking shield. And whether that same spell was also why Beau couldn't sense her magic clearly.

"Kai Win," Blackwell said. He honestly sounded as if he was glad to see her.

I realized I was staring at him with my mouth hanging open, like an idiot.

He gestured for my grandmother to join us at our table, offering her his seat.

"Mot," she said. "A pleasure. I understand that it has been far too long since we chatted."

"May I get you a coffee?"

"Tea." She clasped arms with Blackwell, then turned and slid into the booth across from me.

Blackwell moved toward the counter to order tea. Apparently, my grandmother wasn't even remotely worried about being poisoned by the other sorcerer.

Win was smiling at me, but I couldn't read anything into her expression. My mind was numb, and I was struggling to maintain my equilibrium. Something about seeing my grandmother and Blackwell in the same space made the day all the more real. All the more impossible to ignore. All the more filled with impending terror and doom.

I wondered if everyone felt this way about their families. Maybe this was utterly normal, and I just didn't have any experience with it. Beau would certainly have agreed.

"I'm interrupting," Win said. It wasn't an apology. "I was looking into the Dairy Queen ..." — she overpronounced the two words again — "... and I saw you here."

"It's, like, a block away."

"You are as literal as your mother. I felt you here."

I glanced over at Blackwell. He was paying for the tea. "I ... was thinking that Vietnamese might be better for dinner."

"Oh, yes. That would be better."

I thought for a moment that my head might explode.

Blackwell returned to the table, placing the tea in front of Win but not sitting down.

"Thank you," my grandmother said, smiling up at the sorcerer. "How long have you two known each other?"

I opened my mouth, then didn't know what to say.

"About two years," Blackwell said smoothly. "Rochelle, you wanted to get those donuts back for afternoon tea?"

I had no idea what afternoon tea was, but I knew an out when I heard one. "Yeah ..."

I slid out of the booth. Blackwell reached across the table to close the boxes of donuts, then pressed them into my arms. I hadn't taken my satchel off, so I was good to immediately flee the vicinity.

"I'll walk your grandmother back."

"Okay."

"Still seven o'clock for dinner?" Win asked.

"Vietnamese," Blackwell said, grinning with gleeful anticipation.

"Yeah," I said. "Sure." Feeling as though I wasn't completely in control of my own body or mind, I slowly wandered toward the entrance. My hands were full, and I couldn't open the door.

I glanced back.

Win and Blackwell appeared to be chatting pleasantly to each other.

I had absolutely no idea what was going on.

Yet every instinct I had was screaming at me to run and hide.

Another customer opened the door, holding it for me.

I nodded my thanks and exited. I didn't look back.

FIVE

As I made my way back down Solly toward the Thompsons' acreage, I forced myself to keep my mind blank. Not wanting to think about anything until I was back with Beau and could talk everything through with him. It didn't work, though, and by the time I hit the driveway I was thinking about how bad I was going to feel when the news broke that the Tim Hortons in Summerland had exploded due to a leaky gas main or some other cover-up story.

But then I started wondering. If Blackwell couldn't talk about my grandmother — couldn't share anything about her, really — could he kill her? Or attempt to kill her?

Maybe I should have led with that question.

The vision welled up when I was a few steps off the driveway, just within the apple tree section of the orchard. I could actually feel the magic surge beneath my feet as I walked. Then it shot up my legs, torso, and neck to wipe out my eyesight.

If I hadn't been stumbling around blind and worried

about dropping two boxes of Tim Hortons takeout, I probably would have wondered at the timing and location.

Instead, I hunkered down right where I was standing, then slowly slid my ass backward until I came up against a tree.

Once I was positioned safely — as long as Eddie didn't run me over with the lawn mower — I put the donuts down to one side and opened my sketchbook across my bent knees. Then I waited for the white mist occupying my mind to resolve into whatever the magic wanted me to see.

My vision cleared. It was night and possibly deep into it. Hushed, shadowed fruit trees spread out from me in all directions ... so I was deeper into the orchard, or maybe in another orchard altogether. If pressed, I wasn't sure I'd even be able to distinguish between apple, pear, and plum trees in the moonlight. But I was fairly certain I wasn't standing among the cherry trees.

Speaking of the moon, I leaned forward in an attempt to peer up at the sky through the leafy branches, a piece of broken charcoal gripped tightly in my left hand. The moon hung off to one side, about half-full with wisps of sooty clouds clustered around it.

"Same night," I muttered to myself.

Then someone was moving through the trees to my left. I tucked my knees tighter to my chest, barely giving myself enough room to draw if the compulsion hit me. It wasn't as though I was actually in the vision, and I knew that nothing could trip over me, but —

Blackwell stepped into a patch of moonlight. He was armed with a dark pool of magic in one hand. He glanced around, slowly and carefully continuing to cross in front of me. His footfalls were silent in the trimmed orchard grass, but I picked up other faint sounds of his passing. Leaves brushing against his arm. The quiet huff of his breath. He'd been running.

What the hell would a sorcerer as powerful as Blackwell run from?

Win stepped into the pool of moonlight Blackwell had just been occupying, glancing around her as he had. If not for her pale skin, I'm not sure I would have spotted her standing among the trees in her dark cloak. If she'd pulled up the hood, I might not have seen her at all.

Except this was a vision, I reminded myself. I was supposed to see. I inhaled deeply, focusing on the feeling of the charcoal I held poised over the smooth paper of my new sketchbook. I was anchored to the real world. The world outside my head. "Observe and record," I muttered to myself.

I thought for a moment that Win might be stalking Blackwell. Except her gray-eyed gaze was looking everywhere but at him.

A shadow split off from the trees to my right, then slammed against Blackwell's chest without further warning. Teeth and claws flashed as the sorcerer stumbled backward.

He fell directly in front of me, no more than a foot away from my sneakered toes.

The charcoal crumbled in my hand. I stifled a scream.

The demon lifted its face, locking its crimson gaze to mine and opening its blood-smeared maw to reveal rows of sharklike teeth.

The scent of carrion mixed with fresh blood hit me, filling my nasal passages and triggering an adrenaline rush I couldn't quell.

I screamed.

Something flashed across the demon's neck, and the creature was yanked away from me by Win. She was wielding some sort of platinum-colored weapon. My grandmother shouted something, viciously cursing in Cantonese or Mandarin. I didn't know the difference.

Blackwell was dead at my feet. His throat was … gone. His dark eyes were sightless.

I screamed again.

Then someone was touching my arms and attempting to press something into my hands. I slammed my head back against the tree behind me in an attempt to escape the new threat.

Endless white mist blanked out the vision, smoothing away the image of Blackwell's murder. But I couldn't forget the demon's claws or the swift hopelessness of the sorcerer's final moments. I was now condemned to capture it over and over again, pouring the oracle magic into the paper of my sketchbooks in the desperate hope of never having to see such a thing again.

"Rochelle?" a soft, tentative voice asked.

Krista. The young shapeshifter was in the orchard with me, trying to pass me something. I had to try to behave normally. She didn't need to witness my terror any more than she already had.

"It was just a vision," I said, reassuring myself.

"I know. Here."

I opened my hand, and she placed a cool, smooth, round object into my waiting palm.

"I was careful. I watched," she said. "Like Beau told me. But then … you screamed."

"It's okay."

An apple. She'd given me an apple. I took a bite,

allowing the crisp, sweet flesh to draw my senses back into the real world.

My vision cleared enough that I could see her hunkered down in front of me. Her head was tilted quizzically.

"It's okay," I said again.

"I know," she said matter-of-factly.

"Where's Calvin?" I took another bite of the apple, chewing slowly. I wasn't completely sure that my stomach could handle any food.

"Looking for Beau," she said. "But you have your sketchbook already." She backed off a few steps, giving me space. "So I'll stay until Beau comes."

An emotion welled up in my chest. But I couldn't place it, so I pushed it away and took another bite of the apple.

"Good thing I didn't eat it. Conserving supplies is an important survival technique," the towheaded girl said proudly. "It's a Royal Gala. Last year's crop, of course. But they have a great shelf life."

I grinned. I felt like crap, but I couldn't help but smile at my earnest savior.

Krista grinned back at me, brushing her hair behind her ear and drawing my gaze to the half-dozen plastic cause bracelets she always wore.

"What charity is it this weekend?" I asked, attempting to regain some sense of normalcy. "For the apple juice stand?"

Every weekend, Krista and Calvin set up a juice stand at the base of the driveway. Rain or shine. They hauled frozen, fresh-pressed apple juice — left over from when their uncle was alive — out of the massive freezer in the basement and sold it for three dollars a cup, knocking fifty cents off if customers brought cups of their own. They made a killing. Then they donated the proceeds.

"The school library needs new computers," Krista said.

"According to them or you?"

She shrugged.

Pain seared up my left arm. I gasped.

"Rochelle?"

"It's okay," I said, digging around on the ground for a relatively unbroken piece of charcoal.

"Your eyes," Krista murmured.

She could see the oracle magic seeping around the edges of my sunglasses, but she didn't sound scared. Just tentative.

"I have to draw," I said.

Krista nodded, then pulled her backpack off and retrieved a dog-eared paperback from its depths. From the layout and the blurry image, I thought I recognized a Harry Potter tome. My eyesight wasn't sharp enough yet to read the title, though. "I'll stay."

I didn't really have time to argue. My left arm, shoulder, and neck felt as though they were on fire. White mist rolled across my eyes. "Hey," I said, right before I lost track of my surroundings a second time. "Where did the boxes of donuts go?"

"Oh," Krista said. "Calvin and I figured you didn't want them lying around in the sun."

I laughed, not bothering to argue that we were currently sitting in the cool shade of the apple grove.

Time to draw.

"Why Blackwell?" Beau asked.

I looked up from my sketchbook, blinking away the white dots that still swam before my eyes. Beau was seated propped against the tree trunk across from me.

"Sorry?"

He nodded toward my sketchbook where it lay open across my crossed legs. I'd been refining a detailed sketch of Blackwell looking over his shoulder, defining the crisp edge of his shirt collar against the moonlit backdrop of a fruit tree branch.

I frowned. I didn't remember the sorcerer glancing back. Was he looking at Win behind him? Distracted for a moment right before the demon pounced on him and —

"He's going to die," I whispered. Terror constricted my chest. For a moment, I couldn't breathe.

Beau was next to me in an instant, rubbing my back soothingly. Then abruptly slamming the heel of his hand against my lower ribs.

I exhaled in a gasp. "Wow. Was that really necessary?"

"I thought so."

I glowered at him, then turned my attention back to the sketch. I flipped the sketchbook closed and straightened my bent legs, feeling tingles of pain flooding through them. "How long have I been sitting here?"

"Couple of hours," Beau said, rubbing my back again. "Win came by."

"Oh, yeah?"

"Yeah." He snorted. "She wanted me to carry you back to the Brave."

"And you refused." I smirked at him. "You bad boy."

He chuckled.

I sobered, leaning against Beau's shoulder and peering up at the clear blue sky. "What time is it?"

"After five."

"That's more than a couple of hours."

"Calvin didn't find me right away."

"The donuts probably distracted him."

He laughed. "Actually, I don't think he ate many."

Silence fell between us. I smoothed my hands over the almost-silky cover of the sketchbook. Judging by the smudges along its edges, it was now almost half full. Apparently, Blackwell's death was significant.

My throat was threatening to close up again. "Why Blackwell what?" I asked, following up on Beau's first question. "Why is he going to die? I don't know."

"No," Beau said. "And you know he's not going to die. I meant why do you draw him in the first place?"

I twisted away from him sharply, lifting the sketchbook as if it were the bloody murder weapon. "I just saw it, Beau!"

"Yeah. And now Blackwell will study the sketches, and we'll thwart the vision. That is why you get them, right? To try to thwart them."

I looked away from him as I whispered, "We know how well that works."

In the aftermath of the intense vision, with my fingers crusted in charcoal, I felt as if the death of Beau's sister, Ettie — and my inability to figure out the visions of her death quickly enough — stood firmly between him and me.

Beau ran his fingers down my arm, tracing the curves of my ivy vine tattoo until he reached my wrist. Little electric kisses followed in the wake of his touch. He flipped my hand over and laced his fingers through mine.

I squeezed his hand as tightly as I could. He grunted in satisfaction.

"We both know that Ettie was a willing participant in her death," he said quietly. "She not only ignored you, she deliberately put herself in harm's way, wearing that dress ..." He trailed off. We'd already had this conversation — probably more times than was ultimately healthy. Talking about it didn't change the facts. "Blackwell will fight to the bitter end."

"Fight?" I scoffed. "Wait until he sees the sketches. He'll be gone two seconds later."

"He's seen them. He knows. He was with Win. He's probably waiting for you at the Brave, ready for a second look."

"He stayed?"

"Crazy, huh?"

I thought about Blackwell. About him sipping his coffee, then placing it carefully on the table at Tim Hortons. "He doesn't like being out of control," I said.

"None of us do."

"No, I mean, he already feels out of control. Because of Win. She's holding something over him."

"Of course she is."

"Do you think you and I are doomed to hate each other's families?"

Beau laughed harshly, then rose fluidly to his feet and held out his hand for me. "I think it's a good thing our families are small."

I let him haul me upright, brushing off my jeans as best I could. My ass was covered in dirt from having scrambled around like an idiot when the vision hit.

"What is it?" Beau asked softly.

I shook my head. "Other than Blackwell dying?"

"Yeah."

I wrapped my free hand around his, then we meandered back in the direction of the Brave. My eyes were glued to the ground.

"These visions are different," I finally said, trying to articulate a feeling I hadn't quite figured out myself. "I feel ... vulnerable in them. Like the demon can see me. Talk directly to me."

"But you're not there. You're not seeing yourself."

"No. I don't think so. But it is. It sees me. When I see it in the future, it can look back at me."

Beau's grip tightened on my hand, momentarily crushing my fingers. His magic rolled over him. Then with a quick exhalation of breath, the energy and his grip both eased. "We need to call Jade."

"And have her come up here to hunt a demon? And possibly Blackwell? Or my grandmother, for that matter? Because if Jade thinks Blackwell is evil, what the hell is she going to think about Win? No. Or not yet, at least."

"Not to fight, no. But Jade puts us in contact with Drake, and Drake puts us in contact with Chi Wen, who you can ask about the visions."

"Not in two days."

Beau looked at me, confused.

"You said the half-moon that I've seen in the visions is only two or three days away."

"Maybe one day now," he murmured.

We didn't speak for the remainder of the walk to the Brave.

Blackwell was sitting out front at the patio table, reading a local newspaper and sipping an apple juice that he'd apparently bought from the twins' juice stand. I handed him my sketchbook without speaking. I brushed my fingers against his shoulder and climbed into the Brave to shower and change.

I probably should have said something. I probably should have insisted on refining the sketches further. But one or two days wasn't a lot of time. If we were even putting the clues together correctly in the first place.

And I really wasn't going to face my grandmother over dinner, along with whatever her yet-to-be-revealed agenda was, with a dirt-crusted ass. Even I had more respect and dignity than that.

I WAS SOAKING WET, MY HAIR DRIPPING WITH soapsuds, when I realized I hadn't answered Beau's question. *Why Blackwell?*

Why had I experienced visions of Blackwell dating all the way back to when I was thirteen years old? He wasn't my father. He hadn't known my mother. He hadn't even known I'd existed, because Win hadn't known. Because no one had known.

Chi Wen once said he thought I was influenced by the most powerful people around me. So living in Vancouver, that should have been Jade and her family.

Blackwell was from Scotland.

He'd found me through my Etsy shop. Years later.

Hadn't he?

So why Blackwell? Why not my grandmother?

Why was he the very first Adept I had ever seen?

"GOI CUON, HALF TOFU, HALF PRAWN. ENOUGH for the table. Pho dac biet, four large bowls. We'll share. Two servings of com hien thap cam, and one com chay tham cam with tofu." Blackwell looked up from the menu to address our waiter directly. "We'll keep a menu."

"That's salad rolls, beef soup, and rice," Beau whispered to Krista and Calvin, who were seated on his left. We were all occupying a round table in the very back corner of the spartanly decorated Vietnamese restaurant.

It was sweet of him to pretend to be filling in the kids, because I had no idea what Blackwell was ordering either.

"Bubble tea?" Win asked from across the table.

"Ah, yes." Blackwell consulted the menu again. "Mango, strawberry, taro, peach, blueberry, or honeydew?"

"Taro," Win said dismissively, unfolding her napkin and placing it in her lap.

Beau made a disgusted face for the kids' benefit.

Krista giggled, then said, "Blueberry?" in a hopeful voice to her mother, who was seated beside her.

Leanne nodded. "One blueberry and one strawberry, please."

"And tea for the table," Blackwell added.

The waiter nodded, then made his getaway. He hadn't said more than five words since the ten of us showed up and requested a table. With the restaurant only half full, I assumed he appreciated the business. But I suspected he could sense the uncomfortable tension that ten Adepts — all relative strangers to each other — brought with them, even as someone nonmagical.

Yes. Beau had invited everyone to dinner with my grandmother.

Win hadn't been amused. She'd insisted on a table at the very back, though we'd been offered another just off the windows. All the other diners were seated at least two tables away from us.

Henry was having a blast, of course. He was grinning from ear to ear, as if he was cataloging every little awkward moment.

Ember was glued to her phone in an intense fashion, which made it clear she'd rather be anywhere else than eating pho with a bunch of strange Adepts.

Blackwell had attempted to settle beside me when we initially sat, but Win redirected him to sit next to her. He had obeyed without question.

That wasn't weird at all.

Silence fell as we waited for the drinks to be delivered. I wondered if any of the other customers were staring at us, but my back was to the room so that I couldn't see. Ironically, my grandmother couldn't mask herself from nonmagicals and still get served dinner.

I found myself imagining what it might look like if a fight broke out at our table.

I wondered who would win and who would die.

Blackwell caught my gaze from across the table. He tried to smile. He didn't pull it off.

Beau slipped his hand into mine underneath the table. "Krista and Calvin raised fifty-one dollars for the school library in two hours this afternoon. That has to be some sort of record."

"Yeah," Krista said. "Sorcerers and witches should come to stay all the time. Right, Calvin?"

Calvin looked utterly put on the spot by the question — and more than a little terrified at voicing an opinion that I assumed was contrary to his sister's.

Henry threw his head back and laughed. Ember covered her smile with a sip of water.

"I thought we would talk," Win said to me, as if no one else was sitting with us. Her expression was coolly blank.

I opened my mouth, but then found I had nothing to say.

"I thought a family dinner appropriate," Beau said. "Don't you, Win?"

Win's lips twisted, but instead of replying to Beau, she glanced over at Blackwell. "You encouraged this?" she asked.

Though he responded to Win, Blackwell didn't look at her. "You'd have Rochelle here without protection?"

"I'd have her home. With me." She eyed me for a moment. "Well fed, and taken care of properly. Studying her craft in a focused and meaningful way. Needing no concern for her safety. And not mixing with lesser beings."

I straightened my spine, exceedingly aware that their conversation wasn't about our choice of restaurant or dining companions.

"Good luck with that," Blackwell said.

Win smiled smugly. "I've never needed luck."

Leanne and Eddie were leaning into each other and quietly discussing something about the B&B's schedule for the next day. Calvin was playing with his tablet. But Krista, Ember, and Henry were all listening to Win and Blackwell intently.

"Was that some sort of racial slur?" I asked, locking eyes with my grandmother. There was no way I was going to let that comment slide.

Leanne and Eddie fell silent.

The waiter dropped off the bubble tea, then topped up our water. The tension pervading the family get-together grew smothering as cubes of ice plinked against our glasses and threatened to slosh water onto the table.

"Thank you," Blackwell murmured.

The waiter crossed over to a party of four seated along the wall three tables away.

"Well?" I narrowed my eyes in Win's direction. "I'm not big on games."

"I have no issue with anyone's race," my grandmother said haughtily.

I opened my mouth, gearing up for a fight. A massive, all-out brawl in public would send Win scurrying away as quickly as she'd shown up at my door. No one wanted to deal with a pissy, mouthy orphan on any sort of permanent basis. It was a technique I was well versed in, and had successfully used to thwart numerous bonding attempts by foster parents and social workers. The trick was to not overdo it, though. Lay it on too thickly and people got angry, then somehow that anger transitioned into guilt, which made them even more clingy. No, making someone uncomfortable was a much better —

Beau squeezed my hand.

I shut my mouth.

"I'm interested in the activities of the sorcerers League in China," Henry said, attempting to defuse some of the tension. "In North America, we're looking to create a more responsive collective."

Win didn't respond.

"Oh?" Ember said, stiffly but politely filling the awkward silence. "Are you a member? I mean ... it's not like covens, is it? Where membership is a requirement?"

"I'm a newly elected director, actually."

"It's a good thing there aren't any membership purity requirements, marshal," Blackwell said drily. "Such as with the pack. Otherwise, after Southaven, they wouldn't have accepted your application."

The table fell silent again. Only this time, Leanne,

Eddie, and Beau were sending death glares in Blackwell's direction.

The sorcerer frowned, as if he was unaware of how his insulting Henry would also insult the shapeshifters at the table. But presumably, he had no way of knowing the pack's position on Krista and Calvin being some sort of shifter hybrid, rather than either a true wolf or coyote like their parents. Therefore he had no way of knowing that the Thompsons had been encouraged to leave Portland for reasons of 'purity.'

"I am the Chinese League," Win said blithely.

"Sorry?" Henry said. "You're the chair of the Chinese chapter?"

"No," my grandmother said. "Any sorcerer who practices in China must swear allegiance to me."

Henry looked dumbfounded. "That's ... unusual. And I'm sure I would have heard of such a ..." He glanced over at Blackwell, who shook his head almost imperceptibly.

"What does 'membership purity requirements' mean?" Krista asked.

"We'll talk about it later," Leanne said, looking pointedly at Calvin.

The boy immediately cued in on his mother's wishes and tried to draw his sister into a two-player game on his tablet.

The waiter hustled out of the kitchen with armfuls of salad rolls and peanut sauce. His timing was impeccable.

I leaned into Beau, pointedly whispering more than loudly enough for the shapeshifters at the table to hear me, "It means we're sitting at a table with a bunch of bigots from the nineteenth century."

"I wish that were true," he whispered back. "Racism is

alive and well in the twenty-first century, especially among the Adept. And it has nothing to do with skin color."

He snagged a plate of tofu salad rolls, then offered it to me. After I'd taken a roll, he passed the plate to Krista, who instantly rejected the 'fake meat.'

Everyone eagerly embraced the distraction the food provided, eating voraciously. After all, it wasn't polite to talk with one's mouth full.

WE MADE IT THROUGH DINNER WITHOUT FURTHER incident, but only because the shapeshifters first inhaled the food Blackwell had ordered, then used Krista's and Calvin's bedtime as an excuse to leave pretty much the second the serving dishes were empty. Before dessert, even. Though given that I'd seen no sign of my boxes of donuts from this afternoon, that part of the meal might already have been taken care of.

Blackwell insisted on picking up the bill. No one offered any protest over him paying or leaving early.

The sun hadn't even fully set. But then, we had just passed the longest day of the year. The evening had cooled slightly, though, so I was happy I'd brought the lightweight, long-sleeved hoodie I'd purchased off Etsy earlier that spring. The top was reconstructed out of a series of garments, sporting gray sleeves and black cuffs that I folded back when I was sketching, and a patched-together deep-navy-and-charcoal torso.

Ember was the only one who had driven to the restaurant, and she had room for only one other person in her rental Smart car, so Henry went with her back to the B&B.

The rest of us walked home in small groups, marking the fourth time I'd taken that route since Blackwell and I had gone up the hill to Tim Hortons earlier that day. Though the few hours between then and now felt like days to me. The dinner had aged me easily two years.

I wasn't cut out for stilted conversations and tension-filled family gatherings.

My grandmother strode ahead of me, moving nothing like I would have imagined a woman in her sixties could move. Though I was still just guessing at her age. Blackwell walked between us, maintaining a few steps of distance between Win in front and Beau and me behind.

Krista and Calvin darted back from beside their parents up ahead, clamoring around Beau.

"Piggyback, Beau," Krista said.

"Both at the same time," Calvin added, more demanding than asking.

Beau chuckled and leaned down without breaking stride, offering a bent arm to each twin. Krista and Calvin wrapped their hands around his flexed biceps, then Beau straightened, lifting them off their feet while Krista squealed gleefully and Calvin grinned like mad.

I laughed quietly. Though it had technically only been ten years ago, I couldn't remember being eleven. Not in the way the twins were eleven. That mixture of child and adult, and the way they were able to enjoy both aspects of their lives.

"Faster," Krista cried.

Beau flashed me a grin, then jogged off down the road with Krista and Calvin swinging off his arms. The feat of strength was effortless for him. The twins' grip would give out way before his arms would.

Blackwell shortened his stride, allowing me to catch up with him.

"That's quite a display," he said quietly.

"Nothing anyone his size wouldn't be able to do," I said.

"For a few minutes, perhaps."

"And as far as the neighbors know, that's as long as the game lasts."

Blackwell fell silent. The houses on either side of the road were quiet, but still well lit. The chickens wouldn't have cooped themselves yet, but with the sun setting at our backs, the street was darkening before us.

"How long until we talk about everything we need to talk about?" I said.

"You are not prone to verbosity yourself," Blackwell said.

"But some clarification is needed, yes? Like, why you?"

"Why me?"

"Why did I see you? When the visions manifested, I saw you first. Stealing your amulet from the dragons."

Blackwell touched his chest protectively. I had never sketched my first vision of Blackwell, so that was something he hadn't known. The sketching had come later, in the form of shrink-mandated therapy. Then it had stuck around as an outlet for what I'd thought was a psychotic disorder, but which had turned out to be oracle magic.

Some days, it would be easy to think that I'd simply traded one type of crazy for another. That I was actually hallucinating everything and everyone around me, while in real life I was probably a drooling, lobotomized mess in some psych ward. But not today.

Today, I had to believe.

"When?" Blackwell asked, pulling my attention back to the conversation. "When you were how old? Thirteen?"

"About that."

"I didn't steal the amulet. I simply reclaimed it."

"Then you ran," I said wryly.

Blackwell snorted, but he didn't disagree.

Up ahead, Eddie and Leanne turned left into their driveway. Beau set the kids on their feet, glancing back to see how close I was.

"Rochelle," Blackwell said urgently. "There is a larger scope here. Larger than you having visions of me when you were in your teens."

I stopped along the edge of the road. "So tell me, then."

Blackwell stopped next to me. I couldn't really see his face in the evening light. He was simply a pale wash of skin above the dark lapels of his suit.

"I was hoping to have more time," he whispered. "Before ... this." He looked over at my grandmother.

Win had stopped a few feet away from Beau at the base of the driveway. She was turned to look back at us.

Darkness continued to slowly erode my eyesight.

Nothing else happened.

Win lifted her hand, beckoning us toward her. The gesture parted her cloak momentarily, and a wash of sunset reflected off her ivy brooch. Then she lowered her arm and the cloak fell closed again, snuffing out the oranges and reds that had bloomed briefly on her chest.

Blackwell stepped forward without another word.

Blinking away reflected spots of sunset, I trailed behind him, knowing that I was missing something huge. Knowing that I would just have to wait for clarity. And hoping that insight didn't arrive in a demonic form.

"Maybe we should sleep outside tonight," Beau said, leaning back in a plastic patio chair against the Brave and lifting his face to the sky. The moon was hovering over the horizon, and we were parked in the perfect place to watch it clear the broad expanse of fruit trees between us and the lake. We'd spent the last couple of hours of the deepening evening chatting through all the revelations of the day while the others retreated to their various cottages for the night. Everyone was more than ready for some alone time. Thankfully I got to spend mine next to Beau. It was probably near midnight, but I didn't bother pulling out my phone to check.

I grinned at him. "Bugs."

Beau snorted. "I run hotter than you. I'll draw them all. You'll be unscathed."

"I'll accept that as fact just as soon as you show me —"

A woman shrieked sharply from somewhere along the upper left side of the property. Then her voice was muted out as suddenly as it had sounded.

I froze, listening intently.

Beau was out of his chair before I saw him move, crossing farther into the small clearing and slowly panning his head left, then right.

Nothing else happened.

"It's okay," Eddie called out from somewhere above and behind us, possibly near the main house. "Just the kids punking Leanne."

Beau didn't answer.

"Cool, Eddie," I called back.

Beau continued scanning the trees. His shoulders were set in a block of tension.

"Beau?"

He shook his head, turning back to me. "It's nothing ... just ..." He lifted his head, staring beyond the Brave toward where the main house sat. "There are no sounds."

"What do you mean? It's nighttime."

"The second bat box Eddie set up along the edge of the new apples has occupants." He pointed in the direction of the cottage we set aside for Gary and Tess, below us at the base of the property. "The bats are good for the orchard."

"I know. They eat the bugs."

"At night. Bugs I can't currently hear."

"You can normally hear bugs?"

Beau sighed. "You know what I mean."

"You mean something wicked this way comes."

Beau, still listening to the still night, didn't answer.

"You said we had two days," I whispered, fear blooming in my stomach. "If something had changed, wouldn't the vision have changed?"

"Yeah, maybe." Beau paced back to press a kiss against my forehead. "Go inside. I'll just do a circuit."

I frowned.

"Please?"

"Fine."

Without bothering to see if I was going to keep my word, he stepped off into the deep shadows between the trees, heading toward the main house.

I couldn't really complain about him being overprotective. And it wasn't like I wanted to wander around in the dark anyway.

Something moved at the edge of my peripheral vision,

from the opposite direction than the one Beau had taken. I spun toward it, immediately identifying Henry by his cowboy hat.

The marshal held up his hands and offered me a grin. "Beau with you?"

I shook my head.

Henry nodded, closing the space between us. He lifted his gaze to the moon. "Not the same as the visions you sketched."

"No," I said.

"There's something in the air, though," Henry muttered.

"No bugs, Beau said."

"Yes. A stillness."

"But no magic."

"Not that I can feel. Though I'm not the most sensitive. Ask Blackwell." Henry nodded toward the dark trees behind and to the left of us.

"Ask me what?" Blackwell stepped out of the darkness, but then paused, scanning the area rather than joining us by the Brave.

"Why you obey Kai Win without question," Henry said.

Blackwell didn't answer.

"Were you her apprentice?"

I touched Henry's arm. "He can't talk about it."

Henry whistled. "A geas? That's old magic. Outlawed."

"Not everywhere. Not at the time," Blackwell said crisply, wandering over to stand on the other side of me but facing out into the clearing.

"You're not that old," Henry said.

"Or I was younger than you're assuming."

Though they shared a similar lanky frame, Blackwell

was a couple of inches taller than Henry. They stood there for a long moment, eyes locked in some sort of silent battle, with me sandwiched between them.

I scrubbed my hands in an attempt to brush away the sparks of energy coming off them. "Is this necessary?" I asked, grumbling.

"Yes," they answered in unison.

I sighed. "Can you do it elsewhere, then? I'm seriously tired."

"Why are you here, marshal?" Blackwell's tone was deep and intense.

Henry tugged open the unbuttoned neck of his short-sleeved, collared shirt. Just enough for Blackwell to see the edge of my henna tattoo.

"You're not planning on testing its effectiveness here, are you?"

"We're still a month away from the next full moon."

"And you have a job to do. Don't you, marshal?" Blackwell stressed Henry's title.

"Yesterday, Rochelle had a vision —"

"So I've seen."

"So you think I should leave? Go back to transporting prisoners, protecting witnesses, and apprehending fugitives while a demon manifests in Summerland, British Columbia?"

"I think you have no authority here. Nor are you the most powerful sorcerer in the vicinity. And I believe you'd be very interested in testing the strength of your temporary tattoo, which is not solely constructed to keep the wolf at bay during a full moon. Is it? You're hoping to channel the shifter magic, every day, and without the forced transformation. Rochelle doesn't need you complicating the situation."

"By that logic, we should give the Godfrey coven a call." Henry practically spat the threat in Blackwell's face. "Plus, the situation, as you call it, is the result of your own secrecy and the power you trade in."

"That is absolute, ill-informed garbage."

"Had you informed Rochelle of her grandmother's existence and your connection —"

"That's enough!" I shouted, shoving both of them away from me. I hated feeling crowded that way. Like I was trapped and unable to breathe.

I inhaled, then released a shuddering breath.

Blackwell was staring down at his chest, utterly amazed. I'd shoved him away, but not with my hand. Rather, my ivy tattoo was pressed against him, holding him at bay.

I cranked my neck to look left at Henry. My hand was flat against his chest. The marshal was watching Blackwell, not me, as if waiting for a reaction.

Blackwell's surprise melted into a smug smile. Then he raised his eyes, meeting my gaze. "Care to tell me about this?"

I folded my arms, pulling the ivy tattoo away from Blackwell with the gesture.

"If you'd been around, Blackwell," Henry said, "and not off sulking, you would have noticed that the oracle wasn't only proficient at wielding mind magic."

Blackwell sniffed. "I'm not her mentor."

Branches snapped underneath someone's feet, calling my attention away from the pissing match ramping up between the sorcerers. Again.

Ember stepped into the clearing. She looked as though she'd been getting ready for bed, perhaps showering or washing her face. Then, for some reason, she'd tugged on a pair of the gumboots that were stocked in all the cottages underneath her calf-length cotton nightgown and wandered over. She was also carrying her briefcase. "Something disturbed my wards."

Henry stepped toward her, any and all hints of aggression smoothed away as he clicked into professional mode. "Around your cottage?"

"No," she said as she crossed over to us. "Between there and the RV."

"So you walked over here?" Blackwell asked incredulously.

Ember opened her palm to show him some sort of glowing stone. "It only lit up when I hit the edge of the orchard."

"What does that cover, a five-yard radius?" Blackwell sneered. "The demon that's coming could cross that distance before the stone even lit up."

"I have other defenses, sorcerer," Ember said darkly.

"No one knows what you're all talking about," I said, feeling edgy with their magic angrily sparking all around me.

They all turned to look at me questioningly.

"Okay, so I don't know what you're talking about. I'm the only one who doesn't get what's going on."

Henry nodded toward Ember. "She's holding a magical detector. Still, it was stupidly brave to investigate on her own rather than to text me."

"I tried to text," she said. "You and Rochelle. The messages didn't go through. I have full signal."

Henry swore under his breath, glancing around the clearing again.

"What does that mean?" I whispered to Blackwell.

"Most likely magical interference, but only on your and Henry's phones."

"Stay with Rochelle," Henry said to Ember.

The witch lifted her chin haughtily. "I intend to."

Without another word, Henry and Blackwell stepped away in opposite directions.

"So ..." Ember said. "Do you have any lemonade?"

"Um, no. Apple juice?"

"Almost as good. Especially if it's the juice the twins were selling earlier."

Obligingly, I turned toward the Brave.

Ember stiffened.

I twisted back to follow her gaze. My grandmother was standing where Blackwell had just been.

"Everyone's out for an evening stroll," I said. "Maybe you're all tripping each other's wards."

Win sniffed derisively.

"I doubt your grandmother trips any wards," Ember said quietly. Then she stepped in front of me, adopting a defensive posture.

"I mean my granddaughter no harm, witch," Win said, slowly closing the space between us.

"You certainly were interested in her estate," Ember said.

"Made some phone calls, did you?" Win's question was delivered with a completely neutral tone that I found exceedingly intimidating.

Ember squared her shoulders but didn't answer.

"Apparently, everyone here knows a lot of stuff that I don't," I said pointedly.

"It might behoove you to ask some questions." Win stopped a few steps away.

"Maybe she doesn't trust the answers she'll get," Ember said.

My grandmother looked up, gazing at the night sky.

The moon stood out starkly, not a cloud in sight. Which was good, because I'd sketched wispy cloud cover in the vision of the demon attacking Blackwell. Her voice cut through the deepening darkness. "You think to stand between me and my kin, witch?"

"If necessary."

"Why would it be?"

But before Ember could answer, sudden movement erupted in the darkness as Beau darted out from the trees. Krista and Calvin were hanging off his back. "I can't find Leanne and Eddie."

"What?" I cried.

Beau set the twins down. They were barefoot and wearing Star Wars pajamas. "Get into the Brave," he said.

They obeyed him without question. As I opened the door, I could practically feel the twins' fear as they scrambled up the stairs past me. Calvin pushed Krista ahead of him, then turned back to look at us from inside the RV. "I thought it was a game," he whispered.

"It's okay," Beau said. "Rochelle and Ember will stay with you. Go."

"Beau?" I asked as the twins disappeared inside the Brave.

He shook his head, indicating behind me. The children could still hear us.

"Have you seen Henry?" he asked. "He's not at his cottage."

"He was just here with Blackwell."

Beau nodded, then turned to Win. "Will you stay or come with me?"

My grandmother tilted her head as if considering the question, but I honestly had no idea what she was thinking. Whether she was completely disinterested in the missing shifters, or amused by Beau's protectiveness, or simply dismissive as always. "Any trail, shifter?"

"Two. Both ended without warning."

"You tried the nearby trees?"

"Of course."

"They were just taken?" I asked.

"You aren't wolf," Win said to Beau, ignoring me completely and insulting him at the same time. "Your nose isn't trustworthy."

"It's better than yours," Beau said stiffly.

"Not for magic," she said snidely.

Beau gestured toward the line of trees between us and the main house. "Lead on. Might I suggest we find the sorcerers first?"

Win smirked. "And leave my granddaughter alone with two uninitiated fledglings? Backed only by a witch who deals in contracts, not defensive spells?"

"Your granddaughter is more capable than you know," I said, not feeling terribly capable at all, but bluffing madly.

Win snorted. Then she stepped away, melting into the darkness surrounding us without another word.

Beau swept me forward into a crushing kiss. I forced myself to release his neck and not beg him to stay. Then he followed Win into the apple trees.

I looked up again at the night. There wasn't a cloud in the sky, and the moon was only a few feet above the horizon. "Maybe we were wrong," I said.

"About what?" Ember asked.

I shook my head. Now wasn't the time to fill the witch in on my last two visions. Not with the twins in the Brave. "You placed wards around here?" I asked instead.

"I always do."

"Can you ... I don't know ... seal them up? Create a magical boundary of some sort?"

"They're not those kinds of wards. It takes days to lay enough spells to fortify something as large as a house, or even an RV ... or someone with more powerful warding magic than me."

I touched my necklace, inadvertently drawing Ember's gaze to its raw diamond.

"Yeah," she said. "Someone powerful enough to make something like that."

There was a question in her comment, but I ignored it.

"Mom says there are wards around the house," Krista said from behind us.

I looked up to see the eleven-year-old peering out the window just above my head.

"Inactive," Ember said. "And old. But ... maybe ..."

I shook my head. "Beau expects us to stay here."

Ember shrugged. "I suggest you get some mobile wards, then. They won't be as powerful as they would be if they were tied to land, though. Property under your ownership, specifically. But you've got enough sorcerers hanging around, one of them could throw a few runes your way."

"I'll take it under advisement." Yeah, I was being snarky, but the witch was developing a terrible habit of dispensing unsolicited advice.

I climbed into the Brave, leaving the lights off. The twins were huddled on the bench seat on the far side of the dinette.

My sketchbook was open on the table.

I put my hands on my hips, glowering at them.

Krista jutted out her chin defiantly as Calvin flipped the sketchbook closed, then placed it back underneath the window where they'd found it.

Great. Now I was going to be responsible for their nightmares over the next few weeks.

"I thought it was a game," Calvin blurted, repeating himself. "You know, hide-and-seek, but like for training. But then, when we tried to ... the trail was just ... gone. I think ... I think there might be something here ... on the property."

Calvin whispered that last part. All the hair stood up on the back of my neck, but I brushed away my rising fear. I didn't want them to see me distressed. "It's okay. Beau will be back soon." I crossed toward the fridge, navigating easily in the moonlight coming in the windows. "The moon is pretty bright tonight," I said, opening an upper cupboard. I had to lift up on my tiptoes to snag a box of Oreos. "Even for not being full, I mean."

"The last full moon was a strawberry moon," Krista said, falling into her know-it-all mode — a classic coping mechanism that I had no problem indulging. "It was a rare full moon on the summer solstice. The last time that happened was before my mom and dad were even born."

I turned to the fridge for Ember's apple juice. Then I noticed that she hadn't followed us into the Brave.

Looking back at the open door, I held the box of Oreos out to Calvin. He didn't take it from me.

"Where's the witch?" he asked.

I didn't answer.

I placed the cookies down on the table, dug my left hand into my satchel, and curled my fingers around the tactical pen I kept in the side pocket. The pen that Beau had showed me how to use in case I ever needed to gouge someone's eyes out.

"Ember?" I called softly.

The witch didn't answer.

I crossed toward the door. The twins slipped out from the bench seat to follow me. "Stay put," I said.

They stopped where they were, holding each other's hands. Their eyes were wide and apprehensive.

An unbidden and unwanted anger rose in me, momentarily choking me. I took a deep breath as I tore my gaze from the kids, then pushed the almost-debilitating emotion away.

Then I went to look for the witch.

SIX

"Ember?"

The small clearing around the Brave was empty. As expected, but not as I'd hoped.

I stood at the bottom of the stairs, peering out into the moonlit evening and momentarily wishing I was ... more. More than an oracle wielding just a tactical pen and useless glimpses into the future.

For a second, I wished I were the woman in my mother's drawing. No demon, no malicious force, would even dare to go near her.

"Beau is near," Calvin whispered behind me.

I turned my head slightly. The twins were on the steps, practically pressing against my back. I hadn't even heard them move. Another minus on my scorecard of useless superpowers.

"Can you smell him or hear him?" I asked, speaking as quietly as possible.

"Smell," Krista said, her breath brushing my right ear.

"And Ember?"

I felt, rather than saw, Calvin shake his head.

Something moved within the trees. I waited for the shadow to resolve into an identifiable person. It didn't.

"Who is that?" I breathed.

"Where?" Calvin whispered.

I didn't bother pointing. If it was someone they knew, the twins would have picked up the scent.

The shadow coiled around an apple tree a dozen feet away. I caught a glimpse of a spiked, black-scaled tail. Then a flash of crimson eyes. Then nothing.

It might have been an echo of the visions. Though those usually came with a misty edge.

Or we were being hunted.

"Step back, slowly," I said. "Step back inside." I climbed the stairs backward without taking my eyes off the clearing. The twins moved with me.

I threw the aftermarket lock, but even as I did so the Brave suddenly felt like a death trap around me. A metal box easily ripped asunder by massive teeth and claws.

I moved to the dinette, peering through the windows into the apple grove. I didn't know where to run, where to hide with the kids. Leanne and Eddie had already been taken from the house or at least from the vicinity of the house. We needed to hide. We needed to hope the demon couldn't track us by scent.

"Do you know where the tree house is?" A wooden box only fifteen feet off the ground wouldn't offer any better protection, but it was the best hiding spot I could think of. Plus, it was closer than the house and I wasn't sure we should leave the property.

"Yes," Krista said.

"I want you two to climb over the bed and pull the screen out of the back window. Quietly." I pointed toward the back of the Brave, indicating the window I wanted them to open. "If we have to leave, that's where we'll exit."

Krista nodded. Her eyes were deep pools of fear.

"When I say run, you run. No questions, no hesitation," I said, echoing all my training sessions with Beau. "When I say run, you run."

"Beau said stay here," Calvin protested, forgetting to whisper.

Keeping my eyes glued to the clearing outside the window, I lifted my satchel from around my neck and set it on the bench seat of the dinette. I touched my back pocket, double-checking that I had my phone. Then I gripped the tactical pen before me.

"And what did I say?" My voice was laced with fear and anger. With determination.

"Run," Krista whispered. "You said run."

The twins slipped silently back through the Brave, following my instructions without further protest.

I wondered if Blackwell was all the way over among the cherry trees. I wondered if the sorcerer was about to die. If we'd gotten the timing wrong. Or if we had altered the vision somehow already without knowing.

Outside, a shadow slithered away from a tree trunk, creeping into the wash of moonlight between the rows of apple trees. Then it resolved into crimson-red eyes, a black-scaled body, and four massively clawed feet. It stalked toward the Brave. A malignant, dark energy seeped from it, dampening everything that was good and comforting. Stirring deeply hidden horrors and terrible deeds within my heart and soul.

Calvin whimpered. He'd slipped back to stand beside me without me noticing.

The young shifter had been correct. It was a game.

But it was a game with multiple players. Multiple good guys.

"Beau!" I shouted. "It's here."

I saw him burst into the clearing, his gorgeous tiger form boiling forth to split his skin and rend his clothing.

Henry was with him.

The demon was pinned between the sorcerer and the massive, vicious tiger. Beau's snarling growl shook the branches of the nearby trees.

But I couldn't stay to watch the looming battle.

"Run," I whispered, hoping to slip away without being noticed by the demon.

The twins scrambled over the bed, slithered through the window, and dashed off into the trees. I did my best to follow. Some sort of energy buffeted me from behind, blowing my hair around my eyes. Henry's magic, I guessed.

An enraged, earsplitting shriek followed. So the demon did have a voice. Then a booming sound shook the ground beneath my feet. I stumbled. Two large objects had just collided, most likely Beau and the demon.

But I willed myself forward, not back. I had no super-power that would help in whatever fight was taking place behind me.

I kept my gaze on the pair of moonlight-kissed blond heads in front of me, and I ran.

I was getting good at running.

"Go, go, go." I whispered the mantra over and over under my labored breath. Though I could barely hear myself, the twin fledgling shapeshifters dashing ahead of me through the night-shrouded fruit trees would have no problem picking up my urgency.

We flew past the coop, the chickens safely ensconced within it. The rooster crowed after we'd passed, echoing the mournful cry I'd only ever heard in the snippet of the vision I'd had on the beach. I desperately hoped it wasn't a warning as we scrambled across the paved driveway, darting underneath the boughs of peach, nectarine, and apricot trees.

We ran for safety, leaving the battle behind us to Beau and the sorcerers, and desperately hoping that Leanne, Eddie, and Ember weren't already lost.

We didn't reach the tree house.

We were within a dozen feet of the willow tree when Calvin fell. He pulled Krista down with him, and the two tumbled in a tangle of limbs to slam against a tree on the outer edge of the stone fruit grove.

By the time I'd reached them, Krista was struggling to drag Calvin to his feet. He thwarted her efforts, curling protectively into a fetal position.

"Did he trip?" I hissed, glancing back over my shoulder. I almost missed Krista shaking her head, utterly terrified.

Calvin convulsed. Still trying to hold himself still, he snapped his head back in a painful silent scream.

"Oh, no …" Krista backed away from her brother until she was pressed against the trunk of the tree.

"Crap." I hunkered down by the boy as I desperately racked my brain for possible first aid options. "Does he have seizures?"

"No," Krista moaned. She gathered her knees into her chest, rocking lightly with her gaze locked over my shoulder into the dark night behind us. "He's changing …"

I tugged Calvin's arm, feeling his skin writhe underneath my hands as I forced him to roll farther into the moonlight. He moaned with stifled pain. His cheek, jaw, and forehead were painfully distended as the bone beneath transformed.

"Don't touch him, Rochelle," Krista said. "It hurts."

"We have to go." I glanced behind us, trying to penetrate the darkness between the trees with my meager eyesight. "We have to keep moving."

"We can't move him ... he's stuck."

"What do you mean stuck?"

"He shouldn't be changing at all." Krista choked back a sob. "But ... but ..."

"The tree house is right there," I said. "I can see the willow branches. We just have to drag him."

"No," she cried. "We could hurt him more. We could interfere with the magic. Especially you. You're not a shapeshifter."

"You know what is going to hurt?" I snarled before I could check my fear and frustration. "Getting torn to pieces by a demon."

Krista's lower lip quivered. Her eyes were glowing green around the circumference of each iris. Crap. I didn't need both of them turning halfway.

"You go ahead," I said. "You'll need to scale the tree to grab the ladder —"

"I'm not leaving him."

"Don't make me make you."

The girl jutted her chin out, defiant. "How? I'm bigger and badder than you."

I laughed snarkily. "We can test that theory pretty quickly."

"Leave ... me ..." Calvin groaned, still in pain.

I glanced down at the boy. His arms were covered in patchy fur, but the bones of his face hadn't shifted any further.

I swore just about every nasty word I could think of under my breath.

We were sitting ducks, loitering out at the edge of the peach orchard. And me with two preteens to defend and only a goddamn tactical pen for a weapon.

Terror flooded my chest. I gripped the pen and forced the emotion down.

There had to be some way I could protect us all.

Wards.

Could I draw a protection circle? Or was that just witch magic? I'd seen Blackwell draw a pentagram, but that was so it would contain the magic he'd wielded to craft a tracking device. But could I create a shield of some sort, like when I drew my tattoos?

Like with Henry's tattoo?

I took a deep breath. Digging deep within my senses, I recalled the feeling of the oracle magic when it forced me to sketch a vision. I touched the glass-breaker tip of the pen to the dirt at my feet.

"Your eyes," Krista whispered. "They're glowing."

"Watch the trees," I said. "Stand here with the trunk at your back and turn slowly. If anything moves before I finish, you run for the tree house."

"But —"

"You will listen to me." I pitched my tone low to tell her there was no arguing this time. Shapeshifters followed the strongest pack leader. And right now, that was me. "You will run. I will protect Calvin."

Krista nodded, rising to her feet and scanning the trees behind me.

Grunting in pain, Calvin fought against another wave of convulsions.

I needed to ignore him, reminding myself I was helping him the only way I could. I directed my attention to the packed dirt and loose grass at my feet.

I started to draw a circle, but a wash of magical energy pushed through me, making the line turn wavy underneath my shaking grip. A faint white light emanated from the grooves I'd etched into the dirt. Then I was slowly scrambling backward on my hands and knees, encircling the twins and the fruit tree with a glowing ivy pattern reminiscent of my tattoo.

An ivy pattern scarily similar to the one on the brooch my grandmother wore.

I was halfway done when Krista made, then stifled, a tiny noise of terror.

Not looking up, I drew faster, rounding the tree. I was about two feet from finishing when she cried out a second time.

"Rochelle!"

"Stay in the circle!" I growled.

"But behind you ..."

I could already feel the malignant energy seeping through the night air, permeating every frantic breath I took.

I was inches away from closing the protection circle when the smell of carrion hit me.

Krista dropped down into my peripheral vision, throwing herself across Calvin.

A hot breath blew across the back of my neck. My very tender, very exposed neck.

I closed the circle.

A brighter pulse of white light welled up along the ivy

pattern I'd etched into the dirt. Magic flowed up into the night sky, sealing the twins from harm.

Unfortunately, I was standing on the wrong side of it.

The glow subsided as I shakily rose to my feet, but I could feel the circle of energy beside me. The twins were as safe as I could make them.

And if I was going to die, I was going to do it standing.

I was still gripping the tactical pen. I let my arm fall to my side, slowly turning to stare into the crimson-red eyes of the demon from my vision.

Terror shrieked through every one of my senses. I started shaking. My breathing was suddenly frantic, and my vision was instantly and stupidly compromised by unwanted, useless tears.

The walking nightmare of a beast rose up over me, stretching its long neck and back to stand easily seven feet tall. It flexed its wickedly hooked claws as if testing their dexterity, then curled its black spiked tail around my sneakered feet. A wash of moonlight reflected off the black scales that covered it from head to tail.

A shudder of what might have been pleasure ran through the demon.

Then it lowered its wide, flat head until it was level with mine. All I could feel was terror and revulsion. All I could see was the red of its hell-on-earth eyes. All I could smell was death.

My death.

The demon shrieked, then modulated its tone almost as if it was trying to communicate with me. As if it was struggling to form words, to make itself understood.

I moaned.

Rochelle.

Though it didn't open its mouth, the demon's voice

sounded out in my head as it had in my vision. It wasn't an echo or a memory, though. The demon could somehow speak to me, placing its words in my mind.

Found you.

It snapped its shark teeth closed an inch from my nose. I flinched, willing myself to contain my terror.

I wouldn't scream.

It snickered. The sound was like nails scraped across a chalkboard, only epically worse, ricocheting through my every nerve. It was being playful. Or its own version of playful, at least.

It placed its front claws underneath my chin, pressing upward almost gently but cutting into my skin nonetheless. It cranked my head back, exposing my throat.

Krista screamed.

But I made no sound.

I shook as the tears streamed down my face, but I stood between the twins and the demon. I wasn't sure the magic I'd drawn would hold after my death, so I would stand as long as I could. I would keep breathing as long as I could.

The demon lowered its flat, broad head. It opened its maw to lap at the rivulets of blood running down my neck and seeping into the collar of my T-shirt.

Krista screamed and screamed.

Mine.

Forever mine.

Dear God.

I screamed. I couldn't hold the terror in any longer. I screamed for Beau. I screamed from the pain of losing him. Of leaving him.

He was never going to forgive me.

I swallowed my fear just enough to whisper, "Beau. I love you."

Magic buffeted me. Energy flowed through the trees, raising the hair on my arms and the back of my neck. Henry's golden handcuffs appeared before me, snapping shut on nothing.

The demon was gone.

Then the empty cuffs disappeared as well. The marshal must have tried to apprehend the demon.

I swayed forward as if the beast had been the only thing holding me upright for some time. I fell to my knees.

Krista was sobbing behind me, saying something comforting to Calvin. I couldn't make out the actual words.

I reached up to touch my neck. Then I looked at my hand.

No blood.

No wound.

Had I imagined it all? Had this just been another vision?

"Rochelle?" Krista whispered behind me. "Rochelle?"

"It's okay," I murmured, though I still wasn't sure of that.

"Is it gone?"

A massive form tore through the trees. Its clawed, orange-furred feet landed inches away from me. Its deep, terrifying roar rolled through the orchard, blistering my eardrums.

I didn't flinch.

I knew this monster.

The familiar energy of Beau's magic rolled over him, then he crouched before me in his human form. He was practically naked, though he'd somehow managed to retain his stretched and shredded boxer briefs.

"I lost you there for a minute." He lifted his hand as if

to caress my cheek, but then didn't follow through to actually touch me.

"Yeah," I said. "You almost did."

His chest had been clawed. Four inch-wide slashes across his torso were in the process of healing. I reached out to touch him. To lament his wound.

"Beau!" Krista cried. "Calvin is stuck."

Beau rose in a swift, blurred movement, leaving me on my knees in the dirt. "It's okay, little wolf," he said, moving around me to examine my hastily erected ward. He was limping, favoring his right leg.

The demon was gone. I couldn't sense even a hint of the repulsive darkness it had pulled with it through the orchard.

"Whose ward is this?" Beau growled. "Ember's? And why aren't you behind it?"

I didn't answer. Staring off into the darkness, I felt oddly blind. Lost, even. Disjointed. After a vision, I could go for hours without actual sight. Yet I'd never felt this way before.

Or at least I hadn't felt this way for a long time.

Suddenly Beau was crouching down in front of me. "Rochelle?" His hands were wrapped around my upper arms. He was squeezing too hard, as if he had to stop himself from shaking me.

He had been talking but I hadn't heard him. "Beau?"

He took a relieved breath. "We need to get the kids to the main house. Ember has reactivated the wards there."

Ember. I thought the demon had taken the witch. So that was good news.

But I wasn't sure my legs would support me for the trek to the house just yet. I leaned forward, wrapping my arms around Beau's neck. He was saying something about "shock" and "breaking the ward magic around the twins," but I'd once again missed the words that completed those sentences.

"We need to leave," I whispered into the sweat-slicked skin of his neck. "We have to go."

"No."

No.

Just like that.

Blunt and pointed. He'd never said no to me before. Not like that.

"Listen to me," I whispered. And as I did, I allowed myself to acknowledge what I'd probably known was true ever since I laid eyes on my mother's drawing. Ever since I'd entertained the possibility that I was the woman in the vision, despite the missing tattoos. "It's here for me. The demon is here for me. It belongs to me, somehow ... or maybe I belong to it."

"We aren't leaving. We can't just leave. We have to protect what the Thompsons ... what we are building."

Beau loosened my arms from around his neck.

I let him go.

He stepped forward, hunkering down at the edge of my hand-drawn ward to peer at the twins.

I wanted to follow him, but I was still so numb that I wasn't sure I could operate my legs.

"Whose magic is this?" Beau asked.

The silent and round-eyed twins shifted their gaze from him to me. Calvin had reverted to his human form.

"Mine," I whispered. "It's mine."

Leanne burst into the tiny clearing and rushed up to the twins before I could call out a warning. Her eyes were ablaze with the green of her shifter magic, but she appeared unharmed.

She hit the edge of my ward and cried out in pain. But then she seemed to slip through the invisible barrier, tumbling to her knees to gather the twins into her arms. As if the magic I'd called forth had tested her intent and allowed her to pass.

"Impressive," Blackwell said, stepping through the trees from the direction of the main house. Win was close behind him.

I wasn't sure what he was referring to, but I didn't have the time to stand around figuring it out. The demon was gone, for now. But the visions I'd seen hadn't come to pass, so it would be back.

"Beau." I touched his shoulder, trying to explain myself clearly. "We have to go ... I see ..."

The oracle magic hit me without warning.

"I see ... I see ..."

The power rushed up from underneath my feet, pushing me onto my tiptoes as it swept unbidden and unhindered through my limbs. I threw my arms out and my head back in an attempt to stay upright. I lost what little sight the moonlit dark provided in a wash of brilliant white.

Leanne shrieked, then caught herself.

Behind me, I caught footsteps and muffled, panicked grunting. Probably Henry and Eddie.

Then I lost track of my surroundings.

"Listen to me!" I screamed.

"I'm listening ..." Beau said.

But I was beyond speaking.

The oracle magic flooded my mind and flowed through my veins. Then it showed me a future I was already desperate to change.

IT WAS NIGHT. THE HALF-MOON HUNG AS IF pinned to the dark sky almost directly overhead. Even the stars were muted, swallowed by the soul-chilling gloom and wispy, ashen clouds. I was walking through the cherry orchard, stepping around shattered trees and torn branches. The immature fruit I saw sprinkled throughout the destruction would never grow, never ripen. Never pass on its goodness.

Nothing good would ever grow on this ground again.

The packed dirt and orchard grass under my feet were churned and darkened with the blood of the fallen heroes that littered the vista before me.

I found Beau among the bodies, refusing at first to look at anyone but him. He had a terrible wound at his neck. Not claw or teeth marks, though. A rope burn, maybe. The raw, weeping flesh was cauterized at the edges. His face was pale and gray. All the life had been choked from him.

I fell to my knees beside him.

The deep trough in the dirt leading to his final resting spot told me he'd been dragged there. Dragged through broken, destroyed fruit trees. Dragged to his death.

I wasn't going to be able to go on without him. Kneeling there in that moment, that surety came to me. I would just lie down in this field of death and wait to die alongside him.

I reached for a crumpled, bruised leaf that had fallen on his cheek. Nothing should mar his beauty. I wanted to see all of him. I wanted only him in my mind, filling my sight for the last moments I had in this terribly empty, blood-sodden world.

My fingers passed through the leaf.

Right.

I wasn't there.

This was a vision.

Not the end.

Not the end yet.

Not if I could stop it.

I lifted my head, forcing myself to see beyond Beau's fate. To see it all.

I knew it was destiny I was envisioning, as sure as I filled my lungs with night air from the orchard in which I actually stood, where my body was still firmly rooted to the ground, and the oracle magic danced across my skin.

And that was okay.

Destiny could be foiled.

I just had to be strong enough to nudge it in another direction.

But first, I had to see it.

I needed to see it all to stop it.

The demon was taking its time eating Blackwell's internal organs. With the wide, dark-blue evening sky stretched overhead, it looked smaller than when it had loomed over me beneath the willow tree.

Win had fallen a half-dozen feet beyond the younger sorcerer. My grandmother was facedown as if she'd been crawling to the safety of the trees and not made it. A breeze stirred the shredded ribbons of her black cape.

Ember, sprawled next to my grandmother, had already been hollowed out from neck to pelvis. She was holding something in her hand.

I stepped closer, moving around Henry and ignoring

the demon slurping guts only a few feet away. The marshal was next in line in the demon's feast. He'd lost his cowboy hat somewhere. His shirt was ripped. Claw marks scored the henna tattoo on his chest.

"Something important there," I muttered to myself as I crouched beside the witch.

I would have to connect the clues together when I sketched the vision. And there was something especially important about the ruined henna tattoo.

I peered down at Ember's hand. Her arm was sprawled out, almost as if she'd been holding it before her as she fell. Her fingers were curled around Win's ivy brooch. The platinum pin was pierced through the palm of her left hand, and her blood had darkened the sharp edges of the ivy wreath.

The witch was staring sightlessly up at the darkening sky. And smiling.

Smiling.

Why was she smiling?

Listen to me.

I WAS ON MY KNEES AGAIN, AND DESPERATELY tired. Drained of energy. Exhausted. Once again, the oracle magic had filled me, used me, and then left me devoid of emotion and mobility.

I could feel Beau crouched beside me. I lifted my head to meet his magic-filled, green-eyed gaze, surprised that I could see him so soon after a vision. His fingers were outstretched but still not touching me.

He'd never been concerned about touching me while I was having a vision before. Something was different now. Maybe it was the magic I'd wielded to construct the ward around the twins. Or maybe it was the glimpse of the destruction the demon could craft. A demon who knew my name.

I lifted my hand to his, hesitating just before I made contact, fingertip to fingertip.

"Listen to me," I whispered.

He nodded. His shifter magic settled, leaving his face a dark wash in the night. "I listen," he said. "I always listen. But that's not the same as blindly obeying, Rochelle. We'll talk. Then we'll talk with everyone else."

I dropped my hand into my lap. I couldn't hold it aloft between us, not without his support.

Beau frowned, the expression utterly alien on his beautiful face. Then he lowered his arm as well.

The oracle magic started to tingle in my palm. I curled my fingers into a fist. Soon, my entire left arm would be on fire with the need to sketch the details of the vision.

"Come," Blackwell said. "She'll need to draw now."

I turned my head and caught my grandmother staring at me. She lifted her chin as a tight-lipped smile spread across her face. Smug and proud. Though the moonlight highlighted her pale skin, her eyes were deeply shadowed, like twin black pools of night.

"Rochelle Hawthorne Kai, granddaughter of my blood, oracle, sorceress. You are a true testament to your ancestors' power and legacy tonight."

'Of my blood.'

My stomach twisted, curdling. I wasn't sure if I was reacting to Win's coldheartedness or her attempt to claim a relationship that didn't exist beyond the blood connection she apparently revered.

Another movement caught my attention. Eddie was pacing the edge of the protection circle fretfully. Leanne was still fiercely hugging Krista and Calvin within it.

"I don't know how to dispel the ward," I said, looking over to Henry for assistance.

The marshal stepped out from the deep shadows of the trees, tilted his hat back on his head, and hunkered down beside me. He looked tired, but unharmed. "Erasing or smudging the ivy should do it, by your hand, of course."

I leaned over, reached into the magic, and scrubbed my hand across the still-glowing lines of ivy etched in the dirt. The ward fell.

Krista broke away from Leanne, darted around Eddie, and latched onto my shoulders. "You saved us," she muttered into my neck. "You saved Calvin."

I glanced up at Beau, then over at Eddie and Leanne. Their expressions were uncertain. Wary.

I wasn't exactly the hero type, but it still stung to be regarded with such distrust. I supposed knowing an oracle was camping on your property was entirely different than actually seeing her have a vision. Also, witnessing me wield magic I shouldn't be capable of was probably troubling, especially for shapeshifters, who weren't big on surprises in general.

As I brushed my hand against the back of Krista's head, white oracle magic flooded my mind. And I could suddenly see her in my mind's eye, older and laughing. Turning her impish gaze to her more subdued, grinning brother. They were whole and happy.

I gasped.

"Rochelle?" Beau asked, concerned.

Krista loosened her hold on me, stepping away.

The oracle mist cleared from my eyes, but not before I saw the cheering crowd of people she'd been standing in front of ... on an outdoor stage ... with signs emblazoned with her name behind her.

The young shifter gazed at me, utter trust etched across her face.

My heart squelched oddly.

There was something happening. Something important that was going to play out in these next few breaths, in these next few words. But I didn't fully understand what was going on.

I opened my mouth and let the magic speak for me. "You will live well, Krista Thompson, daughter of Leanne," I said. "You will laugh and love, and live your dreams. You will ... make a difference."

I wasn't completely sure about that last part, but given the preteen's charitable tendencies, I was confident that it was the truth.

"Will I?" she whispered.

"Yes."

She reached up, brushing her fingers against my cheek. The green of her shapeshifter magic was once again flaring in her eyes. "And we shall always be friends, Rochelle ... Oracle of the Brave."

I laughed at the title that had been previously bestowed upon me by Drake. Then I sobered. I wondered suddenly whether 'brave' could also refer to the Adept I saw in my visions and not just the Winnebago RV I called home.

My hand was burning. I needed to draw. "We are well met," I murmured. I couldn't recall where I'd heard that formal phrase, but I knew somehow it was the right thing to say.

Krista nodded, her expression far too serious for an eleven-year-old. But then, it had been an insane evening so far.

I stood, accepting Beau's hand underneath my elbow without question. That we loved each other was never in question. Even if everything else was for the moment.

Leanne and Eddie gathered Krista and Calvin to them. Their faces were etched with a concern that had everything and nothing to do with a demon playing hide-and-seek with us all tonight.

I turned away, praying to whatever magic governed these things, whatever greater power sent the visions, that I'd done it justice with Krista. I prayed that I would continue to see what it willed me to see.

A blindly faithful oracle.

That was some sort of oxymoron, wasn't it?

THE HUSHED, INTENSELY WHISPERED conversations among the group of Adepts gathered outside the Brave filtered through and around my consciousness while I committed the latest vision to paper. I was surprised by my own level of detachment as I applied charcoal to one smooth, unblemished sheet after another. Perhaps my years lost in visions of death and destruction had numbed me. Perhaps I trusted that all the clues I needed had been laid out before me. And I was somehow certain that I could thwart the future I'd been gifted a glimpse of.

I might not know if there was a higher power — a conscious mind — behind the oracle magic. Or, if there was, why it would care about Beau or Blackwell or Henry or Ember in the grand scheme of all the magic in all the world. But I knew myself. I knew I kept moving. I took what I could find, or buy, or create. Then I took tiny, measured steps continually forward.

It had taken me two years of tiny steps to figure out how to turn what I thought were debilitating hallucinations into a profitable Etsy business. It had taken another two years to save enough money to buy the Brave.

It had taken me two minutes to fall in love with Beau.

I still didn't know why he'd chosen that particular night to leave Seattle, to walk along a highway in the rain, to follow my scent to the diner.

Providence, maybe?

Circumstance, most likely.

I could accept both possibilities equally.

So now, faced with another impossible-seeming situation — the deaths of all of the people near and dear to me — I attacked the problem with equal equanimity.

Circumstances could be changed. And providence was already on my side. I just had to figure out the clues.

So I drew.

It was dawn when I finally admitted to myself that the ache in my hand was the result of trying to define precise edges with a small nub of charcoal and not the oracle magic urging me to further refine the vision.

I'd filled two sketchbooks. The first was all rough overview sketches, attempting to articulate the broad aspects of everything I'd been shown. The second was filled with more refined moments, inserts, and close-ups.

I had ten or fifteen pages full of eyes and blood splatter alone. Beau, Blackwell, Henry, and Ember had all died with their eyes open. I flipped back through the sketches and wondered if there was a reason for it. We squeezed our eyes shut when we were in pain, didn't we? We tried to hide from the truth of our current reality. Wouldn't being ripped to shreds be painful?

Were these four watching and focused right up to the moment of death? Were they united in the fight? Or had they turned against each other by the end?

I couldn't tell by the placement of the bodies, two of which — Beau and Ember — appeared to have been dragged to their final resting spots.

As for the blood, it was everywhere. I'd seen gruesome visions before, but I'd never rendered the blood and gore so dramatically. I'd sketched pages of blood splattered across cheekbones, of gaping seething wounds, and of rippling pools in the gouged dirt. Why the oracle magic wanted me to focus on eyes was probably painfully obvious. There was something I needed to see in my sketches. Why the focus on blood? I had no clue.

Then there were the claw marks through Henry's henna tattoo. That seemed deliberate — both the wounds and the fact that I'd seen and interpreted it so specifically.

And the brooch in Ember's hand. Win's brooch. Had Ember been trying to use the magical artifact somehow? Had Win given it to the witch, or had the witch taken it after my grandmother had fallen to the demon?

And where did I fit in all of this? Was I lying there dead among them and simply unable to see myself? Was I somewhere else altogether?

"Too many questions," I murmured. I placed my head in my hands and was rubbing my eyes before I remembered my fingers were coated in charcoal. Well, that was going to sting.

As if he'd heard me speak, Beau opened the door to the

Brave and stepped halfway up the stairs. He'd thrown on clean jeans and a blue T-shirt, but not showered or shaved. He looked dreadfully tired. "Are you ready?"

"Sure. Right after I sleep for eight hours."

"We've been waiting."

I frowned at his brusque tone, then looked down at the sketchbook open on the table. Beau stared out from the page. I'd have to find something to compare it to — if I had the stomach for it — but the marks on his neck made it look as though he'd been hanged ... to death.

I flipped the sketchbook closed. Its edges were stained with the charcoal impressions of my fingerprints.

"Rochelle?" Beau's tone was softer. "I've asked them to distill their concerns down to a few questions. So we can get some sleep."

"There aren't any questions, Beau. There's only a solution. We're leaving."

"The vision is different this time."

I narrowed my eyes at him. "How would you know?"

"I looked."

"While I was drawing?"

"Yeah."

I stared at him, feeling oddly pained by some imagined betrayal. He'd probably just been checking up on me and had seen what I was working on. Why would I feel so put out by that?

It was his tone. His stiff body language was putting me off. But then, he'd just spent hours conferring with my grandmother ... and Blackwell. They weren't exactly his favorite people. I'd be on edge if I were him. Hell, I wouldn't have stuck around that gab session for longer than ten minutes. But Beau couldn't exactly leave when I was in the throes of sketching a vision. Not if he wanted to be there if I needed him.

I was the one who was acting like an idiot.

"What does it matter if the vision is changing?" I asked, softening my tone, as he had moments ago.

"Because ... because you said we needed to leave. You'd made the decision to leave, yes? On your own, when you realized the demon was somehow here for you?"

"Yeah."

"Then you had this new vision."

I ruminated on the implications of what he was saying. "First, I saw the demon in the orchard. Then, after I saw my mother's drawing, I texted Blackwell for an explanation."

"Then you saw Blackwell telling someone to run in a vision. Just Blackwell."

"Then Kai Win shows up," I whispered.

"So you see the demon kill Blackwell with Win in the background."

Fear curled in my stomach as my mind raced ahead to reach the conclusion Beau had already come to. "And now I've seen you, Blackwell, Henry, Win, and Ember all dead."

Tension twisted through Beau's face, then he visibly forced himself to relax. Apparently, he hadn't actually known the full extent of the most recent vision.

Beau thought I was already engaged in changing the future, simply by reacting to what I saw in each stage of the vision.

"It doesn't work like that," I said in response to his unasked question. But my insistence sounded weak even to my own ears. I really didn't know how the visions worked, did I? Only that this set was different. Only that the demon was somehow able to interact with me within the visions. Only that the death toll was mounting.

"It could simply be an extrapolation ... the same vision. Making me see a progression of events, not an actual change."

"Come out. Talk to everyone. Answer a few questions. Then we'll plan."

I nodded, sliding out of the bench seat obligingly before I thought through exactly what Beau had said. "We'll plan, Beau."

He had already turned away, but he looked back at me.

"We'll plan our future. The others won't tell us what to do."

"Sometimes ... they know best."

"Better than me, you mean." Ettie still hovered between us. Hadn't I tried to warn her? Hadn't I tried to thwart the vision? She just hadn't listened. Beau kept saying he didn't blame me, but I couldn't stop blaming myself. This time I would force everyone to take action, to react, and not simply wait for events to unfold.

Beau rolled his head from side to side, then reached out for me. "We're crazy tired. Talking at each other, not with each other. Come outside for a moment. The sunrise is beautiful. Then we'll sleep for a few hours."

I crossed to him without protest, weaving my fingers through his and feeling more grounded the instant I did so.

The two of us were still learning to use our words with each other ... like toddlers. Grabbing for what we wanted wasn't always the best course. I got that.

But words could be misinterpreted in a way kisses couldn't.

SEVEN

Henry, Blackwell, and Win were waiting in the stillness of the dawn. They stood spread out as far as three people could possibly be in the small treed area around the Brave.

Henry was leaning against the trunk of an apple tree, his hat low on his bowed head. I thought he might be sleeping, but he uncrossed his arms and shifted upright as I stepped down out of the Brave.

Win stood with her back to the RV, watching the sunrise. Swathed in her cloak, she was a long sliver of black against the deepening pink sky.

Blackwell was watching Win, but he turned his dark, expectant gaze on me as I approached them all.

"Ember?" I asked.

"She got the wards activated on the main house, then needed sleep," Henry said. "Does she ... will she need to see the sketches?"

I nodded. The marshal looked pained.

"The witch is inconsequential," Win said coolly, not turning to face us.

"She appears in the new vision," I said, not sure why I felt the need to defend Ember.

"Alive?" The deep-seated mockery underlying my grandmother's question was more than obvious.

"With your pin in her hand," I said caustically. "You know, the magical artifact you wear everywhere."

My grandmother spun toward me. Her eyes narrowed, but as if she was intent on ascertaining the truth of my assertion rather than being overly surprised.

Blackwell chuckled.

Win glared at him.

He shut up.

"I get that you have questions," I said, "about the demon that attacked us tonight ... last night ... whatever. I'm not sure I have any answers. Other than I think we need to leave here."

"And possibly draw the demon with us?" Beau asked quietly from behind me. He was leaning back beside the open door of the Brave. "To somewhere more difficult to defend? Somewhere where more innocent lives could be affected? Or what if it doesn't follow? And slaughters the Thompsons and all the neighbors while we're running away with our tails tucked?"

"There's obviously no simple solution," I said. "But ..." I stumbled to articulate my thoughts clearly. I was just so tired. I certainly didn't want anyone to get hurt because of me, but running seemed like the smartest thing to do. We should have run with Ettie. "The vision appears strongly linked to a specific location —"

"Even more reason to hunker down and face it," Beau said.

"There are too many ... innocents here already," I said, stumbling over including the Thompsons in my concern for some reason. Being around Win made me want to be more guarded than I normally was. And I was already more guarded than was probably healthy.

Win narrowed her eyes in Beau's direction. "You question the oracle's assessment, shifter?"

Beau lifted his chin and met her gaze, but he didn't answer her. He didn't need to. His message was loud and clear. Her opinion didn't matter.

"I'm not sure saying 'the demon that attacked us' is the correct turn of phrase." Henry slipped into his poised, collected, professional mode as he casually stepped directly into the path between Win and Beau.

I hadn't even noticed that they were physically facing off against each other. But then, I was seriously drained.

"I agree," Blackwell said.

Henry shifted his hat higher up on his head, then nodded at the other sorcerer. "It seemed more of a game."

"How so?" I asked.

"It snatched Leanne, Eddie, then Ember," Blackwell said. "Placed each of them down, unconscious, in opposite corners of the property. But it didn't cross the fences into the neighbors' properties, or onto the road."

"Grabbed them and carried them?" I asked. "It's strong enough to hold a shifter for an extended period of time? Leanne didn't look hurt."

"No," Blackwell said grimly. "As best as Ember could discern, it was moving through dimensions."

I pressed the heels of my hands to my temples, attempting to massage the tender spots and my growing headache away.

"Must we do this now?" my grandmother snapped.

"Would you rather the oracle be uninformed, Win?"

Blackwell said stiffly. "How will she aid us without all the knowledge we can give her?"

Win frowned at the sorcerer. Even I could pick up that he wasn't just talking about the demon and the mind-boggling idea of moving through dimensions.

"Demons come from other planes of existence?" Beau asked. So apparently, I wasn't the only one in the dark about everything.

Henry shrugged. "It's the prevalent theory."

"With the other being that they're from hell?" I asked. "Then why isn't the world flooded with them?"

"They need an invitation," Henry said grimly. "Usually in the form of a sacrifice. Human sacrifice."

"Right." I'd seen demons before in my mind's eye. I just hadn't seen the process by which they appeared.

"It's unusual," Blackwell murmured, as if he was thinking off the top of his head.

It was a weird attempt at a fake out, because everyone standing in the clearing knew the sorcerer never opened his mouth unless he'd thought through every aspect of what he was going to say. "This demon appears to come and go almost at will."

"Not via separate summonings?" Henry asked.

"How else would it snatch the shifters and the witch, then move them through time and space without effort?"

The sky was brightening, making me uncomfortably aware that I'd left my sunglasses in the Brave. My head was really starting to hurt.

"It takes a powerful magic wielder to tie a demon to this plane," Henry said. "I've only heard of it in theory, not in practice. Some would say it takes the darkest of souls to perform such a feat."

Blackwell smirked at the implication laced through

Henry's words. "Why would anyone here want to hurt anyone else?"

"To get to Rochelle ..."

"Blackwell dies," I blurted out. "You all die. Why would any one of you call a demon, then die at its hands?"

Blackwell and Win looked equally disconcerted in response to my outburst, but Henry didn't flinch. Cowboys were great at playing chicken, apparently. Either that or Beau had already told the marshal about his possible demise.

I glanced back at Beau. He attempted a smile that didn't reach his eyes. We were all drained.

I turned back to the others. "I'll get you the sketches, then I need to sleep. But we should be gone before nightfall. If we want to thwart the vision, we have to change something major. We need to split up and leave."

"It'll be more difficult to defend ourselves while we're running," Beau said.

I whirled around to glare at him, not sure why he was being so stubborn and insistent. "Is that why you're always telling me to run?"

"Yes, Rochelle," he said wearily. "I want you defenseless. Also pregnant and barefoot in the fucking kitchen."

Magic exploded against his chest. It shoved him back against the Brave, which swayed underneath this unintentional assault as Beau curled forward, stifling a scream.

I ran toward him, grabbing his arm. Every muscle in his body was clenched.

"Kai Win, no," Blackwell hissed.

I looked behind me. My grandmother held another starburst of darkly colored magic in the palm of her right hand.

"How dare he," Win said snottily. "How dare he speak to her that way."

"They're mates," Henry said. "They have conversations. Sarcasm is prevalent among the younger generation."

Beau straightened with a groan as I pushed him toward the door of the Brave. A gesture that would have been futile if he hadn't already wanted to move.

I felt shocky. I was shaking. A numbness was threatening to shut down my limbs. I wasn't sure how to react to Win's aggressiveness, to her defense of me, to her hurting Beau.

I just desperately wanted to get away from it all. Quickly. Before Beau retaliated.

Before the vision came to pass.

"I'll get the sketchbooks," I mumbled. "Then we should all sleep."

"Yes," Henry said reasonably. "We can all take a few hours' respite."

The marshal was openly twirling his golden handcuffs, magic glinting from them. Win kept her gray gaze locked to me, though, not sparing him or the cuffs a glance.

Blackwell's back was to me, facing Win with one leg in front of her. Physically blocking her from attacking Beau again, perhaps. Though his hands were spread open at his sides in a gesture of what looked like surrender.

I had felt so in control while I was sketching, but now everything was muddy and unclear. Human intervention made everything uncertain. I turned my back on the drama in the clearing and climbed into my haven.

I made a beeline for the sketchbooks on the dinette. I wanted the future out of my hands, just for a couple of hours of sleep. Then I could convince Beau that we needed to leave ... all of us.

"What about the neighbors?" Beau asked quietly from behind me. "What about everything we've helped build here?"

I picked up the sketchbooks, cradling them against my chest. I turned back slowly.

Beau filled the space between me and the door. He had one arm up and his hand spread across the bathroom door. His head was bowed as if he were suddenly too weary to lift it. His other hand was pressed against his chest where Win had hit him with her magic. He was hurt. He'd heal, but ... I wasn't sure I was processing everything quickly enough. Something was getting lost between us. Shouldn't I be trying to soothe him? Shouldn't I be rallying against my grandmother's actions?

Except he was questioning me. He was going to question me all the way to his death.

"Why would a demon go after the neighbors?" I asked, careful to soften my words as I said them. We were both tired. Tired people fought fights that often got way out of control.

"If it's drawn to you but can't find you, won't it go looking?" Beau raised his head to meet my gaze. He looked ... concerned ... determined ... and something else I couldn't place.

"What aren't you saying? Up to this point, you've always wanted to not get involved. To not be connected to the pack, or even to other Adepts."

"That's politics. This is life and death. Isn't it?"

"If we leave, maybe we draw the demon away."

"But that's not what you've seen, Rochelle." Beau swallowed apprehensively. "Plus ..."

"Plus what?"

"There's your mother's drawing."

A hollow pit opened up in my stomach. "Just say it, Beau. Don't try to lead me somewhere in order to convince me."

"If the demon is yours —"

"You think I'm sacrificing humans and summoning demons? When? In my sleep?"

"No. I —"

"You just heard Blackwell and Henry say that was the only way it works."

"Henry said 'usually.' " Beau's tone was belligerent. "He's heard of it in theory."

"And you know better? With no experience?"

"You do?"

"I know what's in my head!"

"Rochelle, this is getting out of control. I'm talking about responsibility."

"Like me being somehow responsible for the demon."

Beau scrubbed his hand across his face. I clutched the sketchbooks tighter against my chest.

"I can't fight it on my own," he whispered. "If it's coming for you, I can't fight it off."

"You're not alone, Beau."

"I mean we need to stick with the others, if they'll stick with us. This demon tore through me when it wasn't even really trying ... and took Leanne and Eddie without a fight."

"If it wanted to hurt me, I'd be dead."

"Or it's playing with you."

I stared at him, willing my heart to stop racing. We were just having a conversation. The world wasn't ending. I just needed to calm down and articulate my thoughts. I tried to bring us back to the point. Leaving was still the best choice. If we'd kidnapped Ettie right after my first vision of her death, she might still be alive. Wouldn't she? But we hadn't because Beau had a terrible relationship with his family, and he needed something from them that they couldn't provide. Then Ettie had died. And I'd pretty much murdered Cy.

"We've got nothing to prove to anyone, Beau."

"Prove?"

"We don't owe anyone anything. No matter what our pasts are."

"Is that what you think this is? Me trying to prove that I'm a good person? That staying ... is what? A punishment for my sins? Redemption?" He laughed harshly.

I flinched. I didn't ever want to hear a sound that nasty emanate from him ever again.

"I'm saying you feel that way. Not that I think —"

"It's fundamentally the right thing to do, Rochelle. Cutting and running isn't."

Anger flushed my face. For a moment, I struggled to contain it. To measure my words carefully, to make sure I was expressing myself properly. "I'm not suggesting we sacrifice anyone. We draw the demon away —"

"Maybe. Or maybe it returns to eat everyone we've left behind."

"I'm telling you I see you dead!" I screamed, letting the anger have its way.

"I'm telling you I fight, no matter the odds."

"If Ettie had listened to me ..." I said, rashly and without thinking. "If we'd moved quicker. If we'd kept our emotions in check, then we wouldn't be holding our breath around the pack, Henry wouldn't have been bitten, and your sister wouldn't be dead."

As my final words died between us, Beau's face blanked of all emotion. Then he turned and punched through the door to the bathroom. The flimsy paneling crumpled underneath his fist. He yanked it back, ripping the door from its hinges.

Neither of us moved then. We just stared at the destruction he'd wrought in my home.

A chill of some new emotion I couldn't identify washed all my anger away, leaving me frozen and speechless. My arms went numb. My sketchbooks tumbled out of my grasp.

"Rochelle," Beau whispered.

I raised my gaze from the crumpled door still held in his hand. Pain was etched across his beautiful face, but I couldn't feel anything. It was as if he'd ripped out my heart ... as if he was holding it before me. The flesh growing cold as I slowly died from the loss of it ... from the loss of everything.

"Get out," I murmured. Pain sliced through my jaw. My body was reacting adversely even as my mind lagged behind.

Beau awkwardly propped the door against the now-open bathroom. He reached for me.

"Get out," I said.

His arms fell to his sides. He didn't move closer. He didn't cross through the chasm of ice and pain growing between us. "I'll fix it. Rochelle, please —"

"Get out!" I screamed. I couldn't hear him. Not right now. I couldn't think, couldn't process. "Go, Beau."

He left.

He turned, opening the door of the Brave and climbing down the stairs. The RV shifted with his weight. He carefully latched the door behind him.

He left.

And he took my heart with him. A hunk of useless, bloody flesh torn asunder from my frozen chest. I couldn't even feel the imagined wound. Just the numbness it left behind. A terrible, gaping nothingness from the deep pit of my soul.

I'd told him to go.

But he shouldn't have left.

I stared at the crumpled bathroom door. I forced myself to move to it, stepping over my scattered sketchbooks to touch the shattered piece of my home, my heart.

Was I going to place this between us? Was I going to hold it against Beau? Was the Brave worth more to me than he was? Wasn't it just an object, something I owned and maintained? Wasn't my life really with Beau?

Was I going to walk away from everything we'd built, everything we'd found together because of a fight between two people who were too tired to be talking, let alone making decisions?

I dropped my hand, moving to exit the Brave before I'd even come to any sort of conclusion.

I couldn't live without my heart.

I wrenched the door open, suddenly blind with tears I hadn't felt streaming down my face.

I stumbled on the steps. I fell.

And Beau was there to catch me.

He'd been waiting.

He hadn't really left at all.

I clung to him, pressing my wet face to his warm neck, stopping up the sobs that were threatening to choke me.

"I'll fix it," Beau whispered urgently.

I nodded, not trusting myself to open my mouth without bawling like a lovelorn idiot.

Then he cleared his throat. "We aren't alone."

I raised my head, hastily wiping my runny nose on my sleeve. Win and Blackwell were standing ten feet apart among the apple trees. Henry was leaning against the same tree as before. They were still waiting to see the sketches.

I just wanted to take Beau to bed.

And while we made love, the demon might just tear the others apart, spreading its malignant magic across the property. Murdering all of them, one at a time.

So. Not quite the right time for sexual bonding.

I loosened my hold on Beau's neck, locking my gaze to his red-rimmed aquamarine eyes. I cast my voice out across the clearing as I spoke. "Beau and I are staying. Blackwell ... Win ... are you ... Do you know how to vanquish the demon?"

"In theory," Blackwell said.

"Yes," my grandmother said.

Henry opened his mouth, but I cut off whatever he was going to say. "But the Thompsons have to go. And Ember. Henry, you'll take care of them?"

The marshal snapped his mouth closed, shaking his head. "The witch isn't going to like it."

"But the twins will be safe with you and their parents," I said. Forcing the well of emotion threatening to choke me away, I gripped Beau's hand harder. "They're not in the vision now. Let's keep it that way?"

A pained look flashed across Beau's face. Then he nodded stiffly.

I wiped my cheeks, then turned back to the RV to grab my sketchbooks.

I stopped on the top step, reaching back for Beau. "I trust you," I said. "With my home and my heart. I trust you to make the right decisions for us. But I won't obey you unquestioningly any more than you will me."

Beau laughed sadly. "Fair enough."

I looked past Beau's head toward Win. "And, Grandmother," I said, deliberately evoking our familial tie, "I'd like you to lift the geas from Blackwell. The sorcerer has things he needs to tell me."

Blackwell went very still.

A pleased smile spread across Win's face. "For that, we must negotiate."

"No," Blackwell said, sounding as if it pained him to speak. "The geas cannot be lifted with simple words. Kai Win will take it to her grave."

"And perhaps beyond," my grandmother said agreeably. "But the terms can certainly be modified if it is mutually beneficial."

Blackwell's face had darkened in anger, which he turned in my direction. "I do not need rescuing, Rochelle."

I snorted. "I'm not the rescuing sort." I lifted my chin and addressed Win. "We'll talk after I sleep."

"Being well-rested is always beneficial."

I slipped inside the Brave, gathering the sketchbooks from where they'd fallen on the well-worn and well-loved burnt-orange carpet. I passed them through the door for Beau to hand off. Then I crawled into bed, doing nothing more than kicking off my sneakers.

Beau locked the door. Pulling the curtains as he crossed through to the back of the RV, he joined me.

He curled around me, pressing his lips to the back of my neck. "I hate it when you deal with devils," he whispered, referencing my impending conversation with Win about Blackwell.

"Yeah," I answered drowsily. "Too bad I'm getting good at it."

Then I succumbed to a dreamless sleep.

I might not have deserved it. But I needed it if I was

going to have any chance of navigating the myriad of clues that had been so carefully laid before me.

Tess and Gary were standing on the back patio of the main house, sipping hand-pressed apple juice and chatting with Leanne. Beau and I had just wandered past Eddie packing suitcases into the minivan in the carport on the side of the house.

I had completely forgotten that the two of them were driving up from Richmond for the unofficial opening of the B&B.

I tripped, despite there being nothing in front of me to trip over. Beau caught me by the elbow and I righted myself, fully prepared to retreat and talk through our options before —

"Rochelle!" Tess cried. She set her juice down on the top of the patio railing and made a beeline for the back stairs.

"There they are!" Gary crowed proudly, as if Beau and I had just done something much more magnificent than simply wandering up the driveway.

Leanne slipped back into the house, giving us some space to greet our guests.

Even though all my instincts were telling me that just setting foot on the property might put them in terrible danger, I couldn't help but feel a tiny bit relieved to see them.

"Just because they aren't magically inclined doesn't mean the demon couldn't rip them to shreds." My hushed whisper to Beau was made through a pasted-on smile. "Right?"

"Yeah. We should confirm that with Henry," he whispered back, throwing his arms open to intercept the hug that was coming my way from Tess. "But they definitely need to be gone before nightfall."

He effortlessly scooped Tess off her wedge-sandaled feet and spun her around. She giggled with delight. She'd added copper highlights to her mixture of gray and blond ringlets, and was wearing a long, light cotton shirt over beige linen pants.

Gary beamed down at us from the patio. He was lightly tanned and had lost a bit of weight, probably from putting in a veggie garden in the backyard of their home in Richmond, just south of Vancouver.

Beau placed Tess on her feet in front of me, and I stepped toward her for a hug. Surprise flickered across her face — I wasn't exactly known for my love of physical contact — then she enveloped me in the scent of tuberose and sandalwood. She stood only three or four inches taller than me, but in that moment, she felt like a shelter in a storm.

I pulled away before I got too mushy.

Beau had already made it up to the patio and was clapping Gary on the back.

Tess brushed her fingers against my shoulder. "You look tired."

I nodded. "I didn't sleep well last night."

She clucked her tongue lightly but didn't pursue the subject as we joined Gary and Beau. I offered her husband another rare hug.

"You missed lunch," Gary said, patting my back. "I

brought Beau some beer from a local microbrewery, Russell's. Have you heard of it?"

"No, sir," Beau answered cordially.

I slid onto one of the wooden benches beside the bare trestle table. Then the conversation died.

"What is it?" Tess whispered. "What's happened?"

Beau scrubbed his hand across his head. He opened his mouth, then closed it, looking at me.

"My grandmother showed up." The words were out of my mouth even before I'd decided what to say.

"Oh," Tess said softly. She blinked up at her now-frowning husband, then folded herself onto the bench. Not touching me, but available. "Is that ... good?"

"It's complicated."

"I can imagine," Gary said. He sounded angry. But not at me.

"It's okay," I said lamely. "She didn't know about me ..."

And then I was bawling.

Just like that.

My face crumpled as I silently wept. And it had nothing to do with the damn demon or with our impending doom. It had everything to do with my lost childhood.

"Gary," Tess said, "we'll need some water, please. And Beau, Kleenex."

Gary and Beau swiftly fled the patio for the main house, happily tasked with things they could actually accomplish when faced with a bawling woman.

I swiped my hands across my cheeks and got myself under control. "I don't know why I'm crying."

"I do," Tess said. "And it's good to let it out sometimes."

"Only if you can rein it back in."

She laughed softly.

"Did you and Gary try to have kids?" I completely blurted out the deeply personal question, but I'd been working up to asking for months and hadn't figured out how to be less abrupt.

Tess nodded, looking off toward the willow trees that shaded the patio to our right. "We did. Both our own and adopting."

I didn't ask what happened, because it was already obvious it hadn't worked out.

"I don't like her," I blurted.

Tess laughed again. "I think the 'one big happy family' thing is a myth. Or at least, a minority view."

"You and Gary can't stay."

"Because your grandmother is here? Is that why Leanne and Eddie are leaving with the kids? They said they were taking a quick trip to see family, but people aren't usually so tense until after they get back from days in the car with kids."

I snorted, then had to sniff back some snot to keep it from dripping down my face. "No. Something bad is going to happen. We have to stay to face it. But you need to go."

I removed my sunglasses and met Tess's gaze intently. I couldn't tell her about magic. I couldn't explain further. I wasn't sure what would happen if she figured it out, but I knew that the Adept world was exceedingly careful about living parallel lives to the nonmagical people that so vastly outnumbered them.

Tess nodded, glancing up to accept a glass of water from Gary as he appeared through the sliding glass door. She pressed the glass into my hands. "We aren't going."

"But —"

"No. We've driven all the way up here to see you, but

we won't crowd. We can even go to a hotel. So we're near, but not on top of you."

Beau wandered out of the house, carrying a roll of toilet paper. "I couldn't find Kleenex," he said, utterly and amusedly frustrated by that particular failure.

"Tess and Gary won't go," I said, reaching for the roll.

"No," Gary grumbled, crossing his arms over his belly. "They won't. Beau knows."

I wrapped a few layers of toilet paper around my right hand, then wiped my nose while trying to communicate my distress silently to Beau.

"We'll skedaddle for the evening," Gary said. "Let you be with your gran. Maybe go on a date, eh, Tess? That winery tour starts at three thirty, doesn't it?"

"That would be lovely. It ends with dinner in Kelowna, so we'll stay overnight." Tess beamed up at her husband. "I'll call for tickets." She fished her phone out of her bamboo purse.

They had absolutely no idea what we were talking about. Or what kind of danger they might be in. But they would stay ... for us.

I looked at Beau helplessly. He shook his head, shrugged, then clapped his hand on Gary's shoulder. "Let me show you one of the cottages I've been working on before you guys take off." They headed down the stairs, pausing on the path between the house and the garden.

Tess smiled at me. Her phone was pressed to her ear. "Should we meet her? Your grandmother?"

"Her name's Kai Win," I said. "Yeah, probably. Maybe tomorrow. She's ... different. And there's other stuff, like property and money that my mom left me. An estate I had no idea about until this week."

"All right. We can talk about whatever you want." She

turned her attention to the phone. "Oh, yes, hello. I was wondering if you have any room in this afternoon's tour?"

The sun caught on the tiny diamond solitaire of her engagement ring. The gold of its band and the wedding band nestled next to it had deepened in color from years of wear.

I glanced over at Beau. He and Gary were standing a few feet in front of Eddie's kitchen garden, chatting and waiting on us. He looked over at me.

I reached up and tapped my heart, three times doubled, mimicking a heartbeat.

Beau smiled, joy and sadness intermingled in his expression. Then he tapped his chest in response.

WE DIDN'T LAY EYES ON ANYONE ELSE FOR A couple of hours. It felt as though we'd been given a tiny reprieve.

But after showing Gary and Tess the property, and where we were currently parking the Brave, I felt as if I was hiding rather than moving forward.

And I was a lot of things, but I wasn't a coward.

To that end, I texted the picture of my mother's drawing, which I'd already sent to Blackwell, to Henry. It was attached to a note asking him to look at it while he was examining the other sketches. A note that told him what I thought the drawing meant.

Doing so made me feel exposed and vulnerable. Though it made sense that being surrounded by my chosen family — whether or not we'd formally acknowledged that bond — was the best time to do things that scared me.

I wasn't sure how Henry was going to look at me after he'd seen my mother's glimpse into my possible future. But I also knew we weren't getting through the next couple of days without everyone contributing whatever knowledge they had to the problem.

Plus, I was pretty sure that Henry was going to dispute my wanting him to leave, and he needed to know all the ramifications of staying.

Namely, that the demon might somehow be here for me. And that it was willing to slaughter everyone else to get to me.

EIGHT

"I'm sorry," I said, scuffing my sneaker on the edge of the paved driveway in front of the brown-sided garage.

"There's nothing to be sorry about," Eddie said gruffly.

The coyote shifter shut the back hatch of the navy-blue minivan, then reached out to shake Beau's hand. Leanne and the twins were clambering into the vehicle from the other side. We'd already said a casual goodbye, not wanting to make too big of a deal of them heading up to Vernon for a 'mini vacation' before the opening of the bed and breakfast.

"Text me when it's clear," Eddie said quietly to Beau.

"Will do," Beau said.

I glanced over at Henry and Ember. They were waiting further down the driveway by the witch's Smart car. Henry was writing something in a Moleskine notebook on the roof while Ember stood with her arms crossed, scowling at the nearby nectarine and peach trees. They weren't terribly pleased with practically being ordered to leave with the Thompson quartet.

Blackwell and Win were distributing some sort of magical trip wires around the property. Devices that the three sorcerers thought would be sensitive enough to detect the demon's ability to phase through dimensions.

Henry was quiet about leaving, thankfully. He'd just helped Blackwell and Win for most of the day. Ember insisted that if she was to leave, I should be accompanying her. When that demand was met with a blank stare, she insisted on staying. I gathered she was feeling foolish for having me break the seal on the legacy package without fully understanding what that might mean. But I understood that there was no way for her to have gathered more information while everything was sealed. And despite my mother's drawing, I wasn't sure the demon was tied to the legacy package at all. The vision in which I'd seen it for the first time had happened before Ember even set foot on the property.

Of course, I was only ever working with fairly solid guesses when thinking about what triggered the visions. Not certainties.

Anyway, guilt was apparently a powerful motivator for her. Because if an oracle had just seen my grisly death, I'd run immediately.

Except ... I wasn't running. So maybe I didn't know myself or other people particularly well at all.

Good thing now really wasn't the time for personal introspection, though, because I wasn't big on constantly headshrinking myself. Been there and done all that.

I waved to the twins as they buckled into the backseat of the minivan, then wandered over toward Ember and Henry.

"I repeat my objections," Ember said when I was about a half dozen feet away.

"You could go back to Seattle," I said, stepping past the Smart car and into the shade of the trees. "That would be even safer."

The lawyer witch narrowed her eyes at me, but didn't respond.

Henry laughed under his breath, then turned and handed me a sheaf of notes he'd torn out of his journal. "The sketches are on the kitchen table in the Brave."

"Thank you," I murmured.

"Henry can go with the Thompsons." Ember waved her hand in the general direction of the minivan. "I'll stay."

"Or ..." Blackwell spoke from somewhere in the trees behind me. "We could lock you up in one of the cottages and report you to the Convocation for mismanagement of Rochelle's legacy, and therefore your entire branch of magic."

The witch's shoulders stiffened, but she didn't turn to look at the sorcerer as he stepped up beside me.

"Not the sort of mark that a young lawyer wants on her record," Blackwell said, continuing to threaten the witch completely dispassionately. "If she wants to make partner before thirty."

Ember pivoted, opened the driver's side door, and climbed into the Smart car without acknowledging Blackwell's threat. I wasn't completely sure she'd ever addressed Blackwell directly since meeting him. I would have wondered if that was a witch/sorcerer thing, except she seemed coolly chummy with Henry. Or maybe it was a contractual magic thing — as in, the witch wasn't interested in being tied to Blackwell in any way, not even by casual conversation.

That was yet another thing that should have given me

pause about Blackwell. Except it didn't. My relationships didn't need to reflect everyone else's.

"That was a little harsh," I muttered, side-eyeing the sorcerer standing next to me in the shade.

"I agree," Henry said.

"She's leaving, isn't she?" Blackwell stepped back into the trees behind us.

The Thompsons drove down the driveway. Ember started the Smart car.

Henry stepped closer, watching Blackwell leave over my shoulder. "Read my notes," he whispered. "Text me if you have any concerns or anything you want to talk through. And don't trust Blackwell."

I opened my mouth to protest.

Henry stalled me with a raised hand. "The geas makes him even more unpredictable than usual."

"Then what you're really saying is that I shouldn't trust my grandmother."

"Same difference." Henry rested his hand on my shoulder lightly. Then he turned away without another word, waved to Beau across the driveway, and climbed into the car.

I watched the Smart car as it slowly rolled down the driveway, catching up to the Thompsons' minivan at the base of the drive. I would have thought I'd be relieved to see them go. I wasn't. In fact, I was seriously uneasy as I watched them turn on to Lakeview Drive and drive away.

"They'll be safe now," I muttered to myself, shaking off my doubts and jogging across the driveway to join Beau.

I HEADED BACK TO THE BRAVE TO GRAB A NEW sketchbook and gather my most recent sketches from where Henry said he'd left them, before meeting Beau, Blackwell, and Win back at the main house. They wanted us all behind the reactivated wards before nightfall. I didn't really want to draw the demon to the house, but my elders overruled me.

My part of 'operation demon vanquish' was to study the sketches and wait. Brilliant. But then, my plan to run had been overruled by multiple parties.

My mother's drawing was sitting on the lime-green dinette, though I could have sworn I'd tucked it into the pocket of my satchel. Apparently, the sorcerers had thought it germane to their discussion. Or at least Blackwell and Henry had. Though, I supposed I'd added it to the conversation by sharing it with Henry. Then they'd wanted to study the actual image rather than just a picture in a text message. Good to know that one of them could lift it off me so easily.

A handwritten note torn from a Moleskine notebook sat next to the black-inked drawing. I'd seen both Blackwell and Henry jotting notes in pocket-sized black leather journals, but only a single sentence was scrawled across this piece of paper.

How is the demon tied to you?

I pulled out the sheaf of notes that Henry had pressed into my hands before he left, comparing the chicken-scratch handwriting. The new note was a match.

Someone had also numbered the two sketchbooks sitting to the side of my mother's drawing, one and two. Then they had lightly penciled in page numbers on the back of each page.

Henry's notes were organized by topic and page number. I scanned through the ream of paper until I found a lengthy list underneath the demon heading.

1. Lesser demon in appearance. Therefore unable to exist on the earth plane for long periods of time, and certainly unable to manifest without being summoned.

2. Tied to a magical artifact? Usually the sacrificial knife with which it was summoned. No knife appears in the visions, nor in J's sketch of R.

3. Pictured feasting on bodies (typical behavior) throughout R's vision. Blood everywhere. Yet Beau and Ember appear to have been killed by other means.

4. Two different timelines? Same demon (note the four hooked claws, the elongated snout, and shape of the head). The first timeline appearing in J's vision of R's future? The second shown in R's charcoals? If one future has been thwarted (perhaps by J's actions or death), then how is the demon still tied to R?

5. If the demon is tied to R, how is it being summoned by another practitioner? Blackwell? Kai Win? Ember? To what end?

I looked up from Henry's notes, my mind swimming with too many guesses and not enough solid evidence of ... anything. Also, Henry's implication of Blackwell, Win, or Ember being involved was disturbing, because how the hell was I supposed to refute that? But why would the demon kill Blackwell or Ember or Win if it was tied to them?

And if appearing dead in my vision didn't absolve the

others, then even Henry could be involved somehow. And he could be pointing the finger in everyone else's direction in an attempt to fake me out. What if being bitten by Kandy had somehow changed him fundamentally, morally, not just physically? What if in seeking a way to tame the wolf within, he'd unleashed something else, something dark?

Was that even possible? And who could I trust to ask?

My phone buzzed in my back pocket. I was pacing the length of the Brave and hadn't even noticed. That wasn't great. I didn't need to be checking out from reality any more than I already had a habit of doing.

I checked the text message. It was from Beau.

>*Ok?*

Yep. Just getting supplies. See you at the house in ten minutes?

Ember had floated the idea of drawing the demon to a central point on the property, then trapping it in a magical circle, then vanquishing it. Problem was, she would have to physically be on site to activate the circle and vanquish the demon. So, pretty much using herself as bait. The sorcerers believed that the random tripwires distributed around the property were a safer bet. Ember had sneered at their 'low-powered toys.' But three against one carried the argument.

Beau, however, had been intrigued enough by Ember's idea that he wanted to scout the location she recommended. The witch had indicated that the area immediately surrounding an old but still solid-looking lean-to shed along the back of the property was rich with helpful energy. The fact that this location — which Beau thought might once have been used for goats — was just beyond the upper edge of the cherry grove didn't appear to concern Ember in the least. She used the presence of the grove in the visions to support her argument. The fact that she used the phrase 'helpful energy' had just solidified the sorcerers' sneers.

>*I'll be there in five.*

I smirked at my phone, crossing to grab a new sketchbook from my supply shelf. Only to discover that I didn't have any.

Crap. I futilely ran my hand back along the shelf, knocking charcoals and other pens aside, as if I might be able to find by touch what my eyes couldn't see. I retrieved an unopened package of triple-sifted organic rajasthani henna instead of a sketchbook. I'd picked up two boxes and the cone applicators I'd used to apply Henry's latest tattoo when we had driven through Vancouver on our way to the Okanagan.

My left hand started itching.

White mist edged my sight, then cleared as swiftly as it had appeared.

"Henry's tattoos ..."

There was something important about the marshal's tattoos in my last vision. The demon had clawed across them in a way that appeared deliberate. Though that had to be my interpretation. Because logically, how could claw marks appear deliberate? Except by being the only marks on Henry's body ...

Did Henry's tattoo work? Did it give him some sort of extra power that the demon — or whoever controlled the demon — needed to sever?

And what did that matter now that Henry had left the property?

Without really knowing why, I dug around for some cone applicators. Then I added them, the henna, some fresh charcoal, my mother's drawing, and my last half-empty sketchbook to my satchel. Normally I tried to sketch chronologically, completely filling each book before starting another. But grabbing a new sketchbook at Beau's behest before meeting Win had screwed up my system.

Carrying the numbered and completely filled sketchbooks separately, I headed up to the house. I'd read through the rest of Henry's notes and attempt to discern more clues from the sketches before the demon made another appearance tonight.

If the demon was going to show up at all.

But first, Blackwell and I were way overdue for a chat.

I CORNERED THE SORCERER IN THE KITCHEN. THAT would teach him to try to stay hydrated. I shut the sliding glass door to the patio despite the heat, not wanting to risk anyone hearing us through the screen door, then placed my sketchbooks on the round table that sat off to the side of the kitchen. Tiny pots of aloe and basil dotted the low sills of the wood-framed corner windows. The house had been built in the sixties, so its midcentury design was completely legit.

The kitchen was horseshoe shaped, with a laminate counter standing between Blackwell at the stainless steel sink and me in the eating area. The counter was open space, unlike a similar setup in one of my early foster homes that had hanging cabinets over it, fronted on one side with regular cupboard doors and the other with wavy orange glass. The foster mom had stored her crystal wineglasses on the decorative side, though they weren't utilized as much as the regular glasses shelved on the other side.

Still, when an older foster kid had taken a baseball bat to the lot of them, we'd all been relocated.

Later, I'd found out the kid in question had been abused under that roof, and so had guessed that the violent outburst was his way of protecting the rest of us. I could easily imagine how shrink after shrink would have tried to get him to discuss exactly why he'd targeted the wineglasses. But some things were so obvious that it didn't do any good to talk about them ad nauseam. Some things just had to be acknowledged and moved through.

As I watched Blackwell drain a second tumbler of water, I had to struggle to remember the name of that particular foster brother ... Brian. And there'd been four others at that home. Annie, Lynn, James, Terry. I had no idea where any of them were. Alive, I hoped.

"Why you?" I asked Blackwell, shoving the distant memories away. "Why was it you who found me?"

"When a stranger is selling sketches of you online, it's pretty hard to miss." He placed his used glass upside down in the top rack of the dishwasher.

"That's not it."

"No?"

"Nope."

He straightened, raised one perfectly arched black eyebrow, then leaned back against the counter with his arms crossed.

Except Blackwell never crossed his arms. I would know that. I'd been seeing him in my head since I was thirteen.

"Chi Wen says magic sees magic," I said. "Not the mundane."

"Makes sense," Blackwell said evenly.

"So I saw you because you were tied to me somehow."

"Not tied. Not how you mean."

"But it can't be because we're related by blood, because then why wouldn't I see Win? Or if it has to do with destiny and Beau is my soul mate, then why not see him? So I reiterate, why you?"

Blackwell shook his head. "I'm not certain."

"Guess."

"Because I was looking for you."

My belly curled. Not with fear, but with satisfaction. "You knew I existed."

"I knew you possibly existed."

"Because you knew Win?"

Blackwell didn't answer.

I hazarded a guess based on the onset of my hallucinations. "You'd been looking for me for six years. Before we met, I mean."

"Longer. I found you perhaps a month after you opened the Etsy shop. But by the time I was sure you were who I thought you were, I couldn't just show up in Vancouver."

"Because of Jade. And you didn't tell Win?"

Blackwell shook his head.

"Doesn't the geas obligate you to tell her everything?"

"Only if she asks. And we'd parted ways more than a dozen years before that."

"Your apprenticeship ended while you were in your early twenties? Isn't that young? I thought magic usually didn't manifest until the midteen years."

"I'd been with her since I was nine."

I let that piece of information sink in. "Did you know my father?"

"I never met Kai Lei."

"He died before you became Win's apprentice?"

"No. About four years after. But we never crossed paths before his death."

"And my mother's death?"

"Her disappearance, you mean?" Blackwell corrected me, trying to clue me into something underlying our conversation. "No one knew she was dead."

"Why can you talk about this?" But before he could answer, I took another guess. "You can talk about anything that happened before you accepted the geas?"

"Yes." The sorcerer offered me a brief smile.

"And after your apprenticeship? You can talk about your actions, your thoughts, but not anything you know about Win or anything connected back to her?"

Blackwell didn't answer me.

I thought about rephrasing my last question, then decided to move on. "What can you tell me about my grandmother?"

"Kai Win is the most powerful sorcerer I know. More so even than my own grandfather. He had apprenticed with her, so I was apprenticed with her."

That stopped me cold. "She was your grandfather's mentor?"

"Yes."

"How old is she?"

"I have no idea."

"But easily over a hundred."

"Sorcerers live long lives."

The implications of Win's possible age were so staggering that I lost focus for a moment, trying to work all the timelines out in my mind. I really needed to start taking notes.

Blackwell stepped forward, placing the palms of his hands on the counter that stood between us. "Kai Win has crossed lines I haven't even had cause to draw."

I steadfastly ignored the chill that flooded through my chest and limbs at that statement. It wasn't as though it should have been news. Anyone who laid eyes on Win would probably jump to that conclusion. But the fact that someone like Blackwell — who Jade Godfrey loathed and Ember wouldn't even speak directly to — was the one making the assessment was more than a little disconcerting.

I shook off the feeling, stepping forward and deliberately placing my hands down opposite Blackwell's. "Are you calling the demon?"

Blackwell looked genuinely surprised. "To what end? My own death?"

"Henry suspects you, Ember, or Win."

"He said that?"

"In his notes."

Blackwell considered this for a moment. I always liked that about the sorcerer. Whatever else you could say about him, he didn't immediately jump to the defensive.

"The witch wouldn't be capable of calling a demon. Not alone," he said. "And Kai Win ... again, to what end? She wants you by her side, not in the ground. Killing your friends would be a clumsy, rash move."

I eyed Blackwell for a moment, absorbing his words. "Do you think Win killed my father ... or mother?"

"I do not."

"That question you can answer?"

"Apparently. And again, why would she do so? Even for the darkest of sorcerers, or for Adepts in general, blood ties only strengthen magic. Kai Win is made weaker by having no family. And by all accounts, blood tied or not, your mother was a powerful oracle. Rational and articulate. Mind-magic wielders are often less in control of their power."

"Crazy," I muttered.

Blackwell nodded in silent agreement.

"So I strengthen Win?"

"You do. By existing, if nothing else. But you would strengthen her more so if you practiced together, or even cohabited closely."

"So that's what she wants?"

Blackwell shrugged. "Obviously, I can't actually speak her mind for her, but what grandmother wouldn't? Kai Lei was already a late-in-life child. Her only child. You are now her only family."

I sighed. That wasn't really a burden I wanted. "I'm going to look over the sketches. Again."

Blackwell nodded. "Kai Win and I are trading off making circuits of the property, but after nightfall, we will both be on alert from here. The demon won't slip by us."

"I'm not sure slipping by you is the issue."

Blackwell snorted. "What would you have us do, Rochelle? Make a call to the Godfrey coven? The pack?"

"No. Or not yet, anyway. And I wouldn't call Jade ... at least not for her help specifically."

I locked my gaze to Blackwell's as I stepped back toward the kitchen table. I wasn't sure why I felt the need to allude to my ability to contact the guardian dragons — or at least Drake, the far seer's apprentice — through Jade.

Blackwell nodded, stepping around the counter and crossing to the patio door through which I'd entered.

I flipped open my sketchbook and was settling down at the table when the oddity of my weird childhood flashback hit me again.

Those kitchen cupboards. Brian with his baseball bat. I'd come and gone from Leanne and Eddie's kitchen dozens of times, and had never once been reminded of my former foster home, or the foster brother who'd reportedly been abused there.

I looked up at Blackwell as he slid open the patio door. "Wait."

He paused, turning just his head back to look at me. The sun was bright and hot behind him, but his face was deeply shadowed under the wide eaves over the patio.

"Were you ... did she ..." I stumbled around the question, wondering what my subconscious was attempting to tell me about the weird dynamic between Win and Blackwell. "What did you mean when you said Win crossed lines?"

Blackwell smirked. "I meant a lot."

I almost dropped it, but for some reason I had to know. "Did she abuse you?"

He didn't answer. His silence stretched heavily between us.

"You can't answer," I said, not sure if I was relieved or not.

He nodded curtly, then stepped outside and slid the screen door shut between us. He turned back, facing but not looking directly at me. "But ..." His voice was just above a whisper. "I was very young."

"What does that mean?"

"Ask Henry sometime about the magic surrounding a geas. About how that might be cemented and enforced." Then Blackwell walked away.

A dull ache formed in the pit of my stomach. I wasn't sure how to take Blackwell's answer. Not many men admitted to abuse. Not when a woman was the abuser. Not when the abuse was sexual in nature.

I reached for my phone, opening up my text messages with Henry. But then I hesitated, not sure what I wanted to ask him. Not sure whether I wanted to dissect Blackwell's statement any further. Not right now, at least. Not with everything else going on.

Instead, I texted Beau.

I'm in the kitchen. Where are you?

Then I set my phone aside, forcing myself to focus on the notes Henry had made in response to my sketches. I had way too much to figure out about the immediate future, and no time to obsess about the past. Still, a lead-heavy mass of dread was doing its best to set up residence in my stomach.

We were all flawed, weren't we?

I'd pretty much killed Cy eleven months ago. It was debatable, and I certainly wasn't a doctor. But I don't think he would have bled out quite so badly without the puncture wound in his throat. An injury inflicted by my hand. And I knew that if I had to, I'd do it again.

Attempted murder put me on pretty damn shaky moral ground. But child abuse ...

I shook my head deliberately, as if doing so might force the disturbing thoughts out of my mind.

Unfortunately, my grandmother and I were way overdue for a heart-to-heart. I might not be a coward, but I had been hiding from some pretty harsh truths for a couple of days now.

My phone buzzed with a text from Beau.

>Just securing the tree house. Care to join me? ;)

Oh? Did you need help finding something?

>Like your underwear?

I snorted.

I'm working. Plus I know exactly where my underwear is.

>I'll be there in five minutes and we can play hotter/colder.

LOL! I could never be cold around you.

When I was sketching the moment of Ettie's death, I couldn't get her eyes. I couldn't capture them properly. But now, eyes and blood splatter were apparently all I could see.

I flipped through the second sketchbook I'd filled after the most recent vision. After pretty much unloading the horror from my mind into the first book, I had filled the second with increasingly refined bloody details — and with pages and pages of dead, staring eyes.

Beau. Ember. Henry. Blackwell. Win.

Then there was the demon staring out from the page, Blackwell's guts hanging from its sharp teeth. It was watching me from the pages of the sketchbook. Waiting. But for what?

"You capture the images well," Win said.

I looked up, automatically flipping the sketchbook I'd been hunched over closed. It was purely instinctive. My grandmother had already seen both books, though she hadn't left any notes like Henry had.

I leaned back from the kitchen table, noting that the light in the room had dimmed and that my fingers were coated in charcoal. I'd been working on the sketches without realizing it, drilling the images deeper and deeper into my unconscious mind. When they were fully alive there, maybe I'd be able to do more than sit and wait for all the stronger and wiser magic users to do their thing.

My grandmother had spoken from the pocket door that passed through from the dining room into the kitchen. Now she moved farther into the kitchen. She was still wearing her cloak, despite the heat.

I stifled my sudden need to cross my arms defensively.

Win retrieved a red kettle from the stovetop, crossing to the sink to fill it.

"I've had a few years of practice," I said. It was a barbed response, even if it came way too late. But I was still struggling with being neutral around my grandmother.

"The humans are ... interesting," she said, placing the kettle back on the stove and switching on the gas burner.

She was referring to Gary and Tess, who she'd met for about two minutes before Beau had practically carried them and their car off the property.

"Friendly," Win added.

She wasn't asking questions, so I didn't bother answering.

My grandmother opened the cupboard that contained the white ceramic teapot and various types of tea, selecting a box of Earl Grey over the jasmine green. Choosing the correct cupboard was either a lucky guess on her part or Leanne had made her tea. Though I wasn't sure exactly when that would have happened.

"Tea?"

"No, thank you."

After what seemed like forever, but was probably only a few minutes, the kettle whistled. Win dropped three teabags into the teapot, then added hot water. Waiting for it to steep, she leaned back against the far counter next to the stove and gazed at me.

"I understand you have questions," she said. "I arrive out of the blue, why wouldn't you have questions?"

"None relevant to our current situation." I could demand to know everything my grandmother knew about demons in general, or my mother's sketch, or why she'd allowed me to think I was an orphan for twenty-one years, but all of that would open up a dialogue of frustration and pain — if Win even answered my questions truthfully. And none of it would get Beau through the night alive.

Win looked surprised. "No?"

"No."

A flicker of a smile crossed my grandmother's face. Then she exited the kitchen without another word.

Okay.

That wasn't weird at all.

And where was Beau?

I glanced down at my phone, thinking maybe I'd missed a text message. I hadn't.

Win walked back into the kitchen. Her black cloak hung off her shoulders, fluttering in her wake. No, 'fluttering' wasn't the right word. Boiled. Her cloak boiled around her feet as she walked. She was carrying a china teacup edged in yellow roses. She must have retrieved it from the teak hutch in the dining room.

She poured tea into the cup. It looked disgustingly strong. But then, I wasn't a tea or a coffee drinker.

Holding the teacup delicately before her, she settled her gaze on me again. She didn't appear to have any issue maintaining a neutral expression, unlike me. "I understand why you wouldn't like me, with Mot being your mentor."

It took me a second to remember she was referring to

Blackwell. I was reminded suddenly of the evening he'd first introduced himself to me, and my thinking that 'Mot Blackwell, sorcerer of Blackness Castle' suited him perfectly. But then, I'd assumed he was a figment of my imagination at the time.

Too bad I couldn't say the same about my grandmother.

She still wasn't framing her comments as questions, but I answered this one anyway. "Blackwell's not my mentor."

"No?"

"No."

The emotion that flickered across Win's face wasn't amusement. I was starting to annoy her. Thank God. It usually didn't take me so long to wear someone down. And now, feeling a bit pissy, maybe she wouldn't be so guarded.

"I'm surprised you didn't know that," I said. "What with the geas and all."

"I didn't think to ask."

I smiled. "You assumed. And you know what assuming does, right?"

Win narrowed her gray eyes at me, then took a careful sip of her tea. She set the cup back on its saucer and abruptly changed the subject.

"Where did you get the chickens?" she asked. "It's been a long time since I've met a witch capable of breeding magical fowl. I assume they're yours. No one else here is powerful enough to raise them."

She enunciated the word 'assume' bitingly.

For a brief moment, I wondered if I was outmatched. I'd bandied words and temperaments with countless foster parents. And while they all eventually kicked me out — or I requested to be transferred — I'd always had the upper hand. Well, since the point when I'd figured out what having the upper hand meant.

"They're Leanne's," I said, blithely lying. "I wasn't aware they were magical."

"Weren't you?" Win whispered the question.

I wrapped my hand around my raw diamond on its chain, seeking comfort and grounding. I dropped my gaze to Win's hands. Her magic was an even darker blue than Blackwell's, but she wielded her power like he did. It made sense that he must have learned how to cast from her. Except in the brief glimpse I'd had of her in the orchard after she'd hit Beau, her magic had been shaped like starbursts, rather than orbs.

"I was simply suggesting you bring the chickens with you," my grandmother said evenly, filling the silence that had stretched between us. "Either of my estates could easily be made habitable. Did you receive them from a witch in exchange for a seeing? Magical husbandry is a rare gift."

I didn't know what the hell 'husbandry' was, and I didn't like Win's tone. Undeserved pride, and edged with greed.

"You expect me to move with you? To Hong Kong? To live with you?"

"That's what family does."

"To make you stronger," I said pissily.

Win sipped her tea. "To make you stronger."

I snorted. "And Beau? I'm to drag him halfway around the world? For you? Someone I don't even know?"

Win waved her hand dismissively. "The shapeshifter may come if he wishes. Enforcers are always valuable."

I bristled. But before I could formulate another retort, Beau stepped into the kitchen from the hall.

"You haven't even seen what I'm capable of, Win," he

said, perfectly pleasant and perfectly threatening. "Oh, tea. Fantastic."

A grin spread across my face at the sight of him.

He winked at me, crossing into the kitchen, then reached into an upper cupboard for one of the tall, thick plastic glasses Leanne packed for picnics.

Win didn't react, though she tracked his movements.

Beau turned his back on my grandmother as he went to the fridge and the cupboard, adding ice, then copious amounts of sugar to the glass.

Win curled her lip at his concoction, but her face was neutral again as he turned and gestured toward the teapot.

"May I?"

"By all means." Win deliberately and unnecessarily stepped to the side, allowing Beau access to the hot tea.

Yeah, my grandmother wasn't Beau's biggest fan.

And that fact didn't appear to faze my boyfriend in the least.

Beau stirred his iced tea as he crossed into the eating area. He bent down to press a quick kiss to my lips.

"The offer is open," Win said. "A change of scenery is often invigorating."

"We know," I said.

Beau flipped open one of the sketchbooks lying on the kitchen table, then started paging through it as if he was looking for something specific.

"No rush," Win said. "We have years to get to know each other." She offered me a smile. It was just a slight lift of her lips, but despite all the animosity that hung between the two of us, I felt pretty sure it was genuine. "And I have years to make up for."

The dread that I'd been carrying with me since my first

glimpse of the demon — along with varying levels of terror — eased slightly.

Beau glanced between Win and me. He raised his eyebrow as he started flipping through the second sketchbook.

"Have you seen my mother's drawing?" I asked Win, all casual like I wasn't asking my grandmother whether or not she'd seen a picture of me looking all badass and possibly evil. Plus, you know, cozy with a demon that was now apparently hunting us all.

"I have. When Blackwell and I reviewed your other sketches." She lifted her chin, again with that weird undeserved pride thing going on. Like I was anything to be proud of for her. She didn't even know me.

"Then you know that I ... could be ... that."

Win tilted her head. Her smile widened. " 'That,' as you call it, is a very powerful sorcerer. That vision is nothing to be scared of."

"Who said I was scared?"

Win chuckled. "You did."

"Win? Blackwell is trying to find you." As Beau said it, he didn't bother to look at her.

She nodded, carefully placing her teacup down on the laminate counter. Then she crossed out of the kitchen the way she'd entered, pausing in the dining room doorway and speaking over her shoulder. "Beau. When you refill the teapot, I prefer fresh tea bags."

It was a command. Tension ran through Beau's jaw.

"That is, after all, the polite thing to do," Win said. "And you Southerners are so, so polite. It must be all the sugar."

Beau's shifter magic rolled across his eyes. "Yes, ma'am."

He spoke without looking up from the sketch he was studying, laying his accent on thickly. "We do know our place."

Win drifted out of the kitchen.

I stared at Beau, utterly aghast.

He grimaced at me. Though he could have torn Win's head off, he didn't.

"How does she think her racism will endear me to her?" I asked, brushing the back of his hand lightly with my charcoal-covered fingertips.

"She doesn't," he said. "She just doesn't expect me to be around for long."

He tapped the sketch he had focused on from the sketchbook. It was one of the detailed shots of his face, after death.

The memory of the gray pallor of his beautiful mocha skin flashed through my mind, echoing across the sketch as if I'd seen it with my actual eyes, not via magic.

"Don't look at it," I whispered, pained.

"Sorry," he muttered, flipping ahead a few pages. "It's this I wanted to point out. I've been thinking about it."

I glanced down to see a sketch of Ember. A detailed shot of the witch's face, thankfully. Not a sketch of her missing her innards.

"What?"

"Here." Beau hovered his fingers over Ember's jaw, drawing my attention to the shading underneath on her neck. Then he flipped back to the sketch of himself. "Same marks."

"Maybe." I begrudgingly leaned in, looking closer and comparing the two images. Beau flipped back and forth between the sketches a second, then a third time, the pages almost brushing my nose.

"Could just be smudges on Ember's neck," I said. "Shading to make her jawline stand out."

"It's rope burns," Beau said. "Harder to see on Ember because ..."

"Because the demon has literally eviscerated her from neck to pelvis?"

"Yeah. It's been bugging me since I saw it."

"I can see why." It was difficult to be flippant about Beau's impending death, but I could still try.

He snorted, then lifted his head as if scanning for something. "She's gone."

"Win?"

"Yeah. She hung around for a bit, listening."

"Of course she did. Could she mask her presence from you?"

"Sure. But probably not after I already knew where she was. I hope."

He closed the sketchbook, which was good, because it was disconcerting to be sitting around chatting with him alive and vibrant while sketches of his death literally lay between us.

Beau kept his eyes on the sketchbook, though. "I've been thinking."

And the roiling dread in my stomach returned with a vengeance. "Yeah?"

"Henry's back. With Ember."

"What the hell? And where?"

Beau shook his head. "They snuck onto the property. Ember persuaded Henry to let her set a trap."

"A trap they don't want Blackwell or Win knowing about? Hence the sneaking?"

"They were never going to cooperate. Also, I texted Kandy."

"What? I thought we were waiting?"

"We are, but Henry was going to text her anyway."

"He said so?"

"Not outright. I asked her for twenty-four hours. If she doesn't hear from us by four p.m. tomorrow, the wrecking crew will descend on Summerland. Actually, they don't even need to bring a crew. Jade will do."

I sighed. The warrior's daughter in Summerland was a daunting thought, especially if she was coming to clean up my mess.

Beau stood up, leaned over, and plucked a Gala apple out of the bowl of fruit on the counter. He made a show of buffing it on his shirt, then held it out to me.

"It's nice that I'm such an easy read," I said snarkily, taking the offering.

He settled back into the chair beside me, stretching his leg out so it pressed against mine. "It's nice that I know one thing that makes you happy."

I looked up at him, all my pissiness suddenly and cleanly washed away. "You make me happy."

He smiled. "After Ember sets the trap, I want her off the property. She won't go without you —"

"No."

"Rochelle, Henry can trigger whatever spell Ember gets going. But with you and her off the property, the vision can't be realized."

"Henry and Ember were already off the property!" I shouted. Then I softened my tone. "Beau, no. Plus, you already said you think I'm changing the vision just by making the decision to change it. So this ..." — I tapped the sketchbooks with my finger — "... isn't going to happen."

"It's going to try to happen," Beau said grimly. "It's too big. It took you two sketchbooks, Rochelle."

I looked him in the eye. Carefully, willfully, I forced myself to voice my next thoughts. "The demon isn't going to hurt me. Even if I'm not the one calling it, it's … somehow it's … still mine."

"It's not. I've been thinking about it. At one time, maybe it was supposed to be. But right now, it's tied to someone else. It's a weapon. And the second it's turned against you, you will die."

"If whoever's calling it even knows it's here. Maybe it's sneaking off, or maybe it's some kind of rogue."

"No," Beau said grimly. "That's why I led with the rope burns. Whatever confrontation leads to this …" — he waved his hand over the sketchbooks — "… someone else is involved. Someone hangs Ember and me. I wouldn't have thought I could die that way, but I guess if I was dropped from high enough —"

"Dragged," I blurted, desperate to stop Beau from going into more detail. I was already haunted by the visions. I didn't need his remix crammed into my head as well. "Someone dragged you. Or the demon can do it … with its tail or something."

Beau looked dubious. "Still, I want you and Ember gone before nightfall. And I want you to have Blackwell take you. He and I have discussed it. He believes that the fortifications of his castle —"

"No. And since when are you a fan of Blackwell's?"

"I'm a fan of having you safely behind proven wards."

"Again. No."

"Jesus, Rochelle. You promised."

"I did no such thing. I said I'd listen, and that I'd be reasonable —"

"Leaving is reasonable. And Ember won't go if you don't."

"Don't try to blackmail me. And what about your concerns about the demon following me?"

"You already said it wasn't going to hurt you," Beau said, belligerently throwing his argument from earlier out the window.

"We're arguing in circles."

"All right, then. Don't be a liability."

I clamped my mouth shut. Anger overtook the dread that had been dogging me for days. I opened my mouth to rip Beau's head off, then I thought about it. "You're just trying to piss me off, Beau."

"You angry is better than you dead."

"The demon couldn't get through the ward I placed around the twins."

"Did it try?"

"I ..." I had to think about his question for a moment, trying to remember. "I think so ..."

Beau shifted back in his chair, looking at me expectantly.

I leaned over, placing my hands high up on his thighs. "The thing is ... I'm not going. If you're going to die, or almost die, I'm not running. I'll run with you, yes. Without you, no. You don't know what it's like, Beau. You don't know what it was like with Cy and Ettie."

"I was there." His voice was gruff and heavy with emotion.

"Not the way I was," I said, speaking slowly and carefully so I wouldn't give in to the tears gathering at the back of my throat. "Kandy almost killed you and Henry. Blackwell was down. It was just me against Cy and Ettie. I wasn't strong enough. If the drugs hadn't melted Cy's brain in that moment, I would have watched him kill you, Beau. And there would have been nothing I could do about it. But I would have been there."

I climbed into his lap, pressing a kiss against his lips before he could interrupt me. "I will never leave you alone to face anything like that again. Just like you won't leave me. We die together or not at all."

When Beau sighed, a shudder ran through his entire body. "That's insane."

"Maybe. Stupid. Rash. Insane. Yeah, maybe. But you never know when I might have a vision at the perfect time and foil the bad guys with my knowledge of the future. My magic could be our deadly weapon."

Beau laughed, but he sounded shaky and unsure.

"Stop trying to send me away," I said. "I won't go, and it's a waste of time. Getting Ember to leave is a better bet. She's less invested."

"Fine." Beau pressed his forehead against mine. "Just watch out for the truck with the rope attached to it."

"What?"

"That's the only way anyone could drag me away from you. And I'm not even sure that would work."

I laughed. Darkness was descending to swallow all our lives, and Beau was turning his impending death into a cheesy come-on.

He chuckled, lifting me off his lap and depositing me back on my chair. "You keep refining the sketches. I'll check on Ember and Henry."

Ever obliging, I flipped open the sketchbook nearest to me. Completely by chance, the sketch it showed was a detailed close-up of the four claw marks gouged across Henry's chest and the henna tattoo. It felt like centuries ago that I'd applied it for him.

Beau kissed my forehead when I didn't lift my face to

his, as I usually would have. There was something about this image. Some clue that I hadn't figured out yet.

A black butterfly was dancing above and around the charcoaled claw marks.

"Wait ..." I whispered.

The butterfly zoomed away as I tore my gaze from the sketch. Beau, holding the screen door open, stuck his head back into the kitchen. I hadn't heard him step outside.

The butterfly was madly dancing around his shoulder.

"Rochelle?"

"Wait," I said again, desperately trying to sort through my thoughts.

The butterfly tattoo showed me magic, didn't it? I already knew that Beau was magic and that the sketches were some sort of magic, but ...

The butterfly zoomed back, settling on the open sketchbook. It stilled there, perched on the deep gouges scored across Henry's chest.

"What if the henna tattoo works?" I asked, more to myself than to Beau.

"Henry's tattoo? Then you ink it in. That was the plan."

"Yes, but what if it works so well — melding the power of sorcerer and werewolf — that the only way to take Henry down now is to destroy it." I tapped the sketch for emphasis. The butterfly flitted up over my hand and along my right arm, dancing over my tattooed ivy vines.

My left palm started to tingle.

"That's ... good? You want me to mention it to Henry?"

"No ... I ..." I flexed my fingers open and shut. The tingling started to burn. "I need to sketch."

"Now? Without another vision?"

"Apparently."

Beau stepped back into the eating area, grabbing my satchel off the back of the chair even though I could have easily reached it. He held it waist high to my left, and I dug my hand into it without looking.

The crazy butterfly was dancing around Beau's shoulder and chest again. Over the same spot I'd drawn Henry's temporary tattoo.

My fingers brushed against, then rejected, the new package of charcoal. I closed my hand over the box of henna instead. The burning in my palm eased.

I locked my gaze to Beau's.

He was confused, but just as stoically supportive as always.

"Maybe I'm not so useless in battle after all."

"I didn't mean —"

I shook my head, pulling the powdered henna out of my satchel. "Apparently, you need a tattoo as well."

Beau frowned. "It won't hold on me. Not even inked."

"It will if you don't transform. It's okay. Go check on Ember and Henry while I mix the henna up. Then come back and indulge me."

"I always do."

"Yep." I tugged the satchel away from him, noting that the butterfly tattoo had settled on my wrist again. So apparently, it showed me magic and where magic was supposed to be applied or used. Confusing, but good to know.

WHILE I WAS WAITING FOR BEAU TO RETURN, I idly tested the henna I'd mixed on my own right arm, sketching out a snake design I'd been thinking about twining alongside the twists and turns of the ivy vine. I positioned the snake so its tongue flickered through its half-inch fangs against the inside of my right wrist. Next time we went into Vancouver, I'd have Tyler at Get Inked make it permanent. But I hadn't quite decided on the design of the snake's body yet. I applied a simple crosshatch to the henna test model. I wasn't skilled enough with the cone applicator to go for anything decorative, though I was thinking of something Asian inspired, similar to the gold embroidery on Chi Wen's white robes.

By the time Beau returned with Henry in tow, I was applying the lemon, sugar, and clove wash to my arm over the kitchen sink. A glance at the clock at the stove told me it was almost dinner time. Not that any of us had planned any meals.

Henry pulled a bulbous glass jug of water out of the fridge and poured himself a drink. Leanne or Eddie had added slices of lemon to it. I hadn't noticed it was there, simply drinking water from the tap like Blackwell had.

Beau leaned over the sink, examining the snake tattoo on my arm. "Vision?"

"No. Just a thought." I dumped the remainder of the wash down my arm, letting it drip into the sink while I eyed Henry. "I thought you were leaving."

"Yep," Henry replied between gulps. "I've had this conversation three times already."

I glared at him as he poured a second glass, then gave in. It was his funeral and he knew it. So repeating it over and over just made me the idiot. "Your notes were helpful."

"Did you show them to Blackwell ... or your grandmother?"

"No. Did you mention them to Ember?"

"No. But only because the demon isn't tied to the witch."

"How do you know?"

Henry shrugged, then placed his empty glass in the dishwasher. "Black magic has a feel to it."

"And Ember doesn't feel black?"

"I doubt Ember could practice the magic she does, easily and every day, and also practice black magic."

"One negates the other?"

"They're sourced from very different places, especially for a witch. I'm here for more candles." Henry randomly started opening the drawers beside the stove.

"Dining room hutch," Beau said, leaning back against the counter next to me while I waited for my arm to dry. It would be sticky as hell for a while, but it felt right. Solid. I couldn't really explain it, not even to myself. And I'd drawn it.

Henry closed a drawer, then crossed toward the dining room door.

"What about Blackwell and Win?" I asked. "Do they feel like they could perform black magic?"

Henry snorted. "Do you doubt it?"

"But do you feel it?"

Henry paused, looking back at me. Then he dropped his gaze to my diamond necklace. "Blackwell has his amulet."

"And it's not dark."

"No. And nothing he could do to it would make it so."

"Because he's not an alchemist? Or because it's dragon-forged?"

Henry tilted his head back, surprised. "Both, really. But I didn't know the dragon part. My point is, for me, the amulet's power emanates more than Blackwell's magic. But despite that, I can see the darkness that lies just underneath his surface. Some say that at a certain point, a sorcerer can gain more power only by crossing certain lines."

"It's not the same for all Adepts?" Beau asked.

"Witches would insist it's different for them, because they call their power to them, rather than accumulating magical objects with which to express their magic. Then some Adepts, like the dragons who accompanied Jade, are ..." Henry trailed off thoughtfully, perhaps thinking about the events that had brought a small army of powerful Adepts to the door of the Brave last January.

"Infinitely powerful," Beau said.

Henry shrugged. "Perhaps."

"And the vampire?" I asked, just out of curiosity. Though I'd really gotten nothing more than a glimpse of the pale blond stranger who'd arrived in Westport with Jade.

"They have their own sort of balance, I believe," the marshal said. "But then, they have to. Otherwise, the other Adepts would wipe them from the face of the planet."

"Geez," Beau muttered.

"We all have our crosses to bear." Henry grinned as if he'd just cracked some seriously funny joke. He looked put out when we didn't laugh. "Vampires? Crosses? Get it?"

"And Win?" I asked, bringing us back to the present and most pressing concern. Which was to say, was my grandmother a black-hearted evil sorcerer?

Henry locked his cobalt gaze to mine. I couldn't read his expression. Concerned ... confused ...

"Nothing," he said quietly. "I get nothing from Win. Not a drop of power."

"Is that bad?" I asked, not really sure if I wanted to know.

"It just is." Henry exited the kitchen.

I looked over at Beau.

He opened his hands, holding his palms up in an exaggerated shrug. "I never really wanted to go to Hong Kong or China anyway. I like the food, but I'm not a fan of flying. Now, where do you want me? And should I get naked?"

I snorted. "Here, like this. And removing just your T-shirt will be fine."

I reached past him for the second cone of henna.

Beau nuzzled his face in my neck. "Too bad," he murmured. "But next time, let's see what other stretch of canvas I can provide."

I giggled like a lovelorn idiot. Sometimes I couldn't help being girly around Beau. And honestly, I didn't really try to stifle it anymore. It was obviously a war I was doomed to lose.

Beau tugged off his shirt.

I kept my gaze off his abs, focusing solely on the section of his shoulder and chest the butterfly had directed my attention to.

"What are the candles for?" I asked, squeezing the first line of henna out across Beau's lovely skin. "The demon trap?"

Beau grunted in acknowledgement.

"And Blackwell and Win know Henry and Ember are back?"

"Kind of hard to miss, once they'd figured out someone got past their wards."

I joined two curved lines to create a leaf. Energy rose up underneath my hand.

"Your eyes," Beau whispered.

Then I allowed the power simmering underneath my hand to have its way, letting the oracle magic control my mind and body. I heard and saw nothing more while I gave Beau the only fortification I could offer.

We might both die tonight. I was following every clue I saw, every clue I unearthed, and every clue magic gifted to me.

I wasn't a coward, but I wasn't a hero either. And that meant I would exploit all the help I could unearth, and then some.

Hell, I'd cross my fingers, toss salt over my shoulder, and even swear my utter, unfettered belief in whatever providence governed the whole damn world if that was what it took to walk away with Beau.

NINE

"How much longer are we just going to sit here?" I asked, as if I were some sort of badass ready to barrel into battle.

"As long as it takes." Henry grinned at me from the overstuffed armchair he'd turned toward the low, wide picture window in the wood-paneled living room. From my viewpoint from the couch, he appeared to be perched over the top boughs of the peach trees in the front yard. We'd spent the last few hours idly watching all the light seep from the sky and the stars come out.

Blackwell snorted while pacing through the formal dining room, like he didn't get the joke. But then, I wouldn't have expected him to know anything about mundane life or rote 'adult' responses.

Win didn't bother to look up. She had both of my sketchbooks open, side by side on the seventies-style teak dining room table, and was comparing the detailed drawings with the rough sketches. A glass-and-teak hutch filled with china ran the length of the wall behind her. My grandmother handled the sketches differently than Blackwell and

Henry did. As if they and what they revealed already belonged to her, rather than being something to respect or believe in. I kept stopping myself from charging over and ripping them out of her hands.

I pulled my gaze away from her bowed head for what had to be the tenth time. Henry caught my look and lifted his chin in an upward nod. He got it. My frustration and my anxiety.

Ember had mountains of paper spread out across the teak coffee table, and every fifteen minutes or so she asked me to sign something. The witch's energy was almost frenetic. I could feel her magic sparking off her every time she passed me her gold pen. I'd stopped reading whatever I was signing over two hours ago.

I turned my attention back to the sketch I was idly working on so I didn't nod off, recalling the lines of Beau's henna tattoo. I'd only gotten a glimpse of it after the vision had passed but before the others had returned to the house and the bickering between them all had begun anew. I'd combined two of my own tattoos — a twisted wreath of ivy around the butterfly — for Beau's design. But there were subtle differences in the patterning on the wings and the curl of the leaves that I wanted to recall in case I had reason to henna them on Beau again.

"Bathroom," Ember murmured, shifting out of the second armchair by the front window. She tucked the last of her paperwork into her briefcase, which she snapped shut and left on the coffee table. Then she crossed through the living room toward the main hall, hesitating before me.

I looked up at her. She started to speak, then glanced back at Blackwell, who was leaning over Win's shoulder. Both of them had their heads bowed, discussing one of the sketches quietly.

Ember bit her lip, then glanced over at Henry. He lifted his shoulder in a shrug.

I really had no idea what was up with either of them.

"Rochelle," Ember finally said, casting her voice louder than necessary. "If anything happens to me, everything is filed now, and a senior partner at Sherwood and Pine will take care of you."

"Nothing is going to happen to you," I said belligerently.

"Right," she said loudly, then lowered her voice to a whisper. "Just ... be ready. Henry and I have a theory."

She walked away without another word.

Great. I loved being kept in the dark when a future was unfolding I was desperate to change.

I glared at Henry. He smiled back at me, nonplused. I pulled out my phone, texting Beau instead of walking back to the kitchen, where he was putting together a snack for us.

Henry and Ember have something up their sleeve.

He texted back right away.

>Goat shed.

Right. They'd been working on the containment spell for the demon all afternoon and evening. Though that wasn't exactly news, so maybe Ember was trying to clue me into some other plan or some part of the main plan that she and Henry didn't want Blackwell and Win to know about. Great.

I glanced down at the sketch I was working on, tracing my fingers lightly over the charcoal lines of the ivy wreath that was eerily reminiscent of Win's brooch. Had I used it in Beau's henna tattoo design because I'd seen the magical artifact in Ember's hand in the vision? The rope burns, clawed tattoo, copious amounts of blood, and brooch were all clues, or maybe signposts.

Blackwell abruptly stopped pacing right in front of me, blocking my view of the room.

"Where's Ember?" His tone was blunt, far beyond even his usual edginess.

"Bathroom," Henry said. Then he added sarcastically, "For the last five minutes. Good eye, Mot."

Blackwell spun to glare at Henry. Or so I assumed by his stiff posture, because I couldn't see his face. "Where is the shifter, then?"

"Kitchen," I offered. "Fueling up."

Blackwell tilted his head as if listening.

"What?" I asked, struggling to rise from the overly soft brown corduroy couch. "He's not in the kitchen?"

Henry shot to his feet, crossing to me in a blur of movement.

Win slowly stood as well.

"The remote sensors," Henry murmured.

"The remote sensors, what?" I cried.

Then the lights went out. A flurry of movement exploded around me. I tried to dart toward the kitchen, but Henry grabbed me, shoving me back onto the couch.

The stench of carrion rolled through the pitch-black room.

"Beau!" I shouted, struggling to get away from Henry's hold. "It's here."

Rochelle.

The demon's soul-wrenching voice rolled through my mind, weakening my limbs and making my heart rate spike painfully.

Blood of my blood.

The lights flickered on.

Momentarily blinded, I frantically shoved the marshal away. Shaking, with the echo of the demon's words reverberating through my mind, I struggled to sit upright. Henry let me go.

Blackwell stepped back through the kitchen and into the dining room, catching Win's eye, then turning to look at me.

I scanned the room. Nothing was out of place. Not a thing was knocked over or ripped asunder.

"What the hell was that?" I cried. White mist edged my sight ... blood splatter superimposed on the wood-paneled walls. I blinked rapidly, willing the echo of the vision away.

"I'll find Ember," Henry said, ignoring me and stepping back through the hall deeper into the house.

Blackwell strode forward, holding his hand out for me. "Time to go."

"What?" I snarled, scrambling off the couch and stepping out of his reach to call into the kitchen. "Beau!"

"The demon just got through our sensors and waltzed through the hastily re-erected house wards." Blackwell enunciated his words carefully and slowly as if I were an idiot child. "The shifter requested that I take you to safety."

I darted around him, making a beeline through the dining room, passing Win, and crossing toward the kitchen.

"Rochelle," Blackwell said in warning.

I ignored the sorcerer, crossing through the darkened kitchen. I noted the open box of Triscuits and the block of cheese on a wooden cutting board on the counter as I stepped through the screen door and onto the back patio. Again nothing was disturbed, and not a thing was out of place. If the demon had snatched Beau from the kitchen, he hadn't had a second to fight it.

I tamped down on the fear roiling in my belly.

Blackwell was right behind me. I paused by the trestle table, glancing around the dark garden and checking for any movement among the fruit trees beyond. A gradual incline rose from the back of the house, through the cherry tree grove and toward the back edge of the property. The evening had partially clouded over. I couldn't see the moon, and the starlight wasn't bright enough for me to really see anything in detail beyond the railing and the first rows of pea plants.

I pressed the heels of my hands to my eyes, thinking furiously. 'Blood of my blood,' the demon had said. What the hell did that mean?

"Maybe he's doing a circuit," Blackwell said, unconvincingly.

I pulled out my phone, opening my messaging app. "Right. In the middle of putting snacks together for us and without mentioning that he was leaving the house."

I texted Beau.

Where are you?

Stepping past Blackwell into the eating area, I retrieved my satchel from where it was hanging over one of the kitchen chairs.

"I absolutely forbid you to go out there," Blackwell said.

"Stop me, old man."

"I'll go with you," Win said, crossing through the kitchen toward us.

"No, thanks."

"Stop me," she retorted.

I almost laughed in her face, except she wasn't being funny. Henry appeared on the other side of the screen door behind me. I flinched.

"Sorry," he said. "I circled around front. Ember's gone too."

"The demon is playing hide-and-seek again," I said, utterly frustrated that I'd been forced to play by the sorcerers' rules and plans. "It can bypass all your wards and sensors."

"Maybe," Henry said. "Maybe someone let it in."

"That is why we need to go," Blackwell said. "You need to be behind stronger wards."

Win kept silent behind us all.

I shook my head. All I could do was seriously hope this was just a game, like it had seemed the first time the demon had snatched Leanne, Eddie, and Ember.

"Fine," I snarled. "We get Beau and Ember and go. That was my idea in the first goddamn place."

"Absolutely not," Blackwell started to say.

I cut him off. "We all know where Beau and Ember are," I said. "Where the demon would take them. I've already seen how this plays out. You stay here and debate."

I turned to push past Henry, surprised when he moved to block me. I paused, glancing back at Blackwell. "I'm the only one who can go out there without getting harmed."

"You can't see yourself in your —" Blackwell started to say.

I cut him off. "Yeah, yeah. Tell me something I don't know. I might have been lying there dead with the rest of you. Except I wasn't. I'm not." As I said the words, the missing clues started clicking in place for me. "Because it's my demon."

Blackwell said nothing, his gaze meeting Henry's over my head.

"I'm not as stupid as you all apparently think I am," I said. "Blood of my blood? I get what that means."

"Blood of my blood," Henry murmured.

"Who called you that?" Blackwell's tone was carefully modulated, but I could tell when the sorcerer's interest was piqued. "Kai Win?"

I snorted. "Please."

I glanced over Blackwell's shoulder at my grandmother, who offered me one of her creepy-proud smiles again, as if I were making some brilliant deduction. I had to figure out how to stop her from doing that.

"The demon," I said.

"The demon spoke to you?" Henry asked. "In the visions?"

"Yeah. And when I was in the orchard with the twins. And just now, when it snatched Beau and Ember."

"When you were having a vision," Blackwell said. It was a statement not a question. "Oracle, if there was any dialogue, it would have been helpful to note it alongside the sketches."

"Right. I'll add speech bubbles next time."

"Rochelle," Henry said. His tone was heavy with warning. "Demons don't speak English. I'm not sure they speak any language at all." He looked questioningly at Blackwell, who shook his head, then glanced back at my grandmother.

Win just widened her weird smile in response.

"Right," I said in sarcastic agreement. "I'm so creeped out by the creepy demon talking in my head, so I'll just be a good little girl and curl up on the couch while you all go and take care of everything. Then, when the moon rises and you're all missing, I'll take a stroll around the cherry orchard and make a nice bonfire with your picked-over bones."

"Well, that's a little harsh," Henry muttered.

I thrust my left hand toward him, barely brushing my

fingers across his chest before he reeled back from me. I wouldn't have hurt him. But obviously, he didn't know that.

I stepped around him, jogging down the back stairs and calling over my shoulder. "No worries. You guys stay here. I got this." Apparently, I could be a totally glib asshole. I just needed practice. Or for Beau's life to hang in the balance.

"You could have tried your handcuffs," Blackwell said to Henry behind me as I hit the ground running.

"Rochelle's necklace has been fortified by the alchemist, Blackwell," Henry said. But his voice was getting closer, rather than farther away. "I'm not sure the magic of the cuffs would hold her."

They were following me. Which was a bitch, because I really couldn't see much, and my bravado was bound to falter as soon as I was stumbling around in the dark.

"If she knows how to use that new power," Blackwell countered, acting as if he'd already noticed my newly amped-up necklace.

Of course, I didn't have any idea what Henry was talking about. Jade had put some spell protection on the necklace in exchange for my seeing last January in Westport, but I had assumed it would only repel malicious magic. I didn't see Henry's handcuffs as having evil intentions.

I passed the garden, then slowed my pace as I stepped between the first of the old-growth cherry trees that spread up the back slope of the property.

"What alchemist?" Win asked coolly. I glanced over my shoulder to see her following as well. Lovely.

Neither sorcerer answered her, so she rephrased the question. "Mot Blackwell, what alchemist is the marshal speaking of?"

A chill breeze brushed against me, though a second ago,

the air between the shadowed trees had been still. Almost stuffy.

"Jade Godfrey," Blackwell said. I could hear the anger in his voice, the name sounding as if it had been torn from him.

I stopped abruptly. It had been magic, not a breeze, that I'd felt. I dug into my satchel for my keychain, remembering the tiny Maglite that Beau had attached to it.

Henry ran into me from behind.

I stumbled, catching my footing before I fell.

"Sorry," he muttered.

"I assumed you would have noticed the white hair, marshal," Blackwell said. "It's a rather bright beacon." He sounded strangely amused, considering how angry he had been just moments before.

I pulled the flashlight out of my bag. Twisting it on, I kept it carefully pointed at the ground so as to not ruin the night vision of everyone standing behind me.

"Great way to alert the hunter to our location," Blackwell said.

"I think your bickering is doing that just fine," I said snottily.

Win laughed.

I couldn't see her any longer in the dark, but her laughter ran up and down my bare arms with an eerie cool energy as if her magic was licking out from behind the magical barriers that normally concealed it. I shoved my concerns about my newly discovered grandmother away. I had Beau possibly being mauled by a demon to worry about first.

I angled the light farther into the grove of cherry trees. Henry stepped up beside me.

"Where's the trap you and Ember set up?" I asked him quietly. "I don't know this part of the property well."

"On the other side of the trees," he answered. "Closer to the north than the south."

"Helpful," I said. "Left or right?"

Henry barked out a laugh. "Right. About ten yards from the back fence line."

"Try meters, marshal," I said pertly. "I might understand you better. Plus, isn't metric supposed to be more accurate?"

"Well," he drawled, laying his Southern accent on thickly, "when you're about to wander into a killing field, I'm not sure it really matters much, missy."

I didn't answer. But as I stepped deeper into the cherry tree orchard — walking exactly where we weren't supposed to be — I was exceedingly aware I was leaving the sliver of bravado that I'd cobbled together out of anger, indignation, and fear behind me.

BEAU WAS LYING IN A CLEARING NEAR THE UPPER edge of the cherry orchard, where the old trees had been removed in the spring but not replanted yet. Eddie had been systematically culling fruit trees that were too diseased, malformed, or ancient to rehabilitate into peak production.

Even with the wash of starlight overhead and my tiny flashlight, I couldn't see much of Beau's face. But his skin was warm to my touch and his breathing was even.

Blackwell and Win stayed within the deep shadows of the mature trees. If not for the occasional kiss of starlight on their pale faces, I wouldn't have known they were there. The moon would be rising in a few minutes, if it wasn't already well on its way.

Henry crouched down beside me. "It's a side effect of being grabbed by the demon. Ember, Leanne, and Eddie were all knocked out briefly. I gather being pulled through dimensions shuts down a person's mind for a few minutes."

I looked over Henry's shoulder, then around the clearing. "No Ember. Where's the lean-to? The goat shed thing. She might be there."

Henry shook his head, then echoed Ember's words from before the demon snatched her. "Just ... be ready."

"For what?"

Beau groaned awake. Henry straightened, stepping away without clarifying his statement.

"Rochelle?" Beau muttered, rolling to his side. "What the ... are we in the cherry orchard?"

"Of course. Where the hell else would we be?"

Beau sat up, holding himself upright for a breath before attempting to stand. "They just let you out of the house? Some great backup there, guys."

Henry laughed from somewhere behind us. He sounded awfully amused for someone who was about to be eviscerated. Well, possibly eviscerated. If tonight was the night the demon amped up its hide-and-seek game to maim-and-mangle.

I tried to lift Beau's arm over my shoulders and help him up, but he waved me off, then heaved himself up from the patchy grass.

"Ember is still missing," I said. "I'll get you back to —"

"She's not missing," Beau said, rolling his neck, then his shoulders, as he did before his training sessions with Audrey or Kandy. Like all the shapeshifters did before a fight. "Or, at least, I hope she isn't because that wasn't the plan."

"Oh, yeah? Everyone is keeping secrets, eh? About more than just the goat shed?"

Beau looked chagrined. "It's still about the goat shed, just we weren't sure who the bad guy was. Blackwell. Or Win. Or both."

Great.

I glanced around the small clearing again. Henry was situated a half-dozen steps behind and to my right. He currently had his eyes closed and his face lifted toward the half-moon that had just made its appearance. If he cranked his head back any farther, his cowboy hat would probably fall off.

Behind the marshal, I could now see the outline of the angled, cedar-shingled roof over the former goat shed.

Blackwell was slowly pacing around the perimeter of the clearing. He eyed Henry coolly as he came parallel with the other sorcerer. "Is the call of the moon going to be a problem, marshal? Perhaps the oracle misread the visions from the beginning. Perhaps you are the aggressor we should all be wary of."

It was weeks away from the next full moon, so I knew Blackwell's taunts were hollow. I opened my mouth to tell him off, but Beau brushed his fingers against my lower back. I swallowed my bitchy protest.

Henry smirked, then tugged open the neck of his cotton shirt. For a brief moment, I swore I saw the henna tattoo beneath his collarbone reflect the moonlight. "Apparently not."

"So this supposedly secret plan of yours is to stand here, out in the open, waiting to be attacked?" Blackwell said stiffly.

"I'm surprised you came out at all," Henry said without looking at the sorcerer. "But no, unless you somehow knew that Beau would be snatched from the house, this wasn't exactly the contingency plan."

"I protect my investments."

"I gather you learned that from your mentor."

As if in response, Win took a step into the clearing.

"Beau," I whispered. "Let's just find Ember, and ... go. It's time to call in Kandy and Jade. "

"No," he said without any force or nastiness. "Not yet. The game started differently than we guessed, but we play it out all the same."

"I'm not in on the game," I said, getting exceedingly frustrated that there was any playing going on at all.

"You are the game, Rochelle," Win said. "And worth the high stakes. Isn't she, Mot?"

Blackwell looked as though he'd tasted something foul. But then he smiled tightly in my grandmother's direction. "Indeed."

Win pushed her cloak back over her shoulders, so that it hung behind her like a cape. The moonlight glinted off the diamond-sprinkled platinum ivy brooch pinned above her left breast. Some object that appeared to be constructed out of a similarly colored metal hung at her hip — a flashlight or hip flask, maybe?

"This was a long game." Win's voice was thoughtful. "One I thought I'd lost when your father died. Accidents do happen when you play with magic, but Lei changed after your mother's disappearance. He withdrew. Began playing with magic beyond himself. I never saw either him or Jane as so devoted. Though I guess it was one-sided. Jane left easily enough. I suppose I know why that is now. A foolhardy, rash decision that hasn't made a bit of difference, even in twenty-one years. Except for her dying."

"Oh, God," I said, digging deep in order to be flip. "This isn't 'confessions in the dark' time, is it? I'd rather do it over pizza."

Beau snorted with amusement.

Henry chuckled.

Blackwell stood motionless a few steps to my and Henry's right, but he didn't take his dark gaze off my grandmother. "So you were manipulating bloodlines. I've suspected as much since our time together."

Bloodlines? My stomach bottomed out. The demon's words echoed in my mind. Blood of my blood. And Win had used a similar phrase after I raised the ward around the twins.

"Unsuccessfully," Win said.

"Until Rochelle."

"Apparently," Win said agreeably. "I wasn't sure when I arrived. I suspected she was holding back. Or was being held back." She eyed Beau disdainfully.

"Or she was still learning," Blackwell said.

"Either way, she was behind the curve for an oracle."

"In your view, perhaps. But then you saw the tattoos."

Win tilted her head thoughtfully in my direction, but she didn't answer.

"I don't get it," I said. All my glibness had dissolved underneath this onslaught of information, and my magic being chatted about like casual workplace conversation between colleagues.

"Magical manipulation of hereditary traits," Henry said. "That's not where I thought this was going either. But it explains what I thought was simply a recessive or instinctual access to sorcerer power."

Win sniffed haughtily. "Instinct alone couldn't have held that shield against a lesser demon. And then processing the magnitude of the vision, and settling a prophecy on the shapeshifter child?"

Still confused, I tried to process the veracity of all that —

Then the demon appeared in the shadows of the tall cherry trees behind Win. It had one double-jointed front leg raised and its scythe-like claws wrapped around a branch above its wide, sloped head.

Henry glanced over at me, concerned. Then he followed my gaze but didn't react.

"It changes," I whispered. "Every time I see it, it looks slightly different. Is that normal?"

Beside me, Beau started scanning the shadowed line of trees as well.

Energy bloomed to my right. Blackwell was calling forth one of his dark orbs.

No one else could see the demon.

"No white mist," I muttered, attempting to convince myself I wasn't suddenly standing within a vision.

The demon opened its maw in what I could have easily mistaken for a toothy smile.

Found you. Blood of my blood.

Its voice warped uncomfortably through my mind. I tried to shove it away, or at least deny it access to me, though I wasn't sure that was even possible.

"I wasn't hiding," I said, grinding the words between my teeth.

Win flicked her wrist. Something silver flashed along the edge of my line of sight.

Beau let out a hiss of breath.

I didn't take my eyes from the demon as it slowly slid

out of the darkness behind my grandmother. Perhaps I was watching it manifest. Or perhaps it had been there all along.

"We can't see what you see, Rochelle," Beau said.

I lifted my left hand, pointing over my grandmother's shoulder.

Crimson flared in twin points on the demon's dark-scaled face. The scent of carrion drifted across the clearing. It chuckled at having been identified. At having been exposed.

The noise sent a cascade of terror up and down my spine. "Real?" I whispered.

"Real," Beau said.

"Kai Win," Blackwell snapped. "Step forward slowly."

My grandmother ignored him, keeping her gaze on me.

The demon stepped up behind her.

"Win," I cried. "Run. Now."

She smiled.

The demon loomed behind her, its gaping maw perfectly positioned to rip off her head. She raised her hand, palm up over her shoulder.

The demon rested its chin on her hand.

My stomach lurched at the sight. I felt dizzy suddenly, stumbling. Beau grabbed my arm.

"Yeah," Henry drawled. "This is how I thought it would play out. One possible version at least."

"But ... but ..." I scrambled to orient myself, to realign my understanding of the visions.

Win tickled the demon's chin. In the moonlight, I could see that its mouth didn't fully close, its sharp teeth too long and jagged. Win was holding a long, platinum whip in her other hand. It rippled snakelike at her feet. I'd been so wrapped up in the appearance of the demon, I'd missed the reveal of the weapon.

Kai Win was me. Or she'd somehow appropriated my future. The demon, the whip, the cloak. Only her face and the background were different.

"But ... but ... that was me in my mother's drawing," I said.

"Yes," Beau murmured.

"But this ... this ... is Win."

"Welcome to your legacy," Henry said. Then he casually pulled his badge out of his back pocket and clipped it to his belt. A glow flashed across it that had nothing to do with the moonlight.

"Jesus, Kai Win," Blackwell said, utterly appalled. "Summoning a demon? Allowing it to roam free, and multiple times? Treating it as though it's what? A pet? Using it to hunt your grandchild, let alone whomever else you've set it after. How have you not been caught?"

"Who would catch me, apprentice?" Win laughed smugly. "Plus, you're jumping to incorrect conclusions, as is your proclivity. Once I tied the demon to my bloodline, I didn't have to maintain the connection through spells and sacrifices. I was surprised when the binding endured Kai's death, but now I understand."

Win hadn't taken her gaze from me, not once since the demon manifested.

Blood of my blood. "You injected me with demon blood?" I was utterly unprepared for the revelation — and, therefore, was utterly incapable of absorbing it.

Win laughed. "How? I didn't even know you existed. In fact, after Jane had previously miscarried twice in the second trimester, I'd moved on to other avenues."

"That was the key? Demon blood?" Blackwell asked, sounding more intrigued than shocked. But then, I had a sense that he'd been tracking this mystery for a long time.

Perhaps since I was thirteen. "But Jane wasn't of your blood."

"You are so desperately slow, Mot," Win said with a sneer. "I can't believe I put up with you for so long."

"I aged well," Blackwell said, his voice smoldering with sudden anger. "As in, I came to you too young and I kept my youthful appearance for too long. For my sake, at least."

"But your heart was delightfully open to the darkest of deeds even then."

"That's enough," I shouted, shocking even myself with the force of my outburst. "That's enough." I took a deep breath. "You altered my so-called magical heritage through my father and my mother by injecting them with demon blood. This demon's blood?"

"Trust me, it's not that simple." My grandmother smiled.

"I'm not congratulating you!"

"Why not? Do you think Mot Blackwell would have scoured the earth for you if you were just a simple oracle? Do you think your shifter toy would leave the pack —"

Ember appeared in front of Win. One moment, the space between us was empty. The next, the witch was filling it.

Win flinched.

Ember lunged forward, closing her hand over my grandmother's brooch. She must have been hiding behind some sort of cloaking spell, sneaking up on Win while she was distracted.

Then suddenly, we were in the middle of the prescient echoes of my vision. The actions that would result in the actualization of the terrible future I'd captured on paper.

Magic exploded between Win and Ember, though I

wasn't sure who had wielded it — or if it was actually one of them creating it in the first place.

Ember flew backward, slamming against a tree behind Henry and Blackwell, then tumbling to the ground.

I wanted to run to her, but I was frozen. Mired in the initial echoes of the vision. The events that were fated to accumulate into the deaths of everyone I cared for.

"Kai Win," Henry intoned formally. "You're wanted for questioning regarding the practice of black magic."

Win laughed. "By whose authority?"

"The North American League," Henry said.

Win's whip began to undulate in front of her, creating a writhing barrier between her and everyone who stood arrayed against her. It appeared to shrink and expand as it moved.

"Did you actually think she'd come willingly?" Blackwell asked, amused.

"No," Henry said. "But protocol is in place for a reason, Mot. Even if you choose to ignore it."

"The witch has my brooch," Win said, speaking to the demon over her shoulder. "Kill her, and get it back."

"No!" I cried.

The demon lowered its head, settling onto all fours and wrapping one limb around Win's leg as it eyed those of us that stood between it and its target.

Henry stepped to the side, planting himself firmly in its path.

As far as I could assess from a dozen feet away and practically night blind, the witch was still unconscious at the base of the tree.

Blackwell was grinning oddly. He tightened the space between himself and the marshal, standing shoulder to shoulder. Firmly aligning himself with us against Win.

Beau stepped around me to join the sorcerers.

Demon or not, I had no idea how my grandmother thought she would triumph against us all.

"You ... take the shifter," Win said, drawing out the command. "Mot Blackwell."

The sorcerer flinched. Then, moving spasmodically, he raised his right hand. A black orb of magic pulsed in his palm.

"Damn you, Blackwell," Henry snarled. "If you were going to be a liability, you should have left."

"I thought I could fight it," Blackwell muttered.

"You always were an arrogant bastard." Henry slapped one end of his handcuffs onto Blackwell's raised wrist.

The demon traversed half the width of the clearing in a single leap, driving into the marshal at the waist. As they tumbled away, I momentarily lost track of them in the darkness.

Blackwell looked utterly apologetic. But he still flicked his half-cuffed hand and its orb of dark magic toward Beau.

Beau, who'd been spinning to go to Henry's defense, twisted back to face the sorcerer's attack.

"Don't transform!" I screamed, throwing myself to the ground.

Blackwell's dark orb hit Beau dead center in the chest, shredding his T-shirt as it swirled around him, trying to grab hold of him.

Beau growled, lifting up on his toes and arching back in pain.

A white glow emanated from the henna tattoo on his chest and shoulder. The butterfly and ivy somehow absorbed Blackwell's dark magic, then faded.

Beau shrugged off the residual, squaring his shoulders and widening his stance. He stood firmly between me and Win, but faced the sorcerer tasked with his elimination.

Even as he spun his next orb of darkly tinged magic, Blackwell looked impressed.

"Remember our contract, sorcerer," I cried, desperately voicing the idea as quickly as it came to me. "You won't harm, allow to be harmed, or kill Beau."

Win cackled like an insane person. "You think some verbal contract with you supersedes my geas, child?"

Something inhuman shrieked. I clapped my hands over my ears and pressed my face into the grass, but the sound warped straight through my mind, scrambling my brain.

The demon. This was its actual voice.

No one else reacted. Blinking back tears of pain, I tried crawling forward on my elbows toward Ember. But with my hands still clamped over my ears, it was practically impossible.

Another glow of energy blasted through the trees, throwing the demon tumbling across the clearing. Win dodged out of its path, narrowly avoiding getting shredded by its flailing claws and snapping teeth.

Blackwell threw a second black orb at Beau. The handcuffs disappeared from his wrist, momentarily distracting him.

Beau lunged forward, dodging the magical assault and punching Blackwell in the gut.

The sorcerer keeled over with a grunt.

Beau lifted an elbow over Blackwell's bowed head. But before he could strike, some sort of silver snake appeared around his neck, then tightened. He was jerked sideways off his feet.

Win, still a dozen or so feet away from the main fight, had grabbed him with her whip.

Beau fought her hold, wrestling with the platinum weapon as it slowly dragged him toward my grandmother.

Win hadn't taken a single step. She appeared to control the whip with minuscule flicks of her wrist.

Blackwell looked up to meet my terrified gaze, blood dripping from the corner of his mouth. "Good punch," he said. "Got by the protections on the suit."

Something about his weirdly inappropriate pride in Beau's magical prowess defrosted my limbs.

Henry's handcuffs appeared on Win's wrists. My grand-mother shrieked as she seemingly lost control of the whip, which in turn lost its hold on Beau.

Beau slumped forward, his breath ragged and his hand clasped around his neck. My stomach curdled as I realized that I'd see ropelike burns on his neck when he dropped his hand. It was the whip — and Win — that had killed Beau in the vision.

The marshal stepped into the clearing. He was casually brushing the dirt off his cowboy hat.

"How dare you cuff me!" Win shrieked.

Henry settled his cowboy hat back on his head. He was bleeding from various places on his face and arms. His shirt had been clawed, and the outline of his henna tattoo glowed brightly behind the rends in the fabric. "Actually," he said. "I don't have to dare. I'm the good guy. I have right on my side."

Blackwell straightened, facing off with Beau again. Henry swiftly closed the distance between Win and himself.

Heedless of the battle taking place behind me, I continued crawling toward Ember. I'd done everything I could do to help Beau and Henry — with the henna tattoos — and I had no idea how to help Blackwell. But Win had ordered the demon to get her brooch from Ember, and the witch was still slumped helpless against a tree a dozen feet away.

Someone stumbled around me, careful to not actually step on me as I slowly closed the distance between the witch and myself.

Henry.

Magic flicked across my shoulders, nearly grabbing me.

Win and her whip.

The smell of burnt hair. A pained grunt.

Beau.

Blackwell must be trying other spells. The sorcerer would be out of the fight if Beau got his hands on him a second time.

The demon was coiled in the shadows like a watchful and malignant gargoyle just beyond the base of the cherry tree that Ember was slumped against. Fear twisted through my belly at its apparent complacency.

Perhaps the witch was already dead? Perhaps the demon had already collected the brooch? And now it was waiting for the right time to snack. Or ... or it was waiting for me?

Ignoring it because I had no idea what else to do, I touched Ember's cheek. Her head rolled away in response.

She was alive.

I glanced behind me. Win had gotten halfway out of Henry's cuffs, but couldn't manage to get a firm hold on the marshal with her whip.

Blackwell and Beau were gone, but to where or by what means, I had no idea.

"Rochelle," Ember murmured.

"Hey," I said, turning my attention back to the witch. "It's okay. I think the good guys are winning." If you ignored the demon tracking our every move from the shadows.

Ember laughed as if I'd cracked a hilarious joke. Then she spit up blood.

"Oh, God," I cried out involuntarily.

The demon lifted up on its back haunches, eagerly craning its neck forward.

My heart rate cranked up. I tried to ignore it. It really wasn't the time to panic.

"Move me," Ember whispered. "Move me to the circle."

"Holy crap, no," I said. "You're hurt. Maybe bleeding internally."

"Move me, Rochelle." She lifted her hand with effort, dropping it down on my thigh, palm up. Her fingers were curled around Win's brooch.

White mist threatened the edges of my eyesight. "I know," I growled at the oracle magic, like I might be able to speak directly to it. "I see." The power receded.

"Good," Ember said, choking on the word. "Then you know you have to move me."

"Even if I was willing to drag a possibly mortally wounded person around," I snarled, "I don't even know where the damn circle is."

"There," Ember whispered.

Energy brushed by me. Then light flared behind the witch, settling down into a soft glow. A dozen or so candles of all shapes and sizes were arrayed in front of the former goat shed.

"See the space between the candles? Drag me through there, then seal the circle."

I hesitated. "It's a protection circle?"

"Of sorts."

I glanced over at the demon. It smiled at me. Terror rippled through my mind as I dragged my gaze back to Ember.

The witch frowned. "What are you looking at?"

Apparently the witch couldn't see the demon. That was probably a good thing. "Nothing." I stood, crossing around to grab her underneath her arms.

The clearing among the cherry trees was empty. Which was good, because it was already hard enough dragging a wounded person a dozen feet across patchy grass, gnarled roots, and dry dirt.

Even though I could barely see anything in the intermittent moonlight, I was pretty sure I was leaving a trail of blood behind us. Ember was bleeding profusely.

The vision flashed through my mind. The drag marks leading to Ember's eviscerated body. I stumbled, twisting my ankle painfully. Oh, God. What if I was the one fated to drag the witch to her death? I shoved the thought out of my mind. I couldn't fix it. I just had to keep moving.

I passed through the line of candles, noting that the circle intersected one half of the goat shed but didn't include the entire structure. Pulling her underneath the angled roof, I propped Ember against the nearest corner.

She'd passed out. I arranged her arms across her stomach, only then realizing that her leg was badly broken. She was bleeding where bone had punched through her thigh.

"Crap. Crap. Crap." I looked around helplessly, then saw that Ember was wearing a silk scarf. It was better than nothing.

I tugged the scarf off her neck, then used it to try to bind the open wound.

Ember woke suddenly, shrieking in pain.

"Sorry. Sorry. I've never done first aid," I said. "I mean, not for real. Though the ministry made me take this course before I started driving for the residence —"

Ember pressed her hand against mine. "Stop."

Ignoring her, I cinched the scarf closed over the top of her thigh.

"Listen to me," she said. "I'm sorry. We were supposed to talk, but ... Win ... Blackwell."

"I get that there's some plan Henry and Beau are acting on. Though I'm seriously pissed I was kept in the dark about it. Something with the goat shed? And vanquishing the demon?"

But Ember shook her head feebly. "They're the distraction. You're the plan."

She reached up, her hands shaking terribly. She tried to pin Win's brooch onto my T-shirt.

"Ember," I said, gently trying to stop her. "Just tell me how to close the circle."

"I will. Help me pin this on you."

"I'll do it."

"No," she said sharply. "It has to be me. I stole it. I have to transfer ownership."

I sighed, supporting her wrists to help her with the pin until she had it securely attached above my left breast.

Something crashed through the trees beside us. I scrambled to the edge of the circle, attempting to peer into the darkness beyond the candlelight.

"Listen to me ... carefully ..." Ember mumbled.

"I'm listening," I said, hoping desperately it was Beau I was hearing, but knowing he'd never make that kind of racket.

I stepped back underneath the roof of the shed, crouching by the witch again.

"The demon is tied to you ..." Ember coughed up more blood. It looked black in the sliver of moonlight that illuminated her too-pale face.

"I know. I get it. The demon keeps calling me blood of my blood."

"Yes. I can see it. I can see the ties."

"But it's not actually my demon, Ember! It answers to Win."

"But your grandmother has tied it to you."

"Yeah, she was saying something to that effect earlier. Something about magical bloodlines, miscarriages, and my father's death."

"Solve that part later. Right now, you have to vanquish the demon. You have to claim the contract, claim the blood connection, then free it."

"Free it?" I hissed. "Are you crazy? It's already trying to slaughter you all."

"How long do you think your grandmother has had it bound? It doesn't belong here ... in this dimension. Break the tie, claim the bond, and send it home."

Ember's eyes fluttered shut.

She went so still that for one heart-stopping moment, I thought she'd died.

"Ember? Ember?"

"I'm still here."

"You think I can take control of it away from Win because we somehow share a blood connection? That, what? That it wants to be with me? Jesus. And the circle? You want me to seal the demon in here? With us? Then what?" I was fairly certain I'd figured out the witch's plan and why she'd snatched the pin from Win, but I really, really hoped I was wrong.

"Yes," she whispered. "You lure it into the circle. If I'm right, it will probably come willingly. As long as Win doesn't command it otherwise. Lock it in here with you."

"You know that's completely insane, right?"

Ember laughed, then winced with pain. She fell silent again.

Whoever was crashing through the trees veered around behind us. So not Beau. Probably Henry, who likely couldn't sense where we'd holed up.

"You have the pin ... because it was in the vision ... I hope I'm right," Ember whispered. "Usually it's a knife or dagger ... and a sacrifice ..."

The witch was fading fast. I scrambled to piece together the information she was trying to convey.

"Sacrifice?"

"A bloodletting ... an offering ... a summons and a release of magic."

"A human sacrifice?"

"For a demon of this power? Probably more."

"No. No, Ember. I won't do it." My voice was shrill with tension. A mounting fear was blooming in my chest. In my stomach. Throughout every part of my being.

"I'm the sacrifice."

"Absolutely not!"

"I'm already dying, Rochelle. You just have to draw the demon to us, then release the tourniquet so I bleed out."

"You're fucking insane."

"I'm dead either way, aren't I? You already drew it. I've been dead since you set charcoal to paper. Since magic showed you."

I shook my head vehemently. Then I kept shaking it. What Ember was suggesting was beyond insane. It was cold-blooded murder, and I wasn't murdering anyone.

Well, besides Cy. I wasn't murdering anyone else.

"I don't fulfill visions," I snarled. "I thwart them."

Ember didn't answer. Her eyes were closed again. Her breathing was shallower than it was before.

Someone crashed through the trees again, only a few feet away.

I stifled my need to call out for help. Though I was fairly certain neither Blackwell nor Win would ever call attention to themselves in such a way.

Unless it was Blackwell. Unless he was doing it deliberately. So Beau could avoid him, maybe? Maybe the sorcerer was trying to heed the terms of the contract we'd forged in the parking lot of the barbershop what felt like eons ago.

Whoever it was moved off again.

I opened my mouth to call out.

"Thwart it, then ..." Ember whispered. "If you're clever enough to distract destiny ..."

I stood up. "Blood heeds blood," I whispered. "Doesn't it?"

Ember didn't answer, but I was already brushing and smoothing the dirt between the gap in the circle of candles the witch had created.

I wasn't sure I could grab witch magic, or even command it.

But once I had a blank canvas, I could draw.

I might not have the power of the predators in the dark, but I had my tattoos and my sight.

And I was damn good at bluffing.

I drew a twisted vine in the dirt, just inside the circle of candles.

By the time I returned to the gap, the demon was waiting for me.

A cool calmness washed through me.

"Blood of my blood," I said. Then I stepped back and invited the demon into the circle.

It slid through the gap, moving to crouch beside Ember.

"No!" I said firmly.

It tilted its head, but it didn't touch the witch.

I closed the circle, connecting the ivy vines. Magic bloomed around us in a brief wash of white similar to the vision mist. Then it settled as a low hum around my feet.

I faced off against the demon.

It rose before me, matching my height though it could stand much taller if it chose to do so.

Blood of my blood, it said in my mind. *Free me from the sorcerer's will. Claim the binding.*

"Why me and not Win?" I whispered. I knew it was stupid to delay with Ember dying at my feet, but there were things I needed to know.

The demon didn't answer, though.

"Did you kill my mother?"

I whispered the question, dreading the response.

The demon tilted its head, then hooded its crimson gaze in a slow blink.

I came for you.

"Did Win tell you to kill my mother?"

No. My blood belongs to me.

It leaned closer, reeking of carrion and an oily, malicious magic that ran over my hands and up my arms. Like it might be caressing me.

And now only you.

My stomach churned. "I need to know how my mother died."

Running. In a moving steel box. Difficult to track. I found. Steel box fell, rolled. People came. I lost you.

"She was running from you?"

The demon tilted its head in the opposite direction, but its hellfire gaze continued to bore through me, delving deeply into my soul.

I shuddered. There were too many unanswered questions, but I was out of time. And, even if I had all the answers I'd never had as a child, I knew it wouldn't make any difference anymore.

Recalling the way the pin had pierced Ember's palm in the vision — because there was no way I was sacrificing the witch as she'd instructed me — I unpinned the brooch from my T-shirt and stabbed it into my hand.

I hissed as the pain ricocheted through all the nerves of my hand and fingers. I tried to not think about what kind of germs might be currently finding their way into my bloodstream.

The demon tilted its head questioningly. It glanced down at Ember, then back up at me.

I yanked the pin out of my hand, watching blood well up in my palm. A lot of blood. More than I'd expected. I felt a little faint —

"No!" Something slammed against my magical barrier.

Pain exploded in my head. I lurched, spinning to find Kai Win pacing along the edge of the candlelit circle.

"Not yet, Rochelle." Her voice was tight with anger. "You aren't ready."

The demon wrapped its claws around my forearm, strangely gentle as it tugged my bleeding hand toward its mouth.

Win slammed a starburst of magic against the barrier a second time.

Agony reverberated through my entire body, like lightning etched along my bones. Somehow, I was physically tied to the magic of the circle I'd created. I didn't know that was how it all worked.

The demon held me upright, carefully licking the blood from the wound in my palm.

It raised its head. The wound on my hand was gone. The demon's crimson gaze bored through me and into my heart. Which made sense, because I was fairly certain it had just laid claim to my soul. It lifted its palm like it was making some gesture of offering.

I slammed the brooch down, desperately hoping I hadn't miscalculated and that its slender pin was capable of piercing scaled hide.

It was.

It did.

The demon hissed. Its dreadful voice was full of excitement and pain.

Win slammed her fist into the barrier a third time.

The pain forced me to my knees. Could my grandmother actually kill me if she tore down the magic standing between us?

The brooch slowly dropped to the ground before me, as if I were watching it in slow motion.

The demon curled its claws around my head, covering my mouth.

Win shrieked in indignation.

I had completely screwed up. The demon was going to rip my head off. And I was so weak from Win's assault that I couldn't even lift my aching hand in defense.

Wait. Why was my hand throbbing? Hadn't it healed?

The demon smeared its blood across my face, across my lips. It stank like rotten meat. It burned like acid.

Blood of my blood. Forever.

I licked the rancid fire from my lips. "Blood of my blood," I whispered. "Forever."

Win tore down the protection circle.

Darkness edged my vision as the demon stepped

between me and my grandmother. I fell forward, trying to catch myself on my hands.

"What have you done?" Win whispered.

My arms gave out, but I managed to roll onto my back before my face hit the ground. The demon stretched up over me, flicking its claws and gnashing its teeth in Win's direction.

My grandmother hesitated, dropping her gaze to the ground near me.

Barely able to turn my head, I followed her gaze. The ivy brooch was lying in the churned grass and dirt a foot or so away from my shoulder. The demon's clawed feet destroyed whatever surface it walked on. Not a surprise.

Somehow, I gathered enough strength to wrap my fingers around the diamond-studded wreath of platinum ivy. Then I looked up at my newfound and now-loathed grandmother. "My demon," I whispered. "Stalemate."

Win seethed with anger. If she could have gotten past the demon, I swear she would have slapped me. Instead, she backed away. Though I could still feel the roiling, prickly energy of her magic.

Funny that I hadn't felt it like that before. Now, fully unleashed, the sensation was just a little bit shy of dreadful.

The demon nudged me in the ribs, then looked over at Ember pointedly. The witch's chest rose slightly as she inhaled. Thank god. She was still alive.

"No! No eating anyone." Even as I said the words, I was chilled by the thought that I'd immediately known what it wanted permission to do. "Just give me ... a second ..."

I blacked out. I had done it ... even if I wasn't totally sure what that meant yet.

TEN

"Rochelle," Blackwell said. "Rochelle, you need to wake up." His voice was distant, his words carefully formed and articulated. As if he might be talking to a rabid dog.

I opened my eyes.

The demon was hunched over me, blocking my view of ... well, everything except the starlit sky.

I closed my eyes.

Okay, so Blackwell was talking the way someone would talk around a scary-ass demon.

"Where's Beau?" I fought to stay awake, completely drained but exceedingly aware that now was not the time for a nap.

"You need to slowly sit up," Blackwell said, ignoring the question. "Or even better, make it onto all fours and crawl toward the sound of my voice. Try to keep your movements to a minimum."

"Really, Mot," Win snapped from somewhere to the right of Blackwell. "I told you she's bound the demon. We're the only ones in immediate danger."

"Where is Beau?" I asked again. I was slowly feeling more aware — and was therefore more liable to panic if I didn't obtain some much-needed information quickly. "Did you kill him?"

Blackwell didn't answer.

I sat up abruptly, and without completely thinking through the ramifications of doing so.

Blackwell hissed under his breath. I could hear him, but only saw darkness and trees stretched out before me.

The demon lurched back to prowl around me. All the candles that had defined the edge of the circle Win had ripped apart were snuffed out. I couldn't see anything except the moonlit trees and the night sky. As it paced, the demon emitted a low growl that could have almost been mistaken for a rumbling purr. Except, you know, it was coming from a black-scaled, crimson-eyed terror that wanted to disembowel someone ... soon.

"Look at it," Blackwell whispered. "It's changing. Adapting ... to meet the needs of its new master? Does it look more catlike to you?"

"Blackwell!" I cried into the darkness. "Did you kill him?"

"Answer her," Win said. "Did you kill the shifter?"

"No," Blackwell said. "Thankfully Kai Win's instructions were loosely interpretable. I merely relocated him."

Relief flooded through me, pushing my mounting panic away. Strength seeped back into my limbs.

"I might be bleeding internally," Blackwell continued wryly. "But the shifter is most likely on his way back already."

Ignoring the sorcerer's instructions to crawl toward him, I gathered my hands and knees underneath me and slowly made my way over to Ember. The demon continued its languid pacing, simply shifting its path around me as I moved.

The witch was unconscious but still alive. Her breathing was even. I checked her leg, making sure I hadn't tied the scarf too tightly. It was warm to the touch, which I hoped was a good sign.

"We can't just keep waiting around," Win said from somewhere off to my left. "I need my brooch. The girl is too inexperienced to hold the demon."

"Well, I'd say she's performed at an unexpected level of mastery," Blackwell said. "Apparently, she bound the bloody demon without sacrificing the witch. You might want to be asking questions, not making demands ..."

"Blackwell," I said, interrupting their stupid squabble. "I need you to take Ember to a hospital."

"Of course," the sorcerer said. "Just as soon as you dictate terms to the demon as to my untouchability."

"No," Win said. "I forbid it ... for now. Rochelle, bring me the brooch. Then Mot will transport the witch wherever you wish."

Henry stepped into my peripheral vision from the trees that backed the goat shed. He was moving slowly, favoring his right leg. "No, Rochelle," he said. "All of us put ourselves on the line to get that brooch to you."

The demon honed in on the marshal, hunkering down like a cat preparing to strike. It was moving differently than before, and the possible ramifications of that change were terrifying. So I just shoved the observation aside and focused on the here and now.

"No," I said, clearly and with determination. "Henry is a friend."

The demon rotated its head, pinning me with its red-ember slit-eyed gaze.

I shook my head emphatically.

The demon hunched its shoulders, then recommenced its perimeter prowl.

"Jesus Christ," Henry said quietly. "That's not terrifying and thrilling at the same time at all."

Ignoring the sorcerer, I turned to address the night-shadowed trees where Blackwell and Win were concealed. "I'm not an idiot. I'm not giving you the brooch, Win."

My grandmother appeared from between the cherry trees, melting out from the darkness. She was further to the left than I thought she'd been, as if she'd been moving around in the darkness to hide her location. Her face was a thunderstorm of anger and frustration. Her unmasked magic thrummed with a distinct, nausea-inducing energy that I would never mistake or overlook a second time.

The demon eagerly turned its attention to its archenemy, gouging the ground before me with its front claws.

"Marking its territory," Blackwell said, stepping out to stand at Win's side.

Seeing him so enraptured by the transformation of the demon, I realized that it hurt to see Blackwell so easily and casually aligned with my grandmother. I wouldn't have thought myself attached to the sorcerer, but apparently Henry was right. No matter, though. That attachment could be easily undone.

I'd lost so many relationships in my twenty-one years that I didn't bother to count them anymore.

"Apparently, everyone except me has a seriously short memory," I called out, shoving the brooch into my back pocket as I retrieved my phone. "And I'm the only one haunted by the future in which all of you are slaughtered and eviscerated by this very demon."

Henry snorted. "Don't call 911."

"Ember needs an ambulance —"

"I repeat my request." Win flicked her platinum whip threateningly. "Give me the brooch and I won't slaughter your ill-chosen friends. Starting with your mentor, Mot Blackwell."

"Crap," I said. "I'm not supposed to claim the whip too, am I? I'm pretty wiped."

Everyone ignored my glibness. I had no idea why I even bothered trying to be witty. People seemed to prefer me sullen and nonverbal. Maybe I just couldn't pull it off.

"You are misinformed, Kai Win," Henry said, flipping his golden handcuffs in his right hand, "as to the oracle's mentor."

Win cast a withering look at Blackwell.

"I never laid claim to any relationship other than friendship." Blackwell's tone was flat. But on the word 'friendship,' he met my gaze.

I tried to look indignant in his direction. Geas or no geas, I wasn't accepting an offhand remark in lieu of an actual apology.

"Are you going to enlighten me, marshal?" A smug smile had replaced Win's ire. "Before or after I acquire your remarkable handcuffs ... and your only real claim to any sort of remotely interesting magic?"

"The far seer of the guardians and his apprentice have been known to walk the earth at Rochelle Hawthorne's side. Do you think either of them will look favorably on any attempt against her life? Or on threats against the lives of her friends?"

Disbelief flashed across Win's face. Then she barked out a laugh that rang dully through the night-shrouded trees.

Silence fell. I could hear Ember's soft, slow breathing.

Now? the demon whispered in my mind. It curled

around my back, flattening its head in my grandmother's direction.

I shook my head.

Never? it asked.

I didn't answer.

"Dragons!" Win laughed harshly again. "Are you attempting to school me in morality with children's stories and mythology lessons? Ridiculous."

No one responded. She glanced at Blackwell, then looked back at me. The condescension and anger faded from her face. "Mot?"

"The marshal speaks the truth."

"And you are still standing? With the blood on your soul? What mythical guardian would set its sights on you, then walk away?"

Blackwell shifted his head as if he was stretching his neck. "I suppose I must be thankful that I've not come under any guardian's direct gaze. Yet."

"I'll not be lied to."

"A feat you know I'm not capable of."

Beau silently jogged out of the trees to my left, moving for the circle. But he stumbled to a halt as the demon stepped between us possessively.

"Oh," he said. "Hey."

"Hey."

He raked his gaze over me, checking for injuries. He was shirtless and breathing hard, but his henna tattoo was still intact. He hadn't transformed. He cast a measured gaze at Win and Blackwell across the clearing, Henry to my right, and Ember propped up just behind me.

Then he nodded his head. "So ... the demon's on our side now?"

"Apparently," Henry said, heavy on the sarcasm.

"And you're just standing around chatting with them?" Beau jerked his head toward my grandmother and Blackwell.

"No one expects you to speak, shifter," my grandmother said with a sneer. "Your more alluring traits obviously lie elsewhere."

Now? the demon said.

"Not yet," I muttered.

Now!

"Not unless it's a last resort."

"Rochelle?" Though he kept his attention on Win and her undulating whip, concern over my one-sided conversation was laced through Beau's question.

Want blood of enemy. Want now.

I reached out and laid my hand on the demon's head. It curled around me and began to purr, the vibration shooting up my arm to set my teeth on edge.

"Okay there, oracle?" Henry asked.

"Yep," I forced myself to answer. "Time to get Ember to a hospital."

"Past time," Beau growled.

Yes. Now.

I almost let the demon go.

I wanted to let the demon go.

Blackwell met my gaze across the clearing. A look of actual concern flashed across his face. "I'm sorry," he said.

"I don't forgive you," I hissed.

The sorcerer grinned. "I wasn't talking to you."

He grabbed Win's upper arm.

My grandmother was outraged by the unwanted contact. "Unhand —"

"We can't continue this fight, Kai Win," Blackwell said, cutting off the command he'd otherwise be forced to obey.

"Not without fulfilling the vision. And we've already seen who the demon eats first. You."

Win turned her glare on me. She was livid. I couldn't imagine how pissed she would have been if I had set the demon on her ass.

They disappeared. Blackwell had apparently triggered his amulet without Win's approval.

"Finally." Henry pivoted, dropping to one knee by Ember and checking her pulse.

The demon homed in on him as he moved, but didn't leave my side.

"I'm here," she whispered. "I've been awake for a while. Biding my time. You know, until you needed me."

Henry laughed. "I think you've done enough to secure Rochelle's business and undying gratitude. Beyond her lifetime. Your children's children will be dining out on what you've earned tonight."

Ember scowled. "Kids? Ah, that ruins it."

I looked over at Beau. He shrugged, then eyed the demon as it prowled across the clearing and sniffed all around where Win and Blackwell had been standing.

"So ..." he said. "You tamed a demon?"

"Um, no. Not exactly."

"Is it just me, or does it look different?"

"Yes," Henry said, not sounding at all amused.

"I gather that's bad?" I said.

"I have no idea," the marshal said. "But it can't be good. It's a demon."

"Send it home, Rochelle," Ember said weakly. "You need to allow it to return home, then you need to never call it again ... except don't mention that part."

"Just tell it to return home?"

"I would suggest we move out of the way," Ember said.

"So we aren't perceived as an ongoing threat … or dinner. But … I can't actually move myself."

Beau stepped over and scooped the witch up in his arms without effort. She stifled a scream of pain.

The demon whipped its head in her direction. *Now?*

I swallowed, steeling myself against the creature's invasive thoughts. "You're right, it needs to go."

"I'm sorry, Rochelle," Ember whispered.

"What? Why? You seriously saved our asses."

"Except … you're tied to the demon now."

"I'm pretty sure the blame for that lands squarely on my grandmother."

Ember sighed, closing her eyes. "It's worse now. The brooch is a responsibility. A legacy you can't sell or dissolve."

"So we destroy the brooch," Henry said.

I pressed my hand possessively against my back pocket before I'd even thought to move it. Beau eyed me. I forced myself to drop my hand.

Ember shook her head. "Why do you think such things are collected and locked away by the Convocation, or the League, or whomever? They can't be destroyed. So … I'm sorry, Rochelle."

I nodded, ignoring the disconcerting flood of relief that had settled over me at her words. Apparently, the very idea of destroying the brooch made me apprehensive. That couldn't be a good sign.

Beau carried Ember to the edge of the trees. Henry followed. Then they paused, looking back at me.

"You can go home now," I said, facing the demon.

It lifted its wide head to regard me with its crimson eyes.

Blood of my blood.

I shuddered at the satisfaction I heard in its voice.

Blood of my blood, it said again, insistent.

"Yes," I whispered. "Now go. Go home. Don't come back until I call you."

The demon opened its jagged-toothed maw in mimicry of a smile. Then it slowly faded away into the darkness.

I felt oddly bereft for a moment. Then I sought out Beau. Pinning my gaze on him with determination, I crossed through the dark night until I could wrap my hand around his arm and walk away from a vision thwarted.

If it had been thwarted.

WE RACED EMBER TO KELOWNA GENERAL Hospital in Henry's rental car, rather than Ember's Smart car, which couldn't seat all four of us. We immediately nixed the idea of going to the small hospital in Summerland, because we were fairly certain Ember was going to need surgery. Henry sat in the back with the witch stretched out on his lap, singing quietly to her. Turned out that he was muttering healing charms learned from his mother. The spells were customarily used to mend minor bruises and scrapes — such as the ones a hyper kid like Henry had probably dealt with on a daily basis — but the marshal figured any extra healing he could offer would be beneficial.

Beau drove, so the forty-minute trip took only thirty minutes. I kept my eyes off the road, desperately hoping the whole time that he remembered the highway well enough to drive so much over the speed limit.

En route, we tried to figure out how to present

ourselves so as to make it less obvious that we'd all just been in a battle with a demon and two evil sorcerers. Then, when we accepted that wasn't going to happen, we texted Gary and Tess with a list of clothing for Beau and Henry. At Beau's behest and using his phone, I also texted updates to Eddie, Kandy, and Audrey.

Because I was the least bloody and grubby of all of us, I scored a wheelchair for Ember and escorted her through the emergency entrance. It was helpful that my tattoos apparently worked on nonmagicals as well as Adepts to help me avoid drawing attention to myself. Though I had a feeling that was for completely different reasons.

The emergency intake nurses took one look at Ember's leg and carted her off. I didn't even get a chance to offer up the 'we got drunk and tried to climb a tree' story we'd all settled on in the car.

I was pacing uselessly around the tiny waiting area, which was pretty much just a series of mismatched metal-and-plastic-wrapped chairs strung along a sickly green hall, when Tess swooped in. She crushed me in a hug without asking for permission first. Apparently, early morning calls from the emergency ward tore through all those overly familiar barriers pretty quickly. But though I was still feeling numb about everything that had occurred, I definitely squeezed her back.

She held me at arm's length, gave me the once-over, then nodded as if she was satisfied that I'd survive.

"Beau and Gary went back to Summerland to get the Brave," she said. Then, before I could ask for further explanation, she marched off and interrogated the first person she could find about Ember.

I slumped into a chair and continued waiting.

The hospital was quiet, and completely different than

any other city hospital I'd ever had the unfortunate experience of waiting for a foster sibling in before. Except for that weirdly stagnant antiseptic smell and the annoyingly bright lights. Those were apparently universal.

Henry joined me shortly after Tess disappeared. He'd replaced his shredded shirt with a blue short-sleeved T-shirt, but he was still moving slowly, attempting to hide any injuries he'd sustained at my grandmother's hands.

"Shouldn't you check yourself in?" I asked.

He shook his head, carefully lowering himself into the chair beside me. "Nah. Ember should be okay. Tess says they have her in surgery for the break." He glanced around, making sure no one was within hearing range. "They'll have to give her blood, and it'll affect her magic. Dilute her natural healing factors, but not as badly as it would for a sorcerer or shapeshifter. If it wasn't for the leg, she would have just toughed it out until she could find a healer. Like I will."

"Beau?"

"Beau and Gary are getting the Brave and dropping off Gary and Tess's rental car. You four are going to Vancouver. They insisted. Ember and I will stay and call in a cleaning crew if necessary. And a healer for certain. Though I'm not sure there's much to clean up."

Putting aside that everyone was making plans without me again, I zeroed in on my most immediate concern. "What did you tell Tess and Gary?"

"Same story, just more players. That we got drunk, were fooling around, and things got out of control."

"With my grandmother?"

He snorted. "Tempers got heated. Some nasty things were said, and you asked Win and Blackwell to leave." He turned to me, then winced in pain. "You know they can't know, right? It's a fine line you're walking with them."

"Which is why we need to leave before you call any witches?"

Henry grimaced, but nodded.

"What if they already know? Gary and Tess?"

"Explicitly?"

"They aren't stupid. Tess in particular. I don't want anyone screwing around with their heads. In Southaven, Blackwell said something about how witches take care of stuff like this. It sounded as though their taking care of it comes with bad side effects for nonmagicals."

Henry shook his head, thinking. "You'd have to claim some familial connection or prior knowledge ... some magical connection ... or ..."

"Or what?"

"You'd have to ... claim them."

"Claim them, like how. Like ... land or property?"

"Yeah, like servants, really. It's an old loophole, and I'm not sure the Convocation would let you get away with it. Except you do have an in with Jade."

"Jade's on the Convocation?"

"Her grandmother, Pearl, is the chair. Not that I'm really supposed to know that. She's not the sorcerers' League official liaison. And Adepts like their secrets."

"I'm not sure you can call my connection with Jade an in."

Henry side-eyed me. "I've barely met the woman, but Kandy knows her well. She's not going to turn down any request from you. I'd keep your mouth shut around the guardians, though. It's a lifetime contract, and that sort of thing — even if claimed solely to protect someone —

wouldn't fly with them. They'd prefer to remove the problem rather than encourage morally questionable behavior. Honestly, I have no idea how Blackwell still walks the earth."

"He's beneath their notice," I muttered.

"He'd better hope so. But his connection with you ... and Jade ... makes that position very tenuous. I just hope ..."

"What?"

"I hope it makes him a better person."

Tess came hustling around the corner. Henry levered himself out of his seat, crossing toward her. They met a few feet down the hall. Henry bowed his head, listening and smiling as Tess filled him in. Her expression was determined, and her hand gestures were expansive. She was in her element.

I knew that we had put Gary and Tess in a terrible position, just by being friendly and maintaining a relationship with them. But I was insanely glad they were here for us, and for Ember.

I just felt really, really tired. Drained, and with a generous dose of need-to-be-babied. Though I'd never admit that out loud. And I really, really hoped that Beau would show up soon.

When Beau and Gary finally returned with the Brave, it was after eight in the morning. I'd been propped up in the hard plastic chair, sleeping fitfully on and off for over three hours. Beau settled down beside me without a word. I rested my head on his shoulder, wrapped my hand around his bulging bicep, and managed to sleep deeply for another thirty minutes or so.

The scene in the orchard started playing out in my head over and over again, forcing me awake. And the brooch in my back pocket was feeling heavy — malignant, yet compelling. I tugged it free of my jean pocket, wanting to see and touch it, then immediately wanted to throw it away.

"I almost gave in," I whispered to Beau. "I almost used the demon against Win. I wanted to do it." I looked down at the brooch I was rolling between my fingers, jabbing each fingertip with the pointy edges of the ivy.

Beau turned his head to look at me. He'd been leaning his head back against the sickly-green wall of the hospital corridor, trying to nap. "I know."

His acknowledgment only increased the anxiety pooling in my belly.

"But you didn't," he added. "That's what makes us different ... from Cy, from Win ... from Blackwell."

I shifted in my seat so I could shove the brooch away in my back pocket. I wasn't completely certain I was the person Beau was describing. I also wasn't certain he thought so either — since he'd so quickly identified me as the woman in my mother's drawing. But if I pushed the conversation, I knew he would admit as much to me — because when really pushed, we didn't lie to each other.

Even though some part of me wanted to be lied to.

I understood how messed up that was. But first Ember arriving, then Win, had really screwed with our lives. Yeah, it had all been just waiting to happen, but I found myself wishing that the scales hadn't been tipped three days ago. Another year or two of stability would have been nice. Well, my idea of stability.

"I'm actually upset about leaving the chickens," I muttered.

Beau instantly wrapped his arm around my shoulders, tugging me close to his warm chest.

I felt bad, just for a fleeting moment, for playing the woe-is-me card. Then I remembered that Beau liked comforting me as much as I needed to be comforted. And not just about the chickens.

Though they were my responsibility.

"We'll come right back," Beau said. "Leanne and Eddie will look after the chickens while we're away. We'll get Tess and Gary home. Then we'll spill our guts to Kandy, and she'll mediate with Jade. They'll send Win a formal reprimand ... or whatever the guardians do. And we'll be back in time to help Leanne and Eddie open for the long weekend."

"What if Win comes looking for me again in Summerland? And I'm not there?"

"Even if she's stupid enough to look for you while you're in control of her demon, she won't go to Summerland. Most sorcerers aren't dumb enough to tangle with the pack. In fact, we probably played into her hand without realizing it by having the Thompsons leave. We leveled the playing field."

"It got the kids out of harm's way."

"Right." Beau brushed his fingers down the snake henna tattoo I'd drawn on my right arm. The dried dye flaked off underneath his touch. "We'll go back. If Summerland is where you want to be."

"And all the piles of property and money that Ember's uncovered?"

Beau shrugged. "You sell it. Buy yourself a big hunk of land somewhere."

"No. Not me. We. We buy a big hunk of land somewhere."

Beau nodded, swallowing hard.

"We build a house and a chicken coop," I said. "With a garage big enough to get the Brave under cover in the winter."

"Okay." Beau nodded again. "I wasn't going to ask you this ... not right now, I mean. But ..."

Henry and Tess hustled around the corner toward us. Beau shut his mouth and straightened in his chair.

"She's fine," Tess said. "They think the leg will be okay. Months of healing, of course. But okay."

I rose out of my seat, happier than I would have imagined. I'd been concerned about the witch, of course. But still, the degree of my relief surprised me.

Maybe I was unknowingly getting attached to people. That was something to think about later.

"Can we see her?" I asked. "Before we leave?"

"Technically, it isn't visiting hours," Tess said. "They've been trying to stonewall us, but Ember listed Henry as her emergency contact, so they've had to talk to him."

"I think you should go," Henry said. "I know it's early. But, ah ..." He glanced at Tess, who was watching him closely. "I think you should put some distance between you and Summerland."

"You really think that Win will cause a fuss ... again, if we stay one more day?" Tess asked.

"Let's not risk it." Henry eyed me expectantly. "Right, Rochelle?"

I nodded, because I couldn't think of any lie that would smooth the situation. I didn't want Tess and Gary anywhere near Win. Getting on the road, then staying safe in Vancouver, was the best option.

"Though you two could fly back," I said.

Tess lifted her chin. "We're perfectly fine in the Brave, thank you. I have some marking to do, and Gary has his iPad. It's only a four-hour drive. Indulge our nostalgia."

"Yes, ma'am," Henry drawled. Then he tipped his hat in her direction.

She smiled at him, then touched my shoulder lightly. "We'll wait in the parking lot."

Tess hustled off down the hall without waiting for my acknowledgement.

"I like her," Henry said. "You know, for a nonmagical."

"Right. For a human." I laid on the sarcasm.

He grinned. "The Convocation will provide a healer. It's nothing instantaneous, of course, but it'll get Ember walking. A few records will need to be doctored, which, of course, Ember can do herself. This kind of break usually takes multiple surgeries for a nonmagical, but I imagine we'll be in Vancouver in a couple of days." He looked at Beau. "The pack will want to send up a couple of enforcers if you aren't here."

Beau nodded. "Audrey is sending Lara and another wolf I haven't met yet. The Thompsons are already on their way back to Summerland, or about to be."

"So ... we're just leaving?" I was feeling completely unsettled for some reason, even though I was actually getting my way for a change.

"Yep," Henry said. "Your elders have spoken."

I snorted.

Beau shook Henry's hand. The sorcerer leaned into him reassuringly. "Blackwell won't come anywhere near Vancouver."

"Why?" I asked. "What are you worried about?"

"The geas," Beau said. Then he shoved his hands in his pockets and wandered after Tess without elaborating.

I looked at Henry. "He's afraid Blackwell will snatch me if Win tells him to?"

The marshal watched Beau thoughtfully. "Yep. Mot Blackwell traded a lot to train with your grandmother. I hope it was worth it for him, but I would hazard a guess that it was his family that benefited the most and now he's tied to Kai Win ... till death."

"Adepts are always obsessed with the accumulation of power. So there's no reason Blackwell's family would be any different than Beau's, or mine apparently. Other than having more money."

Henry looked surprised. "Not always, Rochelle."

I let the subject drop. Henry, Beau, and I had obviously had very different childhoods and therefore very different understandings of how families treated each other.

"Will the demon come back?" I asked instead. "Say, if I just think about it at the wrong time or place?" Between the skirmish in the orchard and having to race Ember to the hospital, I'd barely been able to think about the ramifications of binding the demon at all. "My expert on contracts is kind of out of commission."

"I doubt it's that easy," Henry said. "But I don't have experience or personal history to reference. The magic in my family is young. Darkness can hit at any time, of course. But I suspect centuries of accumulating power make it more difficult to resist. I'll ask Ember to text you. I'm fairly certain you can't call it during the day. I don't think it can stand sunlight."

"Right." I probably should have known that. From the visions.

"Don't call it, Rochelle," Henry said, terribly serious all of a sudden. "It's not worth your soul."

"Yeah, sure," I said, turning away from the sorcerer and his moral high ground. "But is it worth my life?"

Henry didn't answer. But then, I wasn't really waiting around to continue the conversation.

"Rochelle," he called from a half-dozen steps away.

I turned back to look at him but kept on walking sideways.

He tapped his chest, right over the henna tattoo I'd drawn for him. "Let's make it permanent. Please."

"I know just the place," I said, grinning. "Meet me in Vancouver. We'll get inked together." I lifted my right arm, showing off my henna snake.

"Looking forward to it." He tipped his cowboy hat in my direction. "And oracle? Thank you."

I nodded, turning away and crossing through the glass of the emergency-ward doors into the morning sun.

I had wanted to say something glib about our debt — from when Henry helped us through the situation with Beau's family — being evened out, or void, or something. But I was pretty sure that Henry, along with Ember, had just almost sacrificed themselves attempting to keep me out of Win's clutches.

Yeah, the demon, the whip, and the cloak were pretty bright signposts, even to someone who was supposedly blind to her own future. Or perhaps the correct term was destiny.

A possible destiny envisioned by my own mother, captured in black ink on paper. And possibly thwarted by her death.

Except what if it hadn't been thwarted?

What if it had simply been delayed, and what had

happened last night had been another possible divergent point?

Was destiny like that? Signposts on every corner? A loop back, then around and forward? Over and over, never ending until we died? What was it Chi Wen had said to me in Oregon? *'Destiny is immutable. The future is fluid.'*

So then maybe destiny couldn't be thwarted. Not really. It could just be avoided, each and every single day. Did it come down to the smallest of choices? Or did I have to worry only about the big-picture questions?

Questions like: How far was I willing to go to protect the people I loved? How far was I willing to go to survive?

I already knew I wasn't a hero or a coward. So did that inherently make me a villain? How big a step would it take to cross that divide, to join my grandmother on the other side?

I'd bet heavily that Win would have proclaimed that anything and everything she'd ever done was for her loved ones. For the betterment of her family's lives. That she didn't see herself as the villain, not even remotely.

The Brave was sprawled across four spaces on the far side of the parking lot. Beau was standing near the nose of the RV, looking back toward the hospital for me. He held his hand over his brow, shielding his eyes from the low but already intense sun.

I smiled at him and picked up my pace.

I wasn't sure I could ever pay back the kind of debt I was accumulating — to Henry, to Ember. Even to Blackwell. I wasn't sure I was going to win the war against my destiny.

But I'd keep putting one foot in front of the other until I couldn't any longer. At least I was good at that part.

ELEVEN

"Is that a person in the middle of the road?"

I was leaning over the wheel of the Brave as I peered down the long stretch of highway before me. A tree-covered mountain peak jutted up into the cloudy sky directly ahead of us. The craggy face of another mountain was on my right, interrupted by five lanes of highway stretched out in front of me, beyond which a cliff dropped away to nothing on my left. Well, not literally nothing. But way, way down into the massive tree-lined valley that carved through the mountain range we were currently travelling through.

"Hmm?" Tess said from the passenger seat. She had her nose buried in an ebook on her iPhone. "Maybe one of those sunspot mirage thingies?"

We were on a downward stretch of the Coquihalla Highway, just beyond the summit. The grade was crazy steep through this section, so that on the way north, the Brave had crawled up the hill, nowhere near capable of maintaining even a normal highway speed. Now, heading south, I was having to ride the brakes through many stretches. Picking up too much speed made the RV seriously ungainly.

We'd stopped in Merritt at Starbucks and Dairy Queen, and were currently about three hours away from Vancouver. Though that was dependent on traffic through the Fraser Valley and over the bridges into the city. Being early in the week, the traffic wasn't as bad as it would have been on a Friday. Only a few cars were on the road with us, most outpacing the Brave and disappearing around the curves ahead before I'd even noticed them in my side mirrors.

The highway was carved — literally — through a series of mountains from the interior of British Columbia to Hope, which was just shy of two hours outside of Vancouver. I'd driven the Coquihalla only once, three months ago and in the opposite direction. The road was wide and smooth, but on the way up to Summerland, sticking to the slow outside lane had made me feel as though we were only feet away from dropping off a cliff for most of the trip.

"Seriously, that's a person in the middle of the damn road," I said.

Tess glanced up, turning her head quickly to read a road sign as we sped past it. "We're coming up to a brake check."

"Okay. Not sure why a trucker would need to cross into the road, though ..."

But the figure wasn't crossing the road. It was standing right in the middle of the highway, not much more than a speck. Maybe a half-mile ahead, with nothing but rolling asphalt and yellow line between us. It was also dressed head to toe in black.

"Beau?" I whispered.

Before I could glance back over my shoulder to where Beau and Gary were seated at the dinette, Beau was leaning between the seats and peering out the windshield. His eyesight was better than mine.

"Win," he growled.

"What?" Tess said. "That's ... impossible. Isn't it? How could she know to find us here? And why would she attempt ... she's not unstable, is she?"

Neither Beau or I answered. Blackwell had the Brave tagged somehow, so it would have been easy for Win to have done the same. It was probably a safe guess that Blackwell's magic was how Win had known of my connection to the sorcerer in the first place. She would have felt that magic on the Brave the day she'd shown up. Henry had checked the RV for tracking devices before we'd left the hospital, finding and removing Blackwell's tag but no others. It was an easy guess that Win could hide her spells or magical devices just as well as she masked her personal magic.

I glanced over to Beau just long enough for a brief moment of visual respite, my eyes tracing the lines of his perfectly hewn face. Then I returned my attention to the road.

"Have you got your seat belt on, Tess?" I asked, easing my foot off the brake.

Beau stepped back, muttering something to Gary about 'bracing himself.'

"Yes, of course," Tess said. "But why?"

"We aren't stopping."

I lifted my foot fully off the brake, running a hand across my own seat belt to make sure it was tight.

On the road ahead of us, Win reached up and pushed the hood of her cloak back from her face. I swore she was smirking, though we were still too far away for me to see her expression clearly. It might have been the set of her shoulders, or the magic boiling around her outstretched hands.

I quickly checked both mirrors, but saw no other cars or people in the immediate vicinity, either driving or parked. I wondered if Win had done something to impede traffic, or to magically shield the area. I guessed that she must have used Blackwell's amulet to get ahead of us — then found myself hoping she hadn't killed him for the artifact.

"Rochelle," Tess said, glancing between me and Win. The Brave was eating up the distance between us. "She's obviously desperate to talk. This is not the action of an emotionally balanced person."

We were hurtling toward my grandmother, who was making no effort to clear the way. The distance was difficult to judge as we picked up speed, but she was standing a few dozen meters before a curve in the road. Wide as that curve was, I was going to have to slow the Brave to make the turn after my grandmother got out of the way. But I sure as hell wasn't going to stop.

"Rochelle ..." Tess's voice was anxious now.

"It's okay," I said. "She'll move."

"Rochelle, really ... I think —"

"She's a manipulative bitch, Tess," Beau said from the back. "She'll move."

But Win didn't move.

The Brave's steering wheel began shuddering in my grasp. I placed my foot back over the brake, but didn't give it any weight.

"I'm not stopping," I said, willing Win to read my lips, or even just my expression. "I'm not stopping."

We were almost past the point of no return, and still Win didn't move.

Furious, I tapped the brake.

"She'll move," Beau insisted from behind me.

"Rochelle!" Tess shrieked.

I slowly drifted across the line, moving the RV into the middle lane. Win calmly shifted her position, stepping back in front of us. There were only two southbound lanes in this section. I couldn't go further left without running into the cement barrier, or further right without crashing into the cliff. Stymied, I slammed on the brakes, then started pumping the pedal before they locked.

I'd waited too long. We'd gathered too much speed. I was going to plow right into my grandmother.

Win smiled.

Tess screamed, flinging herself across me to yank on the wheel. We swerved right, toward the empty southbound lane and the cliff face beyond.

Tess screamed again as I shoved her off the wheel, wrenching it in the other direction in an attempt to correct our course.

Win was gone.

But it didn't matter.

The Brave wasn't a sports car. Far from it.

We weaved across the far lane, slammed into the short cement barrier in the middle of the highway, then flipped over it.

My left temple slammed into something hard. Everything went muddled. Out of control.

The Brave slid on its side across the three northbound lanes, thankfully empty of oncoming traffic. There was still no one else on the road. Not slowing one bit, we careened toward the second concrete barrier at the edge of the cliff.

Lying sideways, wrenched against my seat belt, I was still uselessly gripping the steering wheel. Metal shrieked and tore away from the side of the RV, only inches away from my face.

We crashed through the second barrier, slid halfway over the cliff ... and stopped.

My heart was hammering in my chest. I was gasping for air, hyperventilating. I could feel myself losing consciousness. My side window had shattered, and I was staring down through its spiderweb of lines at the endless drop below. I was hanging by my seat belt, over rock and trees and empty space.

Any second now, we were going to tip over the edge and plunge to our deaths.

I felt the Brave lurch, expecting the end.

But it was lurching in the wrong direction.

Inexplicably, we slid back a foot, toward the road. Then another foot.

Something was dragging us back onto the highway, to safety.

The rock face of the cliff appeared through my shattered window. Then gravel.

The Brave went still.

Tess was hanging above me, dangling from her seat and held in only by her belt. I reached up to touch her hand. Her skin was warm but I could see blood in her hair, adding streaks of red to the gold and amber and copper already there.

I thought about trying to move. I thought about doing ... something. Where was Beau? And Gary ...

I reached up and touched the left side of my head. It hurt, and felt disturbingly sticky. I pulled my hand away. It was covered in blood.

Tess moaned. "Rochelle ..."

Adrenaline shot through me in response to her voice. I reached for my seat-belt buckle, getting it unhooked easily enough, then falling the few inches onto what used to be the side of the Brave.

Pain shot through my shoulder, but I tried to ignore it as I scrambled into a crouch, placing my sneakered feet carefully on the crumpled window frame.

I could hear the wheels of the RV still turning, still trying to run. I reached around the steering wheel for the keys, turning off the engine and pocketing them. Then I peered up at Tess dangling over me, trying to figure out how to get her out of her seat belt without getting pinned underneath her myself.

"Beau?" I called out. "Gary?"

No one answered me. I wasn't moving very quickly. Either that or everything around me was happening really, really fast.

Metal wrenched and buckled behind Tess's seat. Then the side of the Brave was ripped outward and Beau was crouched above us, with the bright blue of the sky behind him.

"Hey," he said. His expression was deadly serious. I'd never heard him so angry. But I knew that anger wasn't for me.

"Hey." I tried to smile but failed.

He reached down for Tess, gathering her under the arms while I reached up and unhooked her seat belt. As soon as she was free, he lifted her out of the Brave and disappeared from sight.

I started to climb up after them, using the arms of the passenger seat as a foothold. Then I remembered Gary.

I hunkered back down, trying to peer back through the interior of the RV, but everything was sideways and torn asunder. My refined, saleable sketches had somehow tumbled free from their portfolios, while others had ripped free from my sketchbooks. My visions had been loosely flung around, settling across the destruction. The sight was disorientating and potentially panic-inducing, but I was still riding some sort of adrenaline high that kept my numb brain from absorbing any of it.

Any of it, that was, except for the large hole torn through the back of the Brave, through which I could see the highway. And, farther off, the dark, cloaked figure strolling toward us.

My mother's oracle drawing was lying only a few inches away atop the broken door of the bathroom. Beau had covered the buckled paneling with duct tape and managed to fit the door back into place while he'd been waiting for me outside the hospital, though it wasn't a permanent fix. How the door had remained in place through the crash, I didn't know.

I reached for the sketch, carefully folding it along its well-worn lines and tucking it into my back pocket. The brooch was still secure in my other pocket, but I'd lost my cellphone somewhere.

"Gary!" I called, hoping he'd answer me so I could figure out where he was.

"I've got him," Beau said from above me. "I grabbed him first."

I looked up. He had reappeared at the hole above the front passenger seat. He reached down for me. His hands were ... mangled.

"Beau!" I cried.

"I'll heal," he said. "Come on, Rochelle. We need to move."

I clambered back onto the passenger seat, standing as tall as I could so Beau could lift me out of the wreckage of my home.

My home was ... totaled.

That was really going to hurt when it sank in.

Then it was really, really going to piss me off.

Tess was hunched over Gary, who was sprawled out next to a large concrete structure that stood alongside the edge of the cliff. Maybe some kind of junction box for power lines, I didn't know. Beau set me down in the shadow of the Brave just a few feet away from them. I tried not to look at the underside of the RV, which I'd never seen before and didn't want to look at now.

I grabbed Beau's arms, trying to get a look at his hands. "Why aren't you healing?"

"I am," he whispered. "It's just that pulling an RV back from the edge of a cliff without transforming is ... heavy. Painful."

He shifted his feet in the dirt and rocks that edged the paved road. It all clicked together in my head.

Beau had torn through the back window of the Brave, then had shredded his arms and hands stopping us from tipping over the cliff and dragging us back onto the side of the road.

"Rochelle?" Beau asked. "Are you okay? I need to go for help. I can't believe no one has been by yet."

He was gazing at the empty highway stretched out before and behind us. The Brave was angled across the outside northbound lane. Win had disappeared. Again.

"Have you got your phone?" I asked.

"Yep. No signal," Beau said. "No cars. No cell reception ..."

"Magic," I said glumly.

"Yeah. Magic." Beau sighed. "But I doubt whatever spell she's using has a range wider than I can run in a couple of minutes."

He glanced back at Tess and Gary. Tess was pressing her cotton shirt to Gary's head.

"Rochelle. I wouldn't leave, but ..."

"Gary's hurt."

"Yeah. Badly enough that I don't think I should move him again."

I nodded, swallowing hard. Then, lifting up on my tiptoes, I pressed a kiss against Beau's grimly set mouth.

When I opened my eyes, he was already gone. I moved closer to Gary and Tess, hunkering down in the shade with my back to the underside of the Brave.

I could see the slow rise and fall of Gary's chest, and the huge knot that had been forming in my own chest eased infinitesimally.

"Do you know first aid?" I asked Tess.

She nodded, but didn't look back at me. "Some. It's best not to move him ... again."

"Beau's gone for help."

She glanced back at me, offering a brief smile of acknowledgement. "I heard."

From the corner of my eye, I saw Win step around the crumpled nose of the Brave to my far left.

Tess's tentative smile crumbled.

I wrapped my arms around my knees, looking down at the tattoos etched across my skin. The powdered henna had flaked off the snake I'd twined through the ivy, its deep red lines a sharp contrast now to my pale skin and black ink.

But all of that ink, all of my power, was useless in any fight my grandmother could bring. I was useless.

Except ...

I had a demon in my pocket — possibly literally, because I really didn't understand the whole other-dimensional thing. A demon that was totally lusting after permission to eviscerate my grandmother. Just as soon as darkness fell. In more ways than one if Henry's comment about risking my soul by summoning it proved correct.

I wondered if sunlight was like demon kryptonite. Or whether it was just that light and darkness opposed each other. Two forces that couldn't occupy the same space.

"I thought you'd stop," Win said. She sounded more pleased than shocked.

"What's the endgame, Win?" I didn't look at her.

She stepped in closer. I could see the bottom edge of her cloak and her black leather ankle boots.

"It is as it always was," my grandmother answered. "You come home with me."

"So no 'You hand over the brooch or I'll kill your friends' ?" I said, laying on the sarcasm. "No 'Come with me and you'll become powerful and rich' ?"

Win hunkered down. She was only a couple of inches taller than me in that position, but she stayed too far away for me to reach her. My grandmother wasn't stupid. Evil, yes. Foolish enough to get within reach of an oracle, no.

I kept my gaze on my folded arms.

"You are already rich and coming into your full power," she said, sounding amused. "And you already know the other threat. I would have let you have the shapeshifter. Not to breed with, of course. But if it would have cemented trust between us."

I snorted. "And now?"

"And now ..." Win shrugged lackadaisically, as if we had all the time in the world to discuss her destroying everything I held dear. "Now, he irritates me."

I lifted my gaze finally, meeting her dark-gray eyes. I packed every terrible thing that had ever happened to me into my sneer. "You don't know me at all."

"Ah, but I do now. You tamed the demon, rather than vanquishing it. You didn't stop your vehicle. The human woman did. You're just like me. Genetics is so delightful that way."

Win reached for me, grasping my upper arm.

That was a mistake. Possibly the first one she'd made since we met.

I smiled. Okay, my grandmother wasn't as smart as I'd given her credit for. Or maybe in her previous experience with oracles, she'd never faced one as pissed off as me before.

A look of confusion crossed her face, then her grip tightened determinedly. She was strong for her age. My arm would bear the bruise for days.

Then Tess flung herself between us, managing to startle both Win and me.

"Please," she pleaded. "I can't pretend to understand what's going on. But please. Rochelle has done nothing to you, nothing in her life to deserve being treated this way. You're her blood. You should know better."

Win laughed sharply. "Your human pet is sweet. Does it want to be your mother?"

Tess blinked, then narrowed her eyes at my grandmother. "Take your hands off Rochelle. The police will be here any minute. You should be gone before then, or I will tell them in no uncertain terms that you caused our accident, deliberately and maliciously."

My heart expanded painfully, filling my chest and impeding my breathing for a brief moment. Her husband might have been dying only a couple of feet away, and Tess was threatening a wickedly powerful and most likely evil sorcerer ... for me. Because she thought I was worth fighting for. That I deserved her love.

Win smiled. "You think you can care for an all-seeing destructive force, human?"

"Well," Tess said coldly, "I know you can't."

Win threw her head back and laughed.

So I blasted her with my oracle magic.

Her laughter twisted to a shriek as she released me, scrambling back and clutching her hand.

"You need your hearing checked, old woman," I sneered. "Tess told you to take your hands off me. No one touches me without permission."

Win straightened to tower over us, shaking off my touch with what seemed like little effort. I hadn't gotten a single glimpse of my grandmother's future, and I wondered if she had the ability to shield her mind like she did her magic. If so, that was going to make her practically impossible for me to fight.

Tess pressed back into me, pinning me against the underside of the Brave as if she might be able to shield me from my grandmother.

"This is ridiculous," Win snarled. "Do you want to watch me slaughter them, Rochelle? Is that truly what it is going to take?"

Beau stepped around the nose of the Brave. I could feel his shapeshifter magic rolling up and around him as he walked toward us.

"Don't," I whispered. "Don't transform."

He locked his deep aquamarine gaze to mine. "I love you."

"Beau!" I cried, trying to slip around Tess without hurting her. "Don't!"

A monster built out of claws and fangs and sinew tore through Beau's gorgeous skin. In the space of a single step, a half-man/half-tiger standing just shy of seven feet stood before us. It lowered its head, its orange-furred ears pinned back over its blazing green eyes. It snarled fiercely at Win as it took up a defensive position between her and me.

Without the henna tattoo, which would have been ruined when he transformed, Beau had no protection against whatever magic my grandmother used against him.

Beau's snarl echoed back through the tree-lined valley that rolled out endlessly below the cliff edge, just steps away.

Tess shrieked.

I really couldn't blame her. Beau's warrior form was painful to look at. Hideous. Nightmare fueling ... and utterly beautiful.

Win's whip flashed toward Beau's neck, leaving a streak of silver emblazoned across my retinas.

Beau stepped into her attack, reaching for the whip and allowing it to latch onto his forearm instead.

The stench of burnt flesh and hair hit me hard. Tess moaned and covered her mouth, unable to tear her gaze away from the dreadful scene before her.

Beau snarled in pain, reaching out to grab the platinum whip with his second massive clawed paw. Then, even as it continued searing deeply into his skin, he started slowly dragging Win toward him.

Furious, she wrestled to hold onto the weapon, but inch by inch her feet simply slid out from underneath her.

In his warrior form, Beau was stronger than Win and the whip. Not by much, but enough. She was only a few feet beyond Beau's grasp. She wouldn't be able to fight him, not up close.

I could feel her magic rise, slipping and sliding across my skin. She was preparing some kind of spell.

"Beau." I tried to keep my voice calm, so as to not draw his attention away. "She's going to hit you with something."

He didn't answer because he still couldn't speak in his warrior form, not even after more than a year of training with Audrey and Kandy.

Beau kept reeling Win incrementally closer and closer. The stench of burnt meat intensified.

Tess began to gag, so I reached around her to tug her tank top up over her face. She clung to my arm, forcing me to half-hug her. Not that I protested.

"Mot!" Win shrieked, throwing her head back.

I glanced around, desperately hoping Blackwell wasn't within earshot.

Beau gave the whip one final powerful tug.

My grandmother stumbled forward, slamming her hand against Beau's chest as he grabbed her around the throat.

Magic exploded between them, actually obscuring my eyesight for a moment.

I blinked.

Beau had lost his chokehold on Win. His chest was a mass of bleeding, puckered skin.

I opened my mouth to scream for him.

He stumbled sideways. Then he tumbled off the cliff, dragging Win with him. She was still attached to his forearm by her whip.

I didn't scream.

One moment they were before me. Then they were gone.

I had no idea how far the cliff dropped. I had no idea how far Beau could fall and survive.

Maybe it was only a few dozen feet. On the way to Summerland, I'd seen other roads running alongside the Coquihalla at intervals. It was possible that there was flat ground just below us.

I wanted to crawl to the edge. I needed to see.

Except Tess was screaming. Holding me tight, pinning me in place. Attempting to keep me from harm. Trying to stop me from following Beau.

Blackwell appeared before us, hunching down to catch my attention. "Rochelle."

Tess attacked him. She reared forward, still screaming as she pummeled him with her fists.

He tried unsuccessfully to grab her hands, like he wanted to do so without hurting her.

"Tess." I tried to pull her back. "Tess. Tess. He's here to help." Though even as I declared it, I wondered if he was here to snatch me for my grandmother, as Beau had feared.

That quieted Tess, but she kept one arm out between us, ramrod straight. Protecting me. "Don't touch her," she snarled.

"I have to touch her," Blackwell said. His tone was calm, trying to placate her. "I'm going to take her to safety."

Tess faltered, glancing back at me. Her eyes were wide and wild, yet perfectly clear. The world had just gone crazy before her, but she was focused on protecting me.

"No," I said. "You'll take Tess and Gary to a hospital."

"Rochelle ..." Blackwell began.

"In Vancouver."

"There is no way."

"I won't go," Tess said.

"Then he'll take Gary first," I said. "You'll have to go then."

Tess's lower lip quivered. She glanced over at Gary. I hoped to God he was still breathing, but I didn't take my eyes from Blackwell.

"You'll do this for me," I whispered. "If you can't take them to a hospital in Vancouver, you'll take them to a healer. One you trust. You won't leave them for the witches to take care of."

"They don't have a drop of magic in them," Blackwell said. "Healers need magic to heal ... well, any healers I know. You might have other contacts."

"I'm not going to argue with you." I slowly gathered my feet underneath me until I was crouching. "I have to go make sure the fall killed Win."

"It hasn't," Blackwell said grimly. "I can still feel the geas."

"Which is why you're useless to me here. Take Tess and Gary and don't come back."

"I don't take orders from you."

"You will do this, Blackwell," I snarled in his face. "Not only do you owe me for this shit coming down the way it did, but we have a contract, with a friends clause."

"Which you broke months ago. As we've previously discussed."

"Fine, have it your way. The contract's broken. Which means you'll never get another sketch from me, and I'll do everything in my power to actively use anything I see against you. Even if that means handing each and every vision over to Jade Godfrey."

Blackwell curled his lip at me. Then he glanced over at Gary.

"Please," I said, softening my tone. "Please."

"I can take only one at a time. If I even can take them. The amulet is powerful, but it draws on others' magic as well."

"Gary first."

Blackwell turned away from me without another word.

I straightened from my crouch, woozy and unsteady on my feet. By the time I'd crossed to the edge of the cliff, the sorcerer had disappeared with Gary. Tess stifled a sob, but didn't press me with questions.

I could see the drag marks where Win had gone up to the barrier at the edge of the road, then over it. I could see a trail of broken trees leading way, way down into the valley.

Blackwell reappeared.

"Rochelle," Tess whispered.

I turned back. She was crying, reaching for me. I stepped back, wrapping my arms around her and breathing in her faint perfume. "I'll be okay," I whispered. "I always am. Please take care of Gary for me."

I released her.

Blackwell glowered down at me, wrapping his hand around Tess's upper arm.

"Leave their heads alone," I said.

"Not my problem," he said. "You make it through this, though, you'll have some big favors to call in."

"No worries," I said blithely. "I've got a few banked."

Blackwell shook his head.

"And lift whatever spell you've got holding off the traffic," I said as I turned away.

"I can't. It was done under the geas."

I looked over my shoulder at him. "Don't come back."

He smiled, almost sharklike. "See you soon."

Then he disappeared with Tess.

The sorcerer always did like to have the final word.

I STOOD FOR A MOMENT AT THE EDGE OF THE cliff, looking down into the valley before me. And as I did, I realized with an echo of dread and a trace of empowerment that — minus the demon and the whip — I was standing in the moment rendered in my mother's drawing.

It was this valley of craggy mountains and dark-green trees in the background. I didn't even need to look at the drawing to know it.

I was walking in the future my mother had seen, even though I was a completely different person than she thought I was going to be. This was the future she'd fled from, as far as I could figure.

But, for better or for worse, I was the woman in the vision that I'd tucked into my back pocket. For good or for evil.

And that woman could do anything.

AS I CLIMBED DOWN A ROUGH WALL OF ROCK THAT I shouldn't have been dexterous enough to traverse, I felt my magic gathering up and around me, steadying me on the loose stone. By the time the cliff opened up to the gentler treed slope of the valley, my sorcerer powers were twining through every tattoo etched into my skin in a way I'd never felt before.

I didn't need Win's whip, or Henry's handcuffs, or Jade's knife when I had my tattoos. I didn't need complex spells when I had the future at my fingertips. I was a walking weapon.

I'd just never known it.

It made a kind of sense that the moment before the moment of my death was a good time to find this out. The fact that I would die rather than bow to my grandmother was a forgone conclusion. And not even for any particularly moral reason. But just because no one told me how to live my life or who to love.

It didn't take long for me to find Win deep within the valley. Maybe fifteen minutes. Beau was in his human form, sprawled at her feet.

Win's cloak was shredded. A large bruise was forming on one side of her face. Beau and the fall had hurt her, severely. It seemed a safe bet that she'd be all the more dangerous for it. Wounded animals often were.

The surrounding area was trashed. It was as if two tanks had engaged in a game of chicken, tearing hundred-year-old trees apart and churning rock and soil underneath their metal treads.

Apparently they'd been fighting for the entire time I'd been chatting with Blackwell and climbing down the cliff.

Beau had fallen. And Win was in the process of choking his final breath from him with her platinum whip.

I stumbled at the sight.

My grandmother spun, flicking the whip before her.

I'd startled her.

The whip licked the air, just inches from my nose. Then

Win called it back to her side. It undulated at her feet, moving as if sentient.

"Oh, right," I said mockingly, gathering my damaged soul and all my years of neglect and pain around me, wearing it like a cloak of foolish, sullen bravery. "Is this the part where I say I'll do anything, if only to save my boyfriend's life?"

Win laughed as she stepped away from Beau. She gestured to me to step around her, ceding the way.

I immediately took the opening, attempting to skirt the range of the whip. Though since it apparently expanded and contracted magically, it probably didn't make any difference.

I kneeled down, placing my hand on Beau's chest. I hoped that his reversion to human form had been to unconsciously trigger his healing. His heart beat steadily underneath my palm. I swallowed the rush of relief that threatened to burst through my chest.

Beau was alive.

So all I had to do was buy him time.

I gazed at his beautiful battered face, aware that I might be looking at him for the last time. His left eye was swollen shut. His jaw looked as though it had been broken, one cheek scraped raw. He was missing an ear, and one of his shoulders looked wrong. Dislocated, probably. I squeezed my eyes shut, needing to stop myself from cataloguing his injuries any further.

Then I forced myself to open them again.

I would see him.

I would see Beau as the last thing I ever saw. And I would be blessed to do so. I was blessed to do so.

"I won't go with you," I said, not bothering to look at Win.

"No?" She laughed. "And how are you going to stop me from taking you? It's obvious that whatever offensive power you have can be easily countered by not touching you. I won't bother reiterating my promises. You will come with me."

"Your threats, you mean."

Win stepped into my peripheral vision, but she was keeping way out of reach this time. She shrugged, her blank gaze on Beau. "Say goodbye. You won't be breeding with any animal, no matter how pretty you think he is."

I leaned over and brushed my lips against Beau's, careful not to press too hard. Not wanting to hurt him. I didn't need him to jolt awake right now.

"Rochelle ..." he murmured.

I stilled, holding my breath. But he didn't open his eyes.

When I finally straightened up, I turned to face my grandmother. "Let me reiterate then. You don't know me at all."

Win snorted. "Oh, yes? You'd rather die, would you? And the shapeshifter? You'd be so cavalier with his life?"

I mimicked her shrug, willing my face to be as blank as hers. "He's made his choice."

Win's lip curled as she tilted her head, considering me. "Perhaps you aren't as hopeless as I thought ... what with the running away and the cowering behind the human."

I stepped away from Beau, moving carefully over the loose rock underneath my feet, and trying to avoid tripping over any branches or brush. I could hear water nearby. A creek, by the sound of it. Though that was utterly irrelevant. We were a long way from the Brave, from the road, and from any sort of rescue.

Win followed me with her gaze but didn't move as I widened the gap between me and her. Between me and

Beau. If she went for him, I'd have no chance of stopping her from this distance.

Her whip twisted across the ground between us as if it were tracking me.

"Some people are born heroes," I said as I continued to try to draw her away from Beau. "And no matter what life throws at them — no matter what pain or terror — they make the right choice. The moral choice. They sacrifice themselves for the greater good, for the future, for the lives of others. Beau is one of those people. I'm not. I should know. I've seen heroes. I've seen them stand tall against a greater enemy. I've seen them fall and get back up. I've seen them ... evolve. But I'm unchanged, unchangeable. I survive. And I'm not afraid to survive you."

Win laughed. "I wasn't sure you could string such a large amount of words together at one time."

"Let's just get this over with." I stopped walking, standing firm.

"What will you fight me with, granddaughter? Even your words offer no wit ... or bite."

I lifted my empty hands, epically aware of my mother's vision crumpled in the back pocket of my jeans. "Everything I have."

Win frowned.

"Or did you think I really was just a benign oracle?" I willed my magic to pool in my palms, like Blackwell and my grandmother wielded their power. I pushed past my own bluff, as I willed myself to be the person pictured in my mother's drawing.

White orbs of power pulsed in my hands.

But Win only smiled, proud and snotty. She flicked the whip toward me, delivering a wicked lick to my thigh and slicing through my jeans before I could even react. Magic seared into my skin.

I flinched. Gritting my teeth against the pain, I flung the orb in my right hand toward my grandmother.

She easily batted it away, dispersing its energy with a pop. But the action of doing so forced her a step away from Beau.

I turned and ran, feeling the whip brush the back of my neck as I darted away.

I zigzagged, twisting back to throw my second orb.

Win paused behind me to dispel the attack. She'd closed the space between us, nearer than I'd thought she'd be.

But Beau was in the clear.

I pivoted back, changing tactics completely to run back toward her. Startled, my grandmother stumbled to a halt, allowing me the time to lunge toward her with my left hand outstretched. My fingers brushed her cheek.

The whip wrapped around my waist, almost lovingly. Then it began to lift me off my feet and push me away from Win, constricting and grinding against my lower ribs.

Ignoring the pain and my impeded breathing, I stretched my hands toward my grandmother, who was staying safely out of reach.

Then I watched surprise replace the smugness etched across her face as my ivy and barbed-wire tattoos lifted from my arms, then shot through the air toward her.

If she was close enough to grab me with her whip, then I was close enough to grab her with my tattoos.

Win stumbled back but didn't let go of the whip. She knocked the black tendril of ivy away with the side of her hand, but the henna snake hiding within it struck hard, biting deep into the base of her neck, just above the shoulder.

She shrieked, but more in indignation than pain.

"Have another look, Grandma," I whispered. "This is what you came for. This is why you bred me. This is why my mother died. Take a look."

Then with every ounce of strength I had, I forced my oracle magic through the tenuous connection the henna snake made between us.

Win screamed.

The hold of the whip loosened. My toes touched the ground.

Win reached up, somehow grabbing my henna tattoo. She ripped the snake away from her neck.

As she did, I coaxed my black ivy tattoo to curl around her whip-wielding arm.

She fought me, squeezing the whip so tightly that I almost passed out. I fought through the pain and lightheadedness, twining my barbed-wire tattoo around my grandmother's free arm. Digging the barbs of the wire into her skin, I then lashed it across her belly to pin her arm to her torso.

The henna snake bit her again.

The whip loosened, though it still kept its hold on me. I dropped fully to the ground, losing my balance. Win twisted away from me, dragging me through the dirt and rock behind her.

I slammed my oracle magic into her again, pushing it through the snake, the ivy, and the barbed wire all at once.

My grandmother convulsed, but she was still on her feet.

I could feel her sorcerer magic rising up underneath the connection the tattoos made between us. A powerful pulse underneath my feeble attempt to hold her.

I hit her with a third wave of magic.

She went down.

The whip fell away from me, twisting harmlessly across the ground. But I was certain I couldn't hold her much longer. She was too strong, too skilled, and I only had desperation on my side.

I pulled her closer even as I crawled toward her. I willed the tattoos to keep their hold on her, even as I ordered them to return to me.

My grandmother fought me, punching, kicking, and with rippling pulses of magic — using the connection of the tattoos against me.

She got her arm free of the ivy, then wrenched the snake away from her neck by wrapping it around her hand. Then she snapped the snake in half, tearing it free from my arm.

The bones of my forearm snapped. Though I almost blacked out from the pain, I managed to keep hold of her with the barbed wire somehow.

Behind me, Beau screamed, "Rochelle!"

Though it was strained, the sound of his voice galvanized me. My vision cleared with a blink. My cheek was pressed into the dirt. I lifted myself with my good arm, dragging the other one behind me.

Win had nearly freed herself from the barbed wire as I lunged forward, knocking her backward and crawling up her body to press my hands to either side of her face. My broken arm complied, though it burned.

Pinning her upper body even with what little there was of my weight, I leaned down to lock my gaze to her dark-gray eyes.

"Let's see what we see, Grandma."

I pressed my lips to her cheek.

It was how I would have kissed her. If my life had been different.

If my mother had survived, if my father had been alive. We would have had Sunday dinners and played on the swings in the park.

I pressed my lips against her, grinding them into her cheekbone.

I would have had a puppy, and playmates, and I never, ever would have thought I was crazy.

There would have been clothes in my closet, the best education money could buy, and a grandmother who loved me.

"But no Beau," I whispered.

Then I blasted my oracle magic through Win's mind, shredding her defenses and wiping everything else in its path in a blinding wash of white. It was a brutal, vicious, deep cleaning of every thought, every action, every synapse.

The utter nothingness of her future flowed out of me and through her mind.

I gave it all.

I gave her everything she ever wanted.

Everything I had to give.

She was family, after all. Did she deserve anything less?

Utterly spent, I keeled forward, cracking my forehead against my grandmother's.

Then everything went dark.

WHEN I WOKE, I WAS CRADLED IN BEAU'S ARMS. But when I managed to open my eyes, it was Win I saw. She was kneeling before me. Her hands were folded in her lap. She was staring, but not at me.

Her blank gaze had no malice hiding behind it. Not anymore.

"I'm a monster," I muttered.

"Yeah," Beau said, his chest rumbling underneath my head. "But you're my monster."

I laughed. A terrible, agony-filled noise wrenched out of my throat and chest ... out of my heart.

Beau squeezed me, too tightly.

Pain shot through my right arm, wiping out the inappropriate laughter before it could turn into wails of grief and fear.

"My arm's broken."

"Yeah."

"She's not dead," I whispered.

Beau just grunted.

I could read so much into that response. But I chose not to.

Blackwell materialized within the fallen trees twenty feet away from us. His dark magic was primed in each palm. He spun, seeing Beau and I cuddling before my brain-dead grandmother.

We must have made an interesting tableau.

The magic dissipated in Blackwell's hands. He stepped forward, cautiously skirting Beau and me to gaze down at Win.

"The geas is broken," he murmured. He reached down and retrieved Win's platinum whip. I hadn't even noticed it lying inert on the ground.

Then Blackwell laughed. A sharp, single note full of dreadful satisfaction.

He turned to look at Beau and me. And for a brief moment, I could see something terrible in his gaze. Something hungry and fierce.

Beau growled, a rippling snarl that held a hint of the power I'd felt Desmond wield. Alpha power. The power to quell others' magic. But Beau was still healing, and I suspected that Blackwell could have killed him easily if he'd wanted to. Then he'd snatch me away.

I lifted my left arm, palm up. "Don't make me hurt you," I whispered.

Blackwell's expression blanked. His dark gaze settled on my arm, possibly noting that my tattoos were so faded they were barely discernible even against my pale skin.

I hadn't noticed that yet either.

"Rochelle," he said, as smooth and cultured as always. "You mistake me. I am, as always, on your side. I look forward to renewing our friendship."

Beau's grip tightened, then eased. He didn't trust Blackwell, not one bit.

And neither did I.

That must have shown on my face, because Blackwell frowned.

"Did you do as I asked with Gary and Tess?" I said.

"At Vancouver General Hospital. As you wished. And to my own detriment, when Jade Godfrey discovers my trespass. As always seems to be the way with our relationship."

"That's up for interpretation," Beau said.

Blackwell brushed his fingers against Win's shoulder. She turned her head, looked up at him, and smiled.

My stomach squelched.

He smiled down at her, slowly coiling the whip in his hands.

I thought about asking for the weapon. I could have demanded that he give it to me. Except I was terribly afraid of whatever precipice Blackwell was standing on. I didn't want to push him off. I didn't want to fight him.

And, honestly, I didn't want the responsibility of the whip.

Blackwell looked over at me. Even in the bright, shadowless sunlight, his eyes were a deep black, barely a hint of white at their edges.

I shuddered but didn't look away. "Your magic is black," I whispered, attempting to sound cool and collected.

The sorcerer frowned again. The color of his eyes lightened incrementally. He glanced down at the whip in his hands. Then, completely impossibly, he slipped the platinum coil into a pocket of his suit jacket that was nowhere near large enough to hold it.

"Allow me to continue to clean up your mess," he said, touching Win's shoulder a second time. Still smiling peacefully, my grandmother slowly lifted her hand and placed it over Blackwell's.

He and Win disappeared.

Beau and I both just stared at the empty landscape sprawling out before us.

I could hear running water again. Then birds chattering. I imagined all the nearby wildlife would have been scared off by the Adepts rampaging through the valley. I wasn't sure I was capable of processing the ramifications of Blackwell taking off with Win.

"Beau?"

"I don't know," he said in response to my unasked question. "Except, I guess you can't be found at fault without evidence."

"Fault? She was trying to kill everyone!"

"Well, I didn't say you'd be convicted."

Sirens sounded from far, far above us. Beau gathered me

into his arms, standing and turning back the way we'd come down the cliff.

"I'm sorry about the Brave," he whispered.

I spread my hand across his chest over his heart. "Home is where you are."

He nodded. Then his face twisted into a terrible grimace filled with pain and sorrow ... and possibly joy.

My heart pinched so much that I had to struggle to inhale.

A single tear ran down Beau's cheek. I lifted a shaking hand, wiped it away, then sucked on my finger.

"Hey," I said. "Do you want to get married?"

He laughed, jostling my broken arm painfully. "Hell, yeah."

Then he carried me up to the wreckage of the RV. With the help of whatever magic Blackwell had used to mask the valley below, we talked our way out of the accident, into an ambulance, and all the way to the emergency room in Merritt.

We would figure everything else out later.

TWELVE

"Busy place, huh?" I said. It wasn't really a question.

We stood on a sidewalk in Vancouver, across the street from Cake in a Cup. It was late afternoon, but the sun was still high in the sky. Beau and I had been watching customers coming and going from the bakery for over an hour. He was a quiet sunblock to my left. West Fourth Avenue was busy, full of slow-moving luxury vehicles.

I wasn't a fan of Kitsilano in general. It was too clean, too high-end for my ragamuffin tastes. But after Beau scored me a fresh-pressed apple juice from an organic juice place down the street, then a tasty vegan hotdog from a food cart up a block, I was almost ready to admit that despite being overly trendy, the area might have its uses.

Including being Jade Godfrey's chosen place of residence, and therefore the seat of power in Vancouver. Or maybe the West Coast in general. If not all of North America. 'Seat of power' was Henry's term, and if I hadn't known some of the powerful Adepts who came and went from the innocuous-looking bakery as well as I did, I probably would have scoffed at the sorcerer. But I'd spent too many years with these people in my head. I understood their bravery, their fierceness, and their predetermined sense of right and wrong.

Except I wasn't quite sure where I fell on that moral scale anymore. The platinum brooch in my back pocket — let alone what I'd done to my grandmother — might even put me firmly in the 'wrong' category.

Anticipating the many conversations to come — over and over again in my head — wasn't doing me or Beau any good. And staring at the bakery wasn't getting me anywhere, except possibly sunburnt. I'd have a weird tan line when the cast came off my right arm in six weeks.

Without thinking too much more about it, I darted out between the cars that had paused for the red light on Vine Street, making a beeline for the bakery.

Beau followed me without question or hesitation. We had gone over the plan ad nauseam in the hospital in Merritt, while grabbing clean clothing at a thrift shop, and during the entire bus trip down to Vancouver today. We'd even written out a formal request for sanctuary. The bakery was our first stop.

But my mouth still went dry as I set foot on the opposite curb and instantly felt the prickle of the intense magic that coated the bakery storefront.

I stopped abruptly between a free newspaper box and a full bike rack, both painted different shades of green.

Beau knocked into me, catching me around the waist before I fell forward to be trampled by the shopping-bag-laden pedestrians filling the sidewalk.

A gray-haired woman seated behind the middle French-paned window of the bakery looked up from her laptop. A thick braid was coiled into a bun at the back of her head.

There wasn't a single hair out of place above her high brow. Her eyes were pools of deep indigo.

The exact color of Jade Godfrey's eyes.

And I'd seen this woman before, in my early visions when I lived in Vancouver. Only a few glimpses. But enough to know she wasn't someone I wanted to cross.

"Oh, God," I moaned.

"They can only say no," Beau whispered, loosening his grip on my waist. "That's all they can do. We've done nothing wrong."

The older woman's steely gaze flicked up to take in Beau behind me. Her lips thinned. She lifted her hand and closed her laptop.

The woman seated across from her turned, looking over her shoulder at us. Her strawberry-blond hair fell across her back in a perfect cascade of a perfect wave. Her eyes were also an exact match to Jade's, though I saw no other resemblance.

"Witches," Beau said.

"You can smell their magic through the wards?"

"Jade's family. Maternal."

Right. Apparently, my brain was on strike. Which made sense, since I'd apparently lost any ability to use logic as well. What kind of people attempted to align themselves with the dragon slayer? Warriors ... heroes ... sycophants ...

I was none of those things.

A brilliant smile spread across the younger witch's face. She lifted her hand, beckoning to us.

The magic of the wards shifted, though the prickly energy dancing on my skin intensified rather than dissipated.

"I'm with you," Beau said. "Forward or back. Sideways or ... any direction. Any choice. No matter what."

I reached back and curled my fingers through his. Tugging him to my side, rather than behind me, I hazarded crossing the teeming sidewalk.

We stepped through the open door into Cake in a Cup.

The magic of the wards slid over us, then disappeared. The interior of the bakery smelled like heaven.

And I wasn't a fan of sweets.

I faltered, blocking the doorway.

"We should greet the witches," Beau whispered.

"Not yet," I said, letting instinct guide me. I cast my gaze across the well-picked-over cupcakes behind the glass display cases. The trinkets hanging in the doorway behind us and in the windows to our left chimed softly in a light breeze I hadn't noticed before.

Jade Godfrey entered the bakery through a set of swing doors behind the counter. Her golden curls were clipped up at the back of her head. She was wearing a brown T-shirt emblazoned with a pink-printed Cake in a Cup logo, and a long skirt that looked like crushed rose-colored silk.

I lifted my chin and met her indigo gaze. She didn't seem surprised to see us. But then, I'm sure she'd tasted my magic the instant I'd crossed through the wards. Maybe even before. She probably knew I'd been casing the bakery for an hour already. Just waiting for our next move.

Forcing the expression through my fear, my apprehension, and my anticipation, I smiled.

An answering grin spread across the dragon slayer's face. She stepped past the counter, holding her hand out toward me.

I took it without any hesitation. "We're going to stay for a bit," I said. All the fancy wording and the formal request Beau and I had worked on was discarded without a second thought.

This was Jade. I knew her. I'd seen her do great and terrible things. She would never condemn me. She'd never turn me away.

"All right," she said.

Some sort of magic shifted between our clasped hands, but I didn't try to read or do anything with it.

"Cupcake?"

"Yes. Please," I said. "Do you have anything with apple?"

"Not yet. But I'll give it a try this fall. For you." She looked over my head, smiling at Beau. "And for you?"

"Anything chocolate."

Jade laughed. The sound reverberated around the bustling room, then settled comfortingly across my shoulders.

"Done," she said, releasing my hand. "Go say hi to my gran. Then we'll talk about why your magic is so diminished, and who's chasing you into town."

"We took care of it," Beau said. "And the magic will come back."

Jade sobered for a moment. "It always does." She glanced down at the faint tattoos twining along my arms and underneath my cast. "Most likely stronger than before."

"Stronger?" My voice squeaked on the question more than I would have liked.

Jade pinned me with an intense gaze, then reached up to touch her gold necklace. Though over a dozen wedding ring charms still hung from it, it looked different than the last time I'd seen it. But, oddly, I couldn't really pinpoint those differences. As if the necklace was somehow slowly shifting aspects right before my eyes ...

I grew dizzy, then forced my gaze away.

Jade smirked at me. "That's Mory in the corner." She nodded toward a girl in her late teens, with sunset-dyed hair that tumbled all around her bowed head. She was — literally — pressed into the corner of the storefront. And, even odder, she was knitting. "She's a necromancer. You won't have anything in common. Say hi."

With that odd pronouncement, Jade retreated back behind the counter and started piling cupcakes onto plates.

I glanced up at Beau. People were peering around his broad shoulders, trying to see if we were in line.

"Gran first," he said.

I pivoted obligingly, crossing through the high round tables and brushing by strollers and brown-bagged groceries.

Gran had relocated, and was now sitting with the so-called necromancer. The strawberry-blond witch grinned at us as we crossed through the seating area, but then returned her attention to whatever she was working on. I guessed she was Jade's mother, but she really didn't look old enough to be.

About three steps away from them, and feeling really pissy about being forced to meet new people, I realized that I was stepping into a new chapter. I had endless choices of where to live, and who to invite into my life. I could be whoever I wanted to be.

I wasn't an outsider in the Adept world. And, though I was different than anyone else, I wasn't an anomaly.

I was me.

A genuine smile spread across my face. The sunset-haired necromancer lifted her gaze from her knitting and offered me a smirk.

"Hi. I'm Rochelle," I said.

"Mory," she answered. "This is Pearl Godfrey, Jade's grandmother."

Pearl reached out to shake my hand, frowning fiercely down at my cast for a moment, then lifting her gaze to meet mine.

I removed my sunglasses.

Pearl smiled. "Oracle," she said. "A pleasure to meet you finally."

She meant it. And she didn't flinch at my eyes.

"Cool tats," Mory said. "How did you get them that color?"

"It's a long story," I said.

"Yeah?" She eyed me for a moment. "I've got one of those too."

"I imagine we all do."

"Yeah." Mory laughed as she returned her attention to her knitting. "If you're going to hang around here, you do."

I really had no idea what she was referring to specifically, other than that the people who hung around Jade had a tendency to get pulled into trouble. But if it amused her, that was cool. The future would unfold, as it always did.

I looked over at Beau.

"This is Beau," I said, introducing him proudly. "We're going to stick around for a while."

Beau grinned at me, then reached past me to shake Gran's and Mory's hands.

I SLIPPED BACK INTO THE BAKERY KITCHEN AFTER Kandy arrived to interrogate Beau. Well, as much as she could question him about what had happened while sitting in a bakery filled with nonmagicals.

Jade was baking, though the effort looked casual. As if she was testing out new recipes, maybe. The oven behind her was filled with trays of half-baked cupcakes of various colors. A large fan sucked the heat away from above our heads.

"Do you need me to contact the far seer?" she asked without looking up. She added a tablespoon of what I thought might be cinnamon to a tabletop mixer, which was much smaller than the massive industrial unit currently churning away in the corner of the room.

"I don't think so."

"Well, that's good. We're having a timeout. Or I am ... I doubt he's even noticed, really."

"I need to give you something."

She stepped over to the sink, turning on the water without questioning me further.

I waited, trying to not shuffle my feet, while she washed and dried her hands. Then I pulled my grandmother's brooch out of my pocket.

I held it out to her in the palm of my hand. She stepped around the long stainless steel table situated in the middle of the room, peering down at it.

Silence stretched between us.

"Where did you get it?"

"It's my grandmother's. She used it to bind a demon." I hesitated for only a second before forcing myself to continue. "I took it ... with help. I bound the demon myself. To me."

Jade lifted her gaze from the brooch to meet mine. "And you want me to keep it for safekeeping?"

I squared my shoulders, forcing myself to make the

commitment. To make the choice I knew I had to make for my own sanity. For Beau's safety. Even if it left us vulnerable in other ways. "I want you to destroy it. I want you to sever the connection. You can do that. I know you can."

A slow smile spread across Jade's face. "That's a lot of power to walk away from. Even dampened there in your hand, I can taste it clearly."

"I don't like who it makes me."

Jade laughed quietly, lightly touching her own necklace. "I get that."

She took the platinum wreath, carefully holding it by the pointy edges and turning it in her hand. The tiny diamonds interspersed among the ivy leaves caught the light. Except the angle was wrong for that, so maybe I was actually seeing some of Jade's magic.

I looked away, wrapping my hand around the raw diamond hanging from my own necklace. Waiting for Jade's decision.

"Your grandmother is dead?"

"Not quite."

"She tried to hurt you and Beau?"

I nodded. "And Henry. And Ember, a witch who was helping me."

"Am I expecting your grandmother in Vancouver?"

"No."

"But you came here for protection?"

"From Blackwell."

A sly grin slid across her face.

"But he didn't hurt us," I said hastily, not totally sure why I was still trying to stand between the sorcerer and Jade.

The dowser sniffed. "It's only a matter of time."

"He won't come here."

"Probably not." She sounded disappointed. Then she closed her hand around the brooch. "Energy can't be destroyed. Only transferred."

She opened her hand. A lump of mangled metal and gems sat in her palm.

"That's it? The connection is severed?"

"It is. I guess I make it look easy." She laughed. "The platinum holds some tasty residual, with some hints of tart apple. Shall I add it to your necklace?"

"Um ... can you make something out of it for me instead? For me and Beau? No rush."

"Wedding rings?"

"Yeah."

"I can do that." Jade tucked the lump of platinum into her back pocket. Then she returned to her baking.

I hesitated, realizing that I was shuffling my feet. I stopped. "So, we're cool?"

"Do you need a place to stay?"

"Nah. I actually own a place in Vancouver. It's an estate thing. My mom's, not my grandmother's. An apartment. We're probably going to sell it, though."

"Talk to Gran first, would you? She might make you an offer."

"Okay."

I watched as Jade went back to her baking. A golden curl had come loose and was dancing by her cheek. She ... she looked like magic. Utter magic, measuring icing sugar into a stainless steel bowl.

"How far out of Vancouver do you think I have to be to raise chickens?"

Jade looked up from her mixer, surprised. "You can have a couple in the city now, actually."

"How about more than a couple?" I glanced around the kitchen. "I've got magic deathlayers. You need eggs, right?"

"Do I want to buy magical chicken eggs from an oracle? Totally."

I grinned at her. "Cool. I'll look into it then."

WE LEFT THE BAKERY AND IMMEDIATELY HEADED over to Vancouver General Hospital on West Twelfth Avenue to see Gary and Tess. We could have taken the bus, but we walked most of the forty minutes in comfortable silence, just enjoying the sunny late afternoon and letting our thoughts drift.

I now knew what dark destiny might dog my path, trying to lure me away from the light. I knew what I was capable of. But that didn't mean that I wouldn't breathe in every bit of lightness and love I could find.

I was tired of being alone. Of segregating myself. I was ready to be an 'us.' Me and Beau. Along with Gary and Tess, and whoever else would have us in their lives.

I wanted to see us.

Every day. In the light.

And if the darkness came again, I'd be ready for it. Again. And always.

Destiny might beckon to me, but I could and would choose whether or not to respond, each and every time.

Tess was waiting for us at the nurses' station of the Neurology ICU on the fifth floor. Despite the head trauma, apparently Gary was okay. The doctors had conducted a barrage of tests, and were now keeping him for observation for a couple more days. The second I saw Tess, I picked up my pace until I was practically jogging down the long hospital corridor and flinging myself into her arms like a moron.

She hugged me fiercely, reaching back to tug Beau into the embrace when he hesitated behind us. He'd been worried that Tess would be scared of him, though her text messages over the last day hadn't indicated any trepidation.

"Gary?" I asked.

Tess nodded. Wiping tears from her cheeks with one hand, she tugged me farther along the corridor and into a tiny semiprivate room, chattering the entire way. "I've been texting with Henry. He and Ember will head this way tomorrow. Turns out her break wasn't that bad."

We rounded an open sliding glass door. Gary was in the process of trying to get out of his hospital bed.

"Hey!" Tess said. "You know you're supposed to be resting!"

Gary froze half-propped against the side of the bed, glancing our way. But his guilty expression transformed into a wide, easy grin at the sight of Beau and me in the doorway. "Rochelle! Beau!"

I crossed to him, flinging my good arm around his neck but being careful to not knock him over. He thumped on my back with his good arm. The other arm was in a cast.

"Hey," I whispered, stepping back and showing him my broken arm. "We're cast buddies."

He laughed.

He laughed as if we hadn't just been in a massive accident. He laughed as if he didn't have a large bandage on his head and bruises down the side of his face. He laughed as if I'd just told some brilliant joke and he couldn't wait for the next thing I had to say.

My stomach flipped uncomfortably. Guiltily. "I totaled the Brave. I mean ... you asked me to look after it ..."

Gary nodded, patting my shoulder, then easing back onto the bed. "It was beyond your control, Rochelle. I'm just glad you and Beau are okay. I'm glad everyone is okay."

Tess bustled around the other side of the bed, plumping Gary's pillows and getting his legs tucked underneath the sheets. He gazed at her adoringly, then he glanced back at me. "Actually I don't remember much at all," he said. His tone was too casual.

Tess glanced at him anxiously, then seemed to avoid looking directly at Beau or me. But when the silence stretched between us, she turned to pour him a glass of water from a plastic pink pitcher on a nearby table.

I fiddled with the edge of Gary's blanket. Then looked back at Beau, who was still hovering near the doorway.

"That's ... umm," I said. "That's the thing —"

"It's not," Tess said, interrupting me. "We both hit our heads badly. And concussions can be tricky. That's why we're still here. In the hospital. With the extra tests and ..." She glanced at Gary, trailing off.

I almost took the out she was offering. No one but Blackwell knew that Tess had seen Beau transform. Or that Blackwell had somehow magically transported them from the edge of the Coquihalla Highway to Vancouver.

Except I didn't want an out.

"I was thinking ... we were thinking," I said. "That maybe ... that maybe Ember could draw up some papers ..."

Tess grabbed Gary's hand, visibly clenching it, then pressed her other hand over her chest. Her eyes were shining.

I swallowed my own trepidation. I'd gone over my conversation with Henry in the hospital in Kelowna, talking it out with Beau and looking for a loophole. We needed some guarantee that Gary and Tess wouldn't get their minds wiped because they knew about us, about magic. "If we were family. Formally, I mean. If we were family, it wouldn't matter what you didn't see. What you're pretending to not have seen."

A big grin spread across Gary's face.

Tess started nodding, then continued as if she couldn't stop. "You want us to adopt you? You and Beau?" She lifted her gaze over my shoulder.

Beau stepped up beside me, pressing his arm against mine.

"For goodness' sake, Tess," Gary said. "Say yes before they change their minds. Where do we sign?"

"It might be dangerous," I said. "I mean, I hope not, but ... I don't know what is going to happen with my grandmother. Vancouver is the safest place we could —"

"Yes, yes," Tess cried.

"Yes?" I wiped the tears streaming down my face away. "You know what we are. What we can do. And you still want to be a family?"

"From the first moment we saw you," Gary said gruffly. "And you, Beau." He reached up and clapped his hand to Beau's shoulder.

"From the first moment," Tess whispered, skirting the bed so she could fold us into a four-way hug.

I looked over at Beau, happening to catch the reflection in the sliding glass door of the four of us tangled together.

I saw us.

ACKNOWLEDGMENTS

With thanks to:

My story & line editor
Scott Fitzgerald Gray

My proofreader
Pauline Nolet

My beta readers
Terry Daigle, Angela Flannery, Gael Fleming, Desi Hartzel,
and Heather Lewis.

For their continual encouragement, feedback, & general
advice
Heather Doidge-Sidhu & Ripan Gill — henna info
Joanne Schwartz & Dr. Thalia Field — VGH info
The Office

For their art
Alicia McFadzean (aka Serif and Somnia)
Inked By Chloe
Nicole Deal

ABOUT THE AUTHOR

Meghan Ciana Doidge is an award-winning writer based out of Vancouver, British Columbia, Canada. She has a penchant for bloody love stories, superheroes, and the supernatural. She also has a thing for chocolate, potatoes, and cashmere.

For recipes, giveaways, news, and glimpses of upcoming stories, please connect with Meghan via:
www.madebymeghan.ca
info@madebymeghan.ca

facebook.com/MeghanCianaDoidge

instagram.com/meghancianadoidge

tiktok.com/@meghancianadoidge

ALSO BY MEGHAN CIANA DOIDGE